P9-DHN-399

He takes me to have and to hold. But not to love and to cherish. He wants me close so that he can punish me.

Hope looked up into the rock-hard face of her new husband as a thrill of fear raced through her. "Shall I just go?" she asked.

"No, you have to stay if we are going to make this marriage convincing."

"What are we going to do?" she asked faintly, her heart in her throat. Her body was on fire, her brain a maelstrom of anger and desire.

"Let me start by telling you what we are *not* going to do," Jude said in a flat, hard voice. "We are not going to do what's in your eyes right now."

Dear Reader,

A new year has begun, and in its honor we bring you six new—and wonderful!—Intimate Moments novels. First up is *A Marriage-Minded Man?* Linda Turner returns to THE LONE STAR SOCIAL CLUB for this scintillating tale of a cop faced with a gorgeous witness who's offering him lots of evidence—about a crime that has yet to be committed! What's her game? Is she involved? Is she completely crazy? Or is she totally on the level—and also the perfect woman for him?

Then there's Beverly Barton's *Gabriel Hawk's Lady,* the newest of THE PROTECTORS. Rorie Dean needs help rescuing her young nephew from the jungles of San Miguel, and Gabriel is the only man with the know-how to help. But what neither of them has counted on is the attraction that simmers between them, making their already dangerous mission a threat on not just one level but two!

Welcome Suzanne Brockmann back with *Love with the Proper Stranger,* a steamy tale of deceptions, false identities and overwhelming passion. In *Ryan's Rescue,* Karen Leabo matches a socialite on the run with a reporter hot on the trail of a story that starts looking very much like a romance. *Wife on Demand* is an intensely emotional marriage-of-convenience story from the pen of Alexandra Sellers. And finally, welcome historical author Barbara Ankrum, who debuts in the line with *To Love a Cowboy.*

Enjoy them all, then come back next month for more excitement and passion—right here in Silhouette Intimate Moments.

Yours,

Leslie J. Wainger
Senior Editor and Editorial Coordinator

Please address questions and book requests to:
Silhouette Reader Service
U.S.: 3010 Walden Ave., P.O. Box 1325, Buffalo, NY 14269
Canadian: P.O. Box 609, Fort Erie, Ont. L2A 5X3

WIFE ON DEMAND

ALEXANDRA SELLERS

Published by Silhouette Books
America's Publisher of Contemporary Romance

If you purchased this book without a cover you should be aware
that this book is stolen property. It was reported as "unsold and
destroyed" to the publisher, and neither the author nor the
publisher has received any payment for this "stripped book."

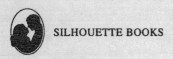

SILHOUETTE BOOKS

ISBN: 0-373-07833-1

WIFE ON DEMAND

Copyright © 1998 by Alexandra Sellers

All rights reserved. Except for use in any review, the reproduction
or utilization of this work in whole or in part in any form by any
electronic, mechanical or other means, now known or hereafter
invented, including xerography, photocopying and recording, or in
any information storage or retrieval system, is forbidden without
the written permission of the editorial office, Silhouette Books,
300 East 42nd Street, New York, NY 10017 U.S.A.

All characters in this book have no existence outside the imagination of
the author and have no relation whatsoever to anyone bearing the same
name or names. They are not even distantly inspired by any individual
known or unknown to the author, and all incidents are pure invention.

This edition published by arrangement with Harlequin Books S.A.

® and TM are trademarks of Harlequin Books S.A., used under license.
Trademarks indicated with ® are registered in the United States Patent
and Trademark Office, the Canadian Trade Marks Office and in other
countries.

Printed in U.S.A.

ALEXANDRA SELLERS

was born in Ontario, and raised in Ontario and Saskatchewan. She first came to London to attend the Royal Academy of Dramatic Art and fell in love with the city. Later, she returned to make it her permanent home. Now married to an Englishman, she lives near Hampstead Heath. As well as writing romance, she teaches a course called "How to Write a Romance Novel" in London several times a year.

Because of a much-regretted allergy she can have no resident cat, but she receives regular charitable visits from three cats who are neighbors.

Readers can write to her at P.O. Box 9449, London, NW3 2WH, England.

Lyrics from "Wake Me Up to Say Goodbye" copyright
1983 by Dorothy Poste. Used by permission.

Prologue

"*What the hell are you doing here?*"

The voice was low, and filled with all the fury she had known she would hear, all the hatred she had feared to face. Hearing it, her head jerked back, but she stood her ground.

"*I had to see you.*"

He laughed. He was changed, frighteningly changed. She would hardly have recognized him; and not just because of the unfamiliar, thick muscles bulging under his T-shirt and all down his arms, not just because of the flatter planes of his face.

He himself was different. Or, he was different in himself. The set of his face was new, the way he now held his jaw seemed to mark a change in the way he faced the world. Once he had been cat-like, able to relax or tense at a second's notice. Now his body, so heavily muscled, looked as though it never relaxed.

She had not imagined that it would be so bad.

His laughter was brief and mirthless and he looked at

her with a cruel grin. He wasn't going to help her over this, of course he wasn't. He was giving nothing. She wanted to ask if they could sit down, but she was afraid to.

Aware of the eyes that watched them, and the ears that perhaps overheard, she stood tongue-tied, gazing at him, telling herself she had been a fool to come. She'd thought she loved him, but who did she love now? The man he had been?

After a moment she said quietly, "You've changed."

He smiled, but his eyes were still dark. "More muscles," he observed softly. "The better to hold you with, my dear. Is that why you came?" His black gaze fixed hers so that she couldn't turn away. She caught her breath as, within her, a flame puffed into life.

"No," she whispered, but he overrode her.

"Jesus Christ!" he spat. "Is that what you came for? You—! What the hell use do you think I can be to you in here? What do you want?"

His anger hit her in waves. He took a step towards her and put his arms around her. They felt unfamiliar. Everything about him was unfamiliar. "Don't!" she began angrily, and he said in a voice so quiet she had to stop breathing to hear, "If you struggle or shout they'll come and take me."

She stilled, and his jaw tightened, as though he'd hoped she would protest, as though what he wanted was violence. Any violence. When she stood quietly in his hold he lifted his hand and clasped her throat.

His hand seemed larger, his skin rough as it had never been. He said, "I could break your neck before they noticed, did you think of that?"

"No," she said.

"No," he agreed. "You thought you were safe here." He was holding her so that she couldn't move, an arm around her back, the hand encircling her throat in a grotesque parody of desire. "Let me tell you something: you're

only safe as long as I care what happens to me. Understand?''

She didn't answer. *"Understand?"* he pressed. He was speaking with a clenched jaw, his lips pulled back from his teeth. *"Guys stop caring in here every day. So if you value that little tail of yours—"* he let go of her abruptly *"—get out of here and don't come back.''*

She stood her ground, gazing at him. She could hear her own laboured breathing. She wished suddenly, fiercely, in spite of everything, that he had kissed her.

"Damn it!" he snarled. *"Get going!"*

She licked her lips. *"I found something,"* she said. *"Something that might help prove that you're innocent.''*

Chapter 1

Hope knew she was going to hate Jude Daniels long before she met him. She had known it, deep in her bones, that moment when, lying drowsily in her bed in the Swiss clinic where she had been made whole at last, she had heard her father say, "I'm going to take Jude Daniels into partnership."

Her father's partner. That place had been hers by right—was *still* her right—for as far back as she could remember thinking about a career. At her father's words she was filled with a hot surge of jealousy, as if something had been stolen from her. And since she could not be angry with her father, she turned it against Jude Daniels.

If she had been honest, perhaps she would have seen what her father had already seen and accepted—that Hope had delayed taking her promised place as his partner because she did not, in her heart, want the job. If she had been honest then...

But she was not honest. She still could not admit to herself that her future lay elsewhere than with her father. So she hated Jude Daniels as a usurper, from that moment. The cuckoo—in the nest that was rightfully hers.

That week when she was twenty-three was not the first time her father had sat beside her hospital bed and given her terrible news. The first time had been when she was twelve, and, frightened and in unbearable pain, had cried for her mother. Then he had told her her mother was dead, killed in the accident that had so hurt Hope. He did not tell her—she found out soon enough—that from now on she would walk only with pain, and with a disfiguring limp.

No doubt that was why she had grown so attached to her father, so dependent on him. Losing her mother and her physical freedom—maybe it had seemed as if he was all she had. Certainly she loved him deeply, desperately. From the time of the accident Hope adored her father. When asked about her future plans, Hope always said, "I'm going to be an architect like Dad," and he always called her "my little partner."

When, five years later, Hope was looking at university and college prospectuses, her father asked if she was seriously considering attending architectural college with a view to joining him in his firm after graduation, and of course she wanted to do it. Of course she did. She was a girl with a natural artistic talent whom her teachers had always encouraged. She had attended the High School for the Visual and Performing Arts. But a career as artist was for the chosen few. The sensible thing would be to utilize her artistic talent within a practical career—architecture.

She was a bright girl, her intelligence well above average. But she did not do well in her first-year exams. Her father looked at her in surprise. "I got stressed out," she explained. "I just need a break. I'll be fine next year, you'll see."

A group of students was getting a trip together that summer to travel Europe looking at the architecture. Hope decided to join them. For three weeks she stared at castles and cathedrals and *mairies* and everything in between. Then, when the others were going home, she and a friend decided to finish up the holiday with a figure painting class in a French château.

"It's being held by Petrovsky," she told her father excitedly. "He's living in the West now." Vaclav Petrovsky was a Russian artist Hope admired a lot. It was an opportunity just too good and too timely to turn down.

Petrovsky liked her work. At the end of the course, he recommended her to a friend in Paris, who ran a very small, exclusive school—only three or four students working in his studio with him...the friend liked her work, too, and took her on.

"It'll only be a year, and I can go straight back to university next fall," she told her father. "It's bound to enhance my future work as an architect; it's not as if it's unrelated."

Her father had not protested then, nor at the end of the year when de Vincennes had offered her another year of tuition. Nor at the end of that year, when she decided to travel and "just take a real, lazy holiday for once, like an ordinary tourist, and get some sun and sea into my system. I'll come home in August refreshed and all ready to go!"

But she had not taken a real, lazy holiday. She had taken her easel and paints with her. In Cannes, sitting in the harbour on a windy day with a pair of binoculars, she had painted a yacht out on the water, struggling to come in against a steady offshore breeze. The picture was full of seaspray and struggle, with the yacht's name just visible on the stern.

Someone, seeing her, had mentioned it to the owners, and before she knew it Hope had sold her first painting, and made some new friends.

August came and went. She painted pictures of their yachts for her new circle of friends and for the first time did not need the money her father regularly deposited into her bank for her. This time she forgot to phone with an explanation. Late in October she called to say that she was going to the Maldives on the yacht of some friends; they would winter in the Indian Ocean. She was looking forward to painting tropical paradise.

It was there, living a life of leisure that her father's money would have allowed her to follow for the rest of her life, that Hope began to take stock. Her life needed direction, or she would wake up and discover twenty years had passed. Some decision had to be made.

One night, invited to drinks on a megayacht, she met Raoul Spitzen, a doctor who ran some kind of clinic in Switzerland. He asked her about her limp and offered to examine her with a view to treatment.

"How old were you?" he asked during the examination.

"Twelve."

"What was the accident?"

"Automobile. My mother was driving us...she was killed."

"Ah. The hip gives you a lot of discomfort?"

Hope only nodded.

"Can you engage in sexual intercourse?"

"I don't—I've always thought I couldn't," she said hoarsely, though there was no reason for her voice to catch. Hope had long ago faced the fact that she was unlikely to lead a normal life.

"There are one or two positions, of course, where it might be possible without pain, but perhaps a young woman does not feel confident about explaining the details to a first-time lover," Raoul Spitzen said, and went on with bluff good nature, "Well, even if we do not get rid of the limp entirely, we can at least normalize your life. You will be free of pain. You will be able to marry and have babies."

So Hope's life suddenly had direction. She was going to be made whole. She was going to be normal.

The operation was only the first step. Afterwards would come months of physiotherapy and exercise, teaching her muscles to move in a new way, while she painted the Alps that so magnificently surrounded the clinic. Then a second operation would make her good as new.

Her father came to be with her at the time of the first operation. A few days later, at her bedside, he told her, "I'm taking Jude Daniels into partnership.

"I'm getting older, Hope. I need a partner," he had said, by way of explanation.

Maybe it was the possessiveness that crept into his tone, as if he had said, "I need a son," but Hope felt a burning, uncharacteristic jealousy, and the first stab of dislike for Jude Daniels.

"But—Jude Daniels?" she mouthed in astonishment, and the floating post-operative fog left her. "Why?"

She knew who Jude Daniels was, of course. Everybody in the Toronto architectural community—and many who were not—knew who Jude Daniels was: innovative, heretic, iconoclast, or burr under the establishment saddle, depending on your point of view.

He followed no particular school in his own buildings. Neither "post-modernist" nor "deconstructionist" nor "traditionalist" himself, he built buildings, Jude Daniels said, according to need. Which meant he could challenge everyone.

When Jude Daniels disapproved of a colleague's building, he said so—sometimes in print—and ruthlessly enumerated its flaws. He regularly broke the architects' unwritten code of silence. Hope knew architects who absolutely hated him.

Not her father, apparently. "Because he's a very fine architect, and I like him," Hal Thompson said. "He doesn't put up with the second-rate. He reminds me of myself at that age, only he has more courage to stand against the crowd than I did.''

Hal Thompson had always himself been considered something of a maverick within the profession. Unusually, he had never gone into partnership of any kind, though it had been offered often enough, and by the biggest firms. He preferred to have complete control. When he won big building contracts, he would take on one of the big multi-partner firms as ''associates,'' but the last word was always his.

She had always assumed the place was there for her in her father's office whenever she wanted it. She had believed he would take on no partner, if not his daughter.

She wanted to say, ''What about me?'' but she did not say it. Instead she thought that Jude Daniels had taken her place when she was weak and unable to defend herself.

It was nearly another year before she came home at last. By that time she was another woman, a new Hope Thompson. She could walk now, virtually without a limp, entirely without pain. She had blossomed into confidence, even into beauty. At twenty-four she was almost newborn, enjoying her female power in a way that girls of sixteen already take for granted.

But she was more practised than a girl of sixteen, more subtle. She had had a long time of watching women's use of their sexual power, without feeling she had any. Her use of it was mature and fresh at the same time. What was even more enchanting, sometimes she forgot she had it. Her eyes would light with joy when something reminded her.

She would lie slouched in a posture never before possible to her, for example, her long legs stretched out in ungainly elegance, and, forgetting herself in the heat of conversation, would notice suddenly that a man was staring at her legs. In such moments her first instinct was awkward embarrassment...and then a smile of remembering would steal across her face: *I am like other women. He is staring at my legs because they are pretty.*

And then, involuntarily, she would smile her surprised joy at the perpetrator, inviting him to share in the wonder of her marvellous legs.

Not many men were proof against something like this.

She came home in the summer before her twenty-fifth birthday. Her father invited Jude Daniels to dinner the day she was scheduled to arrive, so that they could meet for the first time alone. He arranged a dinner party of old friends for a few nights later.

Hope's departure was unavoidably delayed for several days because the framers who were framing the painting of the clinic she had done as a thank-you to Raoul Spitzen screwed up and she had to wait till it was fixed. She didn't arrive until the afternoon of the party.

"I wanted you to meet Jude on his own," her father said sadly, and Hope replied merrily, "That's all right, I'll meet him with the others. It'll be fine."

She met Jude Daniels, and at first sight she knew he was everything everybody had always said: arrogant, sure of himself, and too damned judgemental. The jealousy she had never stopped feeling coalesced into pointed dislike before they had exchanged a word.

He liked her no better. He hardly smiled as they were introduced, and his black eyes were assessing, with a look of hostility that she did not understand, but was eager to match.

He was lean and tall and loose-knit. With a shock of dark brown hair falling forward over his forehead, there was an air of uncut diamond about him. He had a very slight, unplaceable accent, which surprised her. She'd had no idea he was foreign.

Hope was tall, too, though not as tall as he, and looking very European that night. Proud of her new walk and her new shape, she was wearing a short, tight dress in glittering black that left shoulders and legs bare.

Her legs were long and lovely, and more important, they both worked. Her auburn hair, immaculately cut to enhance the soft natural curl, swept her naked brown shoulders. Her makeup glowed, her jewellery glowed. She looked pampered, beautiful, rich. Her father's friends were all bowled over by the transformation. They kept calling her "the duckling." She felt fantastic.

She was acting as her father's hostess that night for the first time in years. He had asked her to put Jude Daniels at her right hand, he wanted them to get to know each other, and though the moment the man entered the room she saw what a mistake it would be, she could not change the seating arrangements without upsetting her father. Anyway, she was a little looking forward to plumbing the reasons for that hostility. *She* had reason enough to dislike *him*—but how dared he look at her like that when he had never met her?

One of the other men at the table that night—another well-known architect and an old friend of Hal Thompson's—did not like Jude Daniels. Knowing it was wrong of her, Hope gently fanned and facilitated Rex Sutton's hostility during the dinner. She allowed him to subtly confront, when her obvious duty, especially as Jude was her father's partner, was to prevent such attacks.

It did not improve her feelings towards him to see that Jude Daniels knew exactly what she was doing and was cynically amused by it—and not a little contemptuous.

"You don't even fight your own battles," he murmured once, leaning in towards her and speaking for her ears alone.

She had an elbow on the table, chin resting on her hand, listening to someone. She coolly swivelled her eyes towards him. "Oh, yes, I do," she promised.

He took her at her word, engaging her as soon as there

was a break in the conversation. "So, Hope," said Jude Daniels, drawling the vowel caressingly, "you've been in a clinic in Switzerland, I understand."

"That's right."

"For a long time. Were you very ill?"

His dark eyes half-smiled, but she knew, and he knew, that the smile was for the onlookers only. Hope felt a ripple of hostility run up her spine, as energising as a cold shower. She *wanted* to fight him.

"I was recovering from surgery."

"You look remarkably well. It must have done you a world of good to really relax."

Every word was barbed, and what the hell business was it of his?

"It does add a certain polish," she said. "You should try it sometime."

"I suppose your career was interrupted," he said, leaning back and watching her out of the corner of his eye. The subtext was that she was an idle little rich girl. "What were you doing before you went to the clinic?"

"I was travelling, and painting."

"Ahhh, you are an artist?" he said largely, as enlightenment struck him.

"I paint, yes."

"And do you sell your paintings?"

She laughed, a rich, mocking trill. "If I had a dollar for every person who asked me that question! It doesn't matter what the person does, I've noticed," she gaily informed the table. "Even an accountant who wouldn't know a Picasso if he stuck his foot through it feels competent to sit in judgement on an artist—without seeing their work, mind you!—by asking that question."

She took a sip of wine, and turned back to Jude, informing him kindly, "I was mostly working to commission for friends." Although that was not the most accurate way to put it. Mostly she had made friends through painting for them.

"Portraits?"

"I painted their yachts."

He smiled in a way that made her want to slap him.

"Is your work shown? Will you have a show here now that you are home?"

He was convinced she was an idler, and she was sure nothing would make him think otherwise. If he saw her on her hands and knees scrubbing a hospital ward it wouldn't change his opinion. A very unfamiliar anger burned in her blood, and her hand shook as she reached for her wineglass.

"I had some pictures in a couple of shows in Cannes the summer before last," she said. Not for the world would she have admitted that the gallery owner was a friend.

He looked admiring over the rim of his glass, took a sip and returned to the inquisition. "In Cannes! And did you sell something there?"

"A couple of seascapes," she told him flatly, not showing him any hint of how thrilled she had been to sell a scene without a yacht in it to someone not a yacht owner, how she had felt it legitimised her as an artist.

"But this is wonderful! I had no idea. Hal," he called down the table, interrupting the older man's not very animated conversation, "you didn't tell me your daughter is a successful artist!"

"Well, you've found it out for yourself," Hal said with a lazy smile, and for the first time it dawned on Hope just exactly what kind of hopes her father was nurturing towards Jude Daniels.

No! she wanted to shout at him. *He's your partner, but he'll never be anything to me.*

"Maybe we can commission the painting for Concord House East's lobby from your daughter. Why not?" he said, and then, to Hope again, "May I see some of your work?"

She was deeply unwilling that he should see her paintings, as though to show him anything so personal would leave her vulnerable. "I haven't even unpacked," she said. "I haven't got a studio."

"But you will set one up, of course," said Jude Daniels. She wondered whether everyone could see what she saw, that he was baiting her, or whether to the others this looked like friendly interest.

"I don't know," she said hesitantly. Her life was so changed, she would need time to absorb who she was before looking at questions like what she would do with her future and where she would spend it. "Things are so different now," she explained, not to Jude Daniels but to the others at the table, people who had known her since before her accident. "I need time...I'm looking for something to do as a stopgap while I get my bearings."

Everyone except Jude Daniels nodded understandingly. "Are you still thinking of architecture?" one of the wives asked. "I remember you were always going to become your father's partner."

The woman glanced at Jude as she spoke, and Hope smiled involuntarily, because the woman was letting her know she had picked up on the hostility between Hope and Jude, and that she was on Hope's side.

"You were going to be your father's partner?" Jude pressed, with an odd emphasis, so that she thought, *You already had that little piece of information. Why are you pretending you didn't?*

"Didn't you know you'd usurped my place?" she responded lightly. To her astonishment his eyes narrowed.

"That is not quite the way I heard it," he said. "I heard that you preferred travel to studying for qualifications, and therefore the place as your father's partner was vacant."

Hope's gaze dropped and her cheeks burned, and though she immediately forced herself to look at him again, there was no doubt that Jude Daniels had won a point.

Another woman leapt into the breach. "Well, I'm sure among us all we can come up with a job for you to do while you're reconsidering your life, can't we, Rex?"

Hope turned to her gratefully. "Yes, I think that's what I need—a job for a few months while I sort myself out. I'm so out of touch with everything. I want to be doing something with routine in it."

As if the gods had decided to take a hand, the phone rang. A few minutes later, her father came back to the table complaining good-naturedly: it had been from the husband of Eleanor, his office manager, reporting that she had had an accident and was in hospital with a broken leg.

"But here is the perfect stopgap!" Jude smiled at her. "Why not come to the office temporarily? Then you will be reminded of the joys of architecture *and* you will have the routine you crave."

It was a dare. His eyes told her that he knew she would not accept his challenge, that she was the sort of rich bitch who talked a lot but didn't intend to get her hands dirty with real work.

Maybe there was a part of her, just in that moment, that was afraid he was right. That she never had done, and never would do, anything worthwhile.

Maybe that was why she agreed to do it.

Chapter 2

The Rose Collection was the life achievement of Isaac
Rose, a wealthy collector of ancient books and manuscripts.
This collection, so important that scholars from all over the
world came to consult it, had been left to the nation when
he died. Several million dollars had also been left for the
purchase of a large library of related works which would
be housed with the collection, and for the building of the
Rose Library.

Jude Daniels, of the new firm of Thompson Daniels, had
captured the trustees' imagination, and the contract, with a
design so unusual Toronto had immediately polarised into
two camps. Most of the city's architects were in the anti
camp.

The architect had taken the instruction literally, and had
designed the Rose Library as a rose, a glass flower on a
cedarwood stem. The stem was composed of four floors
where the precious manuscripts and books of the central
collection were to be kept in perfectly controlled light and
climate conditions; the rose would house three levels of

reading room, as well as the ordinary books in the collection, enclosed in layers of massive glass petals that looked as beautifully fragile as a real rose. Its image would be endlessly reflected in the mirrored walls of two skyscrapers that rose beside it on the south and east, creating the illusion of a forest of roses.

When Hope went to work for her father, the Rose Library was already more than half complete. The stem was standing, and a delicate tree-like network of girders that would hold the moulded glass was already nearly in place. It was a controversial project, and pictures had been appearing in the papers virtually every week while it was building, but it was all new to Hope.

Much against her will, she was entranced by the four-foot-high model of the Rose Library which now graced the lobby of Thompson Daniels' offices, and fascinated by the half-finished building, even shrouded as it was with scaffolding. Not even her hostility for Jude Daniels could make her deny that it was one of the most beautiful buildings she had ever seen. The site was not far from her father's office, and on her lunch hours Hope would stroll over to watch the men at work as, one by one, the massive curving sheets of glass were installed.

She was not alone. It seemed to be the favourite occupation of Toronto's downtown lunchtime crowd, watching the Rose Library go up.

It didn't make her like Jude Daniels any better.

At night her father would talk to her about the younger man as if Jude were his own son, as if she shared his admiration for Jude and would one day share his affection, as if her interest in a man who in fact set her teeth on edge was unquestionable.

It was from her father she learned the past that Jude rarely told people. He had been born in Czechoslovakia. His mother had died as a political prisoner there when he was five, after the Prague Spring had turned to such a chilling winter; Jude and his father had escaped to Canada later. Life had been hard for a child with a father who grieved constantly for his wife and the life they had lost. His father died when Jude was seventeen, leaving him virtually alone.

Perhaps, if her father had not liked Jude so much, Hope might have disliked him less. Perhaps, if she had not felt that in her absence they had formed a father-son bond that excluded her, she would not have resented what she thought of as his arrogance so fiercely. But as things stood, there was antagonism in the air whenever Hope and Jude met.

Which was very often. On her first day, her father, deaf to her subtle pleas that she was too busy learning the ropes to have lunch out, insisted on their all going for what he called "a long, convivial lunch," to replace that introductory dinner they had missed because of Hope's delayed arrival.

"Now, where are we going?" her father asked jovially at twelve-thirty, as the three descended from the offices in the lift. Hope had naturally booked the reservations.

"The Rotunda," Hope said. "I'd like to see it."

The Rotunda was Toronto's newest restaurant, and had been built by a man named Norman Cooper, another one of her father's friends who disliked Jude.

She glanced up at Jude's face as she spoke, wanting him to get the message. She was unprepared for the way his dark eyes flicked to hers, and for the unreadable expression that crossed his face.

"Ah," said her father, and there was a silence, while Hope took in the information that there was more to Norman's dislike of Jude than she knew, and that she had somehow hit a sore spot with her very first shot.

"Is there a problem with that?" she asked innocently.

"Not what you'd call a problem," said Hal Thompson in comfortable reassurance.

Jude was looking at Hope with a calmly assessing look

that made her both nervous and irritated. "You have not been there before?" he asked Hope, in his deep voice.

"No, but I hear it's a talking point, and I wanted to see it."

His long mouth stretched out in a smile, as though he suspected her of deeper motives. Hope was mystified.

The Rotunda was massive, in the post-modern style. On top of a thirty-storey building in the heart of the downtown area, it was built to a circular design under a high glass dome. In the centre of the main floor, she noticed, were the workstations, where the dishes and linens were kept and the waiting staff collected the food that came up on dumb-waiters from the kitchens below.

The tables were set all around the perimeter of the dome on two levels. Coming off the elevator, they were greeted by a wall of sound: only open a month, The Rotunda was a popular lunch spot, and at the relatively early hour of twelve-thirty a third of the tables were already full.

The maitre d' led them in a semi-circle around the edge of the central area to a curvilinear staircase, and up to the balcony level. Here the floor was made of glass. The main area of the floor was of smoked glass, with circles of clear glass at intervals that allowed you to look down at the floor below as you walked, or if you sat near one.

And vice versa. Hope, who was wearing a skirt, was crossing the middle of a circle, gazing interestedly down, when four male diners below lifted their heads to gaze interestedly up. After that she detoured around the clear circles.

When they reached their circular glass table set near an exterior wall of smoked glass, Hope sat for a moment in silence, gazing around appreciatively. Up here, the noise was approaching din, which gave the comforting impression of being in the thick of things. She could see that Norman's theme was circles: there were few straight lines anywhere. The dome itself was composed of bands of glass piled one on top of the other, and where they diminished at the top, what the eye saw, looking up, was a series of concentric circles.

"So, Hope, what do you think?" Jude asked, when she had been gazing speechlessly for a minute or two.

"It's incredibly impressive!" she enthused, leaning over the table to be heard because the background noise was high. "It's Norman's masterpiece, Dad, don't you think? It's a work of art."

Jude's eyelashes fell lazily over his eyes, as though to hide his reactions from her. Hope guessed that he was feeling professional jealousy, and a little flicker of glee smote her. "Look at the way he's dealt with his influences!" she went on enthusiastically, and babbled on in art appreciation style until she realized that what Jude was hiding from her was amusement. He was laughing at her.

"*You* don't like it, I take it," she said with cold fury.

"No, I don't like it," he agreed mildly. She was irritated because she had to lean towards him, straining to hear. Jude did not shout to be heard.

"Why not? Because you didn't build it yourself, perhaps?"

"I'm sure you do not want me to repeat myself."

At this Hope could only stare. "Repeat yourself?"

A waiter came with their drinks, and when he had gone she prompted, "Repeat yourself?"

"You have not read the article that caused so much offense?" Jude asked, with a faint air of disbelief. "I thought that was why we were here."

"What article? I haven't read any article."

Hal Thompson laid down his menu and intervened. "Jude writes an architectural column now and then for the *Globe*. He reviewed The Rotunda when it was unveiled, and I'm afraid Norman didn't take his criticisms in good part."

Hope turned to Jude again, opening her eyes wide. "A

newspaper column now!'' she marvelled. ''Where will it end?''

Her father launched into his usual paean of praise for his protégé. It gave Hope a curious sensation to realize that Hal Thompson really had no suspicion of her dislike of Jude, while Jude was fully aware of it. Just as she was aware of his dislike of her. This fact lent to their exchanges an intimate quality—two people talking in code—that Hope did not recognize for what it was.

''Since I haven't read it,'' she said, when her father had finished, ''perhaps you'd give me a brief précis of your comments, because I really can't see any flaws.''

''When you walked around the edges of those transparent inserts in the floor, no flaw occurred to you?'' Jude prodded gently.

She was startled that he had noticed.

''That's hardly the architect's fault! The maitre d' shouldn't take people right over those areas.''

''It does not occur to you that those circles have no reason to exist?''

''Well, of course they're letting the light through!''

''And yet the dome itself is smoked glass. There is in any case no undiffused natural light in the place.''

''People who look up can see the top of the dome, though,'' Hope tried. The centre of the dome carried a modern design in coloured glass, like a church window.

''And for a consideration like this it is fair to make every woman who dines here uncomfortable,'' Jude said levelly.

''He was trying to make an artistic whole,'' Hope protested. ''You can see that his theme is repeating—''

Jude interrupted without apology. ''It is not the job of an architect to sacrifice the comfort of human beings for the sake of art. The art of architecture is to facilitate living, not to build a monument to an individual artistic ego.''

''I'm sure Norman is well aware of the importance of the end user! He hardly needs you to tell him.''

He looked amused. "I have not told him. I have told you."

When the waiter turned up at her father's elbow, Hope hadn't yet so much as glanced at the menu. Hastily she opened it and ordered almost at random. Beside them, with a screeking of metal chairs on glass, a party of four was arriving. The restaurant was filling up, and the sound levels increased proportionately.

There was the sound of a breaking plate behind her, and Hope involuntarily turned her head, but there was nothing there—their table was beside the smoked glass exterior wall.

"That's strange," she said, half to herself.

Jude handed his menu to the waiter and grinned at her. "Norman's acoustics provide the diners here at the outer edge with the privilege of hearing all the noises from the waiters' workstation. In some positions it is easier to hear a waiter scraping plates down there in the centre than the voice of your companion two feet away."

She was suddenly able to identify the noises she had been hearing for the past ten minutes. Jude was right—she could hear dishes being scraped and stacked, the clank of silverware being dropped in metal bins. Every sound had a high, scraping, treble note that she had not consciously noticed at first but which was becoming slightly uncomfortable over time.

"Next time I'll book a table downstairs," she said lightly. Jude really was making a big case out of nothing. Noisy restaurants were in at the moment, and why should Norman Cooper be blamed for an entire trend?

She had a headache at the end of an hour, but she attributed that to the stress of being in Jude Daniels' company.

Jude had a secretary, as did her father, but, as Hope discovered on her first day, it was the job of the office manager to supervise both of them, as well as their support staff.

She did not really enjoy the work, and was sorry almost immediately that she had agreed to take it on. It was all Jude Daniels' fault, of course: he had dared her, as if knowing she would refuse the dare, and instead of doing the sane thing, she'd been suckered by pride into proving him wrong.

And yet, until she made up her mind what her future was going to be, what else should she do? There was no point setting up a studio here in Toronto if she did not in the end settle here. And one stopgap was probably as good as another. Any woman stepping into Eleanor's job would have had difficulty, and Hope at least had a year of architectural college behind her, so she could console herself that she was being useful to her father.

She was uncomfortable, though, feeling out of her element. Sometimes she wished she had never come home, and yet her life had been too fragmented during her time in Europe for her to feel there was a solid base to return to there. And she was a different person now, as much there as here. Whatever she chose to do now, she would on some level be starting over.

Sometimes on a weekend afternoon she took her paints and easel down to the lakefront or out to the island and painted boats, but without the urgency to commit the images to canvas that she had once felt. Whatever the future held, for the moment her focus was not in her paints.

The one thing about which she felt any urgency at all was men. Hope was dating every night, and loving it. For the first time in her life, men were falling over themselves to get to her. For the first time, too, she did not suffer pain in her hip if she stayed up late, or drank too much, or danced. For the first time she could wear clothes that were sexually enticing without feeling that she looked like a fool or was being a cheat: now she had the right to dress as a woman who assumes in herself the power to attract—and she could, if she wanted to, deliver on the promise of such clothes. Before her operations she had always avoided any hint of sexual potential in the way she dressed. This new freedom to tempt was intoxicating.

Jude Daniels knew about her late nights. He and her father often discussed work over dinner at the Thompson house. Hope usually went in to say good-night to her father before leaving the house on a date, and she made a particular point of it when she knew Jude was there.

Knowing Jude would be seeing her always added a certain extra rush to her blood as she dressed, and although *of course* she dressed for her date, on nights when he was with her father it was Jude's eyes she imagined gazing at her as she pulled on sheer black stockings, Jude's decorum she thought of shaking up as she buttoned a sheer shirt, Jude's negative reaction she imagined as she slipped on a designer dress that left an inch-wide strip of bare skin visible down her side between armpit and hem, or was cut so low her warm, tanned breasts seemed to be on offer on a plate.

She took pleasure in flaunting her beauty in front of Jude Daniels because she was very sure he disapproved of her and her frivolous lifestyle. Jude was one of the worker ants of the world, with an instinctive contempt for those whose function was butterfly, Hope was certain. And he had made up his mind that she was a butterfly.

"We're going to Nina's," she would tell her father caressingly on such evenings, naming Toronto's latest *in* club. "And afterwards Johnny's promised to take us for a midnight sail on that fabulous new yacht he's taking to the Med in September...."

"Enjoy yourself," Hal Thompson would order her with a tolerant smile, though she knew that even he did not understand what it was that drove her now.

"Hello, Jude," Hope would say, opening limpid eyes at

him and making sure he got the full benefit of whatever outfit she had on.

His face when he returned her greeting was always inscrutable. Hope did not have the satisfaction of scoring many points. Since Jude never admitted by so much as a raised eyebrow to disapproving of her lifestyle, her flaunting of it seemed merely gratuitous.

Yet she *knew* she was getting to him. She would glitter and shine and swing her pampered, expensive hair at him, and every now and then there was something deep behind his eyes that told her she had scored. She was absolutely certain that Jude had the urge to slap her, as if he was impatient of her, as if she were living her life half-asleep.

She wasn't. She was wide-awake and alive for the first time, and not even Jude's black gaze could take away the pleasure of it. But sometimes she imagined him trying to slap her, imagined the stinging blow she would give his cheek in return. Sometimes she wished he would say or do something—anything—that would justify such a reaction from her.

Other men did not hide their opinion of her. To her astonished delight, men were falling around her like flies in a room mined by Vapona No-Pest strips. They wanted to sleep with her, to live with her, or marry her and have beautiful daughters just like her, depending on their natures. But Hope was sixteen again and getting permanent with no one. "My father won't let me go steady," she joked with one persistent suitor, and was surprised by the thrill that went through her at the words. It wasn't true that you couldn't relive your life.

She was crossing a magic landscape that had been closed to her before—there had never been any need, or chance, to say those words eight years ago, when she was really sixteen. In those days Hope had always been a popular member of the group, but never singled out by any boy. And she had never tried to single one out, though of course she had had crushes. What had she had to offer? She couldn't even dance. The fear of rejection had always kept Hope determinedly in the buddy category.

No more. She had no buddies now, no pals, only men who wanted her, whether they were her date or another woman's.

Except Jude Daniels. He was not a pal, but nor did he want her. He was the only one in whose eyes she never once saw sexual interest or appreciation. Hope didn't want him wanting her, she'd have hated it if he did, so that was all right.

Jude Daniels was firmly in the category *enemy*.

Chapter 3

Of course her social life took its toll on her effectiveness in the office. She was sometimes late, sometimes inefficient, and her father gave his secretary a raise because she complained she had more of a workload now, and was doing some of Eleanor's work.

For example, Lena had taken over the job when a new draughtsman had to be hired, running the ad and booking and screening the applicants for Hal Thompson to interview. That wasn't in her job description, but Hope had been taking a four-day weekend to take part in a sailing regatta when Hal and Jude decided to hire an extra hand, and then was off sick an extra day, and when she came back it made sense to let Lena continue what she'd begun rather than try to take over the job in the middle.

Small incidents like that made Hope seem more and more merely the boss's daughter. Everybody knew that she'd really been off with a celebratory hangover on the last day. Nobody minded—her father was rich, and the job was only till Eleanor came back, and why should Hope bust her ass over it? As for Lena, she was very happy with Hope's lack of dedication, since it had meant a raise.

Anyway, Hope was great to have around the office. She laughed and joked with them all, and except when Jude was there the atmosphere was easy and friendly, and after a few weeks Hope was firmly in the role of the office pet. They joked when she came in with dark circles around her eyes and groaning every time the phone rang, they loved to hear about the places she went at night, and who had been there, and she painted a terrific portrait of Jude's secretary to give to her mother on her birthday, and now everyone wanted one.

The hot July night of the day that she took the completed portrait into the office to give to Sarah, she was, for a change, at home for dinner.

"Well, hello!" said her father appreciatively, coming into the sitting room to find her lounging on a sofa in shorts and shirt, watching the news. "No parties tonight?"

"I thought it would be nice for a change to have an evening with just the two of us," Hope said.

Jude Daniels appeared in the doorway. Hope's face lost all expression as she turned her head. "Hey, Jude," she acknowledged with a raised eyebrow.

"Good evening, Hope."

"Something to drink, Hope?" asked her father, moving over to the drinks tray.

"A vodka martini, please, very dry."

There was silence while her father mixed the drink for her, and the anchorman talked about starving refugees.

"Shall we have that off, Hope?" her father chided gently as he offered her a glass, and Hope woodenly picked up the remote and the screen went black.

"Jude? Your usual?" asked Hal, just as Hope said with formal sweetness, "Do sit down, please."

Jude nodded at Hal. To Hope he said, "My clothes are dirty."

She looked him up and down. He must have come straight from the Rose Library site, because he was in work clothes—work pants and shirt and boots, and there was dust in all the creases and caught in the curling hair of his forearms and his eyebrows. His dark hair was ruffled and slightly damp with sweat; he'd been wearing a hard hat. He looked like a manual labourer.

"I'm sure Bella is quite used to getting dust out of the furniture by now," she told him. As he sank into one of her father's luxurious armchairs, Hope was conscious of a little thrill of pleasure at the contrast he made with the background of sophisticated wealth.

Her father poured whisky over ice and handed it to Jude, then poured a drink for himself. He glanced at his watch. "I'll make that call to Vancouver now," he said, and carried his drink out of the room across the hall to his study.

Hope's foremost emotion was irritation with her father for having asked her to turn the TV off. She sipped her drink and the silence grew thicker. She hadn't noticed before what a strong body Jude had. Lean, but firmly muscled. The dust of labour emphasised his physicality as a business suit never could. He was very different from the fresh, gym-muscled lawyers and stockbrokers she dated. It only made her like him less, if possible.

The silence went on, but Hope didn't care. She was damned if she would make social conversation with the man. Let him suffer.

At last Jude said, "Sarah showed me a portrait you have done of her."

"Did she?"

"I didn't know you painted portraits."

"I don't, much."

"It's very good."

"Are you surprised?" She carefully kept all trace of the pleasure she felt at his praise out of her ironic inquiry. Why should she be affected by what *Jude* thought?

"I am surprised that you are working in the office instead of painting. What is the reason for this?"

She tilted her head and eyed him. "What's the matter, Jude? You don't like having to revise your opinion of me? I told you weeks ago why I wanted a job—as a stopgap while I work out what I want to do."

He drank some whisky and looked at her, ignoring the challenge. "This was understandable when I imagined you had only amateur talent. You are not sure that you want to paint? Why?"

"There are a lot of ifs in my life at the moment, and I have some adjusting to do. Painting is just not the first thing on my mind right now. There was a time when it was everything to me, and it might be again, but not now."

"I'd like to see your work," he said.

Just at that moment she said involuntarily, "I suppose *you* wouldn't sit for me."

There was a little silence while she hated herself. She could not imagine what had possessed her to ask him. She didn't even *want* to paint him. It was as though someone else entirely had spoken.

He looked at her. "Why not?"

She *did* want to paint him. As he was now, in the silk chair, with the dust of labour on him, forming so strong a contrast to the background of the room. She was silenced by surprise as she realized it. How could she possibly want to paint Jude Daniels? Why?

"I'll get a sketchpad," she said.

She was grateful to find her father still absent when she returned. Hope adjusted the blinds before picking up the pad and pencil. His natural posture was four-square, legs spread, both feet flat on the ground, his arms resting on the chair arms, the glass of whisky held lightly but securely in that long, sensitive, anything-but-labourer's hand.

She wanted to present him head-on, emphasising his impact, and moved a chair to a position directly facing him.

She began and abandoned three sketches. Hope put down her pencil and gazed at him for a moment, then took a sip of her martini. Something wasn't working and she wasn't sure what.

"I'll start with a study," she muttered, and decided on his hand. She picked up her pencil again, and began flicking little glances between his hand and her paper as she worked.

"May I drink?" he asked after a few moments. She looked up to find him half smiling.

"Oh!—yes—no, I'll get another glass." Hope went to the drinks tray and brought another whisky glass, taking the other and offering it to his left hand, placing the empty one in his right hand.

The little transaction ruffled her, she didn't know why. It was the first time she had touched him; they had never even shaken hands before. She was always put into a sense of heightened awareness of anyone or anything she was painting, but she felt now as if an electric field around her had been disturbed. She didn't like it.

She began sketching again. His hands were a curious mix of the sensitive and the practical—they half belonged to the silk chair and the room and half to a work site. An eighteenth-century ruffle around the wrist would not be out of place, and yet there was undeniably a musculature of use over the long thin bones.

"I'm sorry I can't get the sketch done tonight, because I don't suppose you'll have a lot of time to sit for me," she said.

"Not a lot," he agreed. She knew he was working hard on the Rose Library, and now there was some kind of problem with Concord House East. "But I do take Sundays off."

"Can you sit this Sunday afternoon?"

"All right."

Hope nodded, her heart racing, not sure whether they had

declared a truce or not. Not sure whether she *wanted* to declare a truce with him. She wanted to paint him, though, she knew that, so that was what she clung to.

She dreamed about him for the next three nights, tumultuous, difficult dreams that she did not remember in detail. This was not an unusual occurrence when she was engaged in an involving painting, but it was deeply uncomfortable. She felt as though, now that he had invaded her dreams, she had nowhere left to run.

Yet why should she think of *running* from Jude? She didn't like him taking her father's affections, but it wasn't as if he was a personal threat to her.

This was the kind of question her dreams raised, without offering an answer. But there was one problem the dreams solved—the creative one. If only she had the courage to follow her instincts, the painting would go well. If not, she might as well not begin.

On the Sunday she greeted Jude nervously at the door, and led him to the sitting room again. There she had the silk chair exactly where she wanted it, three-quarters facing the window, her easel to one side.

Jude stood casually scanning the arrangement, and then looked at her, waiting for her command. "Shall I sit?" he asked, as she hesitated.

"Yes—no, would you like a drink?"

"Not yet, thank you."

She was nervous, fidgeting, lacking all her usual certainty when she began a painting. He smiled. "Is this painter's nerves?"

"No, no..." She bit her lip.

"If the time is wrong after all, I don't mind. If your father is in, there are things we can discuss."

"No, no, the timing's fine! Anyway, he's not in. It's just—"

"What is it, Hope?"

She took a deep breath, faced him, and said, "Would you let me paint you in the nude?"

Instantly, his eyelids drooped, hooding his thoughts from her.

There was a long pregnant silence and then he looked at her again. His gaze was searching, challenging; a flame flickered in its depths.

"What is it you want to prove that you do not already know?" he said, with dry anger.

The anger mystified her. And there was no way to answer him in words. "I—it's hard to explain, but I don't really know yet," she stammered. "I mean, I don't know how to put it." If she could put it into words, there would be no need to paint, but that was as hard to explain as the rest.

He heaved a breath. "Hope," he began, and she sensed his deep reluctance. She was suddenly desperate for her painting. An urgency very close to the pressure of tears built in her, which was itself extraordinary, because if the need to make this picture was so powerful, why had she not felt it building up, but only the sudden eruption of it?

"Please," she said, before he could go on. "It'll be good if you do." She meant the painting.

He took his lower lip between his teeth and squinted out the window behind her, and she knew he was going to say no.

"Please," she begged again, feeling like a fool, not understanding her own urgency. "If you don't like it when it's finished I promise I won't show it or sell it."

Jude sighed like a man convinced against his better judgement, knowing he is being a fool. "All right," he said.

She was too relieved to smile. "Thank you. There's a bathrobe in the guest bathroom, you know where that is."

He came back a few minutes later, the voluminous black towelling robe covering him. "Good," she said, all business now, to relieve any embarrassment he might feel. "Do you remember the pose you had the other night? Feet apart, arms on the arms of the chair.''

"I remember.''

"Could you—adopt that pose again?''

"Do you want me holding a glass?''

She narrowed her eyes, visualizing it. "Yes, maybe.''

"Give it to me now. I'll have the drink after all. Whisky, please.''

It was a curious about-face, but this wasn't exactly a situation where one had a lot of precedent.

Hope made the drink and handed it to him, and then went to adjust her sketching paper on the easel as Jude slipped off the robe and seated himself in the chair.

"Thank you,'' she said, looking to see that the light was falling on him as she wanted, then adjusted the position of her easel, and picked up her pencil.

"I don't normally do a sketch first,'' she explained, to ease the funny tension in the air. "But because I won't have you to sit on a regular basis I've got to give myself something to work from when you're not here.''

After that there was silence as she worked.

In a very direct way, she was aware of the tension and relaxation of various muscles, the potential power in him that was part of her reason for wanting to paint him. She would need a *trompe l'oeil* technique to give him the quality she wanted, to make him stand out from the canvas the way he stood out from life. She wanted him three-dimensional against a flat background, like a stone lion in front of the wall of a building.

On that level, she was aware of his sex. It was an essential part of the way she would present him, it was part of the reason she had needed to do him in the nude. The sculptors of those old stone lions she had once gazed at all over Europe had almost always carved the lion's sex organs, and now she knew why.

But she rarely painted portraits, and she had not done a

nude man since her time with de Vincennes in Paris. That had been easier than now, because there had been others in the room, and she had known the sitter only as a sitter. Here and now, she was aware of Jude on another level, too, on the level of Jude Daniels the man. She knew it was affecting her, and that it would enter the drawing and her paint, but exactly *what* would be there she would only know as she saw it.

She spent all her time sketching only him, because she could paint the background without him, and she wanted detail. But she hurried, because she was eager to get some paint on the canvas while he was there. After less than an hour, she thrust aside the sketch. "Please take a break," she said, and began to squeeze out oils onto her palette.

Neither of them had spoken after that first explanation. Hope never could chat in that first interpretation of the subject onto canvas, she hated to be distracted and would not stand interruption. Sometimes, when she was painting a seascape and insensitive strangers came too close or became too invasive she would use the most tersely rude expression she knew to get rid of them without affecting her concentration.

Conversation with a subject might contribute to building rapport, but Jude made no such demands on her. He had sat silently, using the time to think, she imagined, or perhaps just to rest from too much stress.

Jude got up and, without resorting to the bathrobe, refilled his glass at the drinks chest. As she covered her palette with the creams and browns and peaches she would need for his skin, she watched him. He stood with his back to her, the light from the window falling on him, and stretched first one and then the other arm above his head; and she wanted to paint him from this angle, too, the long flow of muscle under skin, from neck to ankle. His skin glowed, like a painting of a Victorian child, but the muscles underneath were clearly hard. She would enjoy the chal-

lenge of getting that down on canvas; she could almost feel
the contrast of soft and hard...

He turned and looked at her and there was a curious little
shock as their eyes met. For a long moment neither of them
spoke, nor smiled. Hope felt oddly defenceless, and realized
suddenly that, in sketching him, she had lost the armour of
her dislike for him.

"Ready?" he asked, and she nodded mutely.

She had always been better at putting what she saw
straight into paint: with the pencil there seemed some mid-
dleman officiating between her and the paper, but with
paints the intermediary was eliminated.

Besides, he was not the sort of subject to do in pencil.
His being itself called out to be translated into the thick,
rich texture of oils.

Slowly, slowly, the rapport she needed built up, until she
was so much her eyes that took in the sight of him she
almost became him.

He was tanned almost all over, but he nonetheless had
the marks of the labourer on his skin, of a darker neck and
throat. There were no clear demarcation lines on his arms,
but his forearms, nevertheless, were also a shade darker.
He had been working outdoors on the Rose Library site for
most of a long, hot summer.

The marks on his lower torso were sharp. The line of his
bathing suit was low, and the skin suddenly was pale. That
gave his flesh a natural prominence, as though light just
caught the one area of skin. She would need no trompe
l'oeil effect for that: light and shade would do it.

The underbelly of a sculpted stone lion was more hidden,
but when you looked, it was often astonishing how much
secret prominence the sculptor had given his sex.

Now she cracked the code of what was moving her—
she was standing in front of and just below a monumental
lion. That was the image she had in her unconscious.

And the glass in his hand was wrong. What she needed

was both hands holding the front of the chair arms, like the lion's paws. Hope laid down her palette and brush—she needed a break to relax her tensed muscles anyway—and stepped to the chair.

"The glass," she said softly, her voice cracking as if she had not spoken for days. She had almost forgotten the power of speech. Jude ignored her outstretched hand and bent down to put the glass on the floor beside the chair.

She did not get the message. "Your hands," she said next. "Can you put both hands…" But it was impossible to describe, and she reached for his hand to draw it to the front edge of the chair arm.

"Hope, don't touch me!" he ordered quietly, a second too late: she was already pressing his strong fingers to curve down and grip the silken chair arm.

At her touch, as if it had been waiting for the signal, Jude's body leapt into full, hard arousal.

Chapter 4

Her gasp of indrawn breath was the only sound in the room. Hope stared helplessly for an immeasurable moment of time at that aroused flesh, then, unwillingly, her gaze rose to meet his.

At the look in his eyes her pent-up breath left her with a small grunt, and she realized that she still had both her hands on his. She withdrew from the touch with a spasmodic jerk, and then, trying to keep her eyes from falling again to that engorged flesh between his thighs, licked her lips and swallowed.

She shouldn't be reacting like this. Male models did get erections, it was just something that happened, there was no reason to—

"Hope," he said, in a dry, rough voice.

She closed her eyes and turned her head away. He wanted her. Jude Daniels desired her. Her blood burned and sang with the information, rushing and roaring in her ears, her brain, her body. Chills climbed up her back and around to her breasts like caressing hands. Her legs were hot, melting. Her throat and mouth parched.

The wall of her hostility went down with a roar, and what was behind was revealed to her senses with terrifying directness. The heat of raw desire smoked in her blood, her muscles, her brain.

He had not moved, was completely still with watching her. Now his hand reached and he clasped her wrist in an inarguable grip. Her flesh leapt under his fingers, his touch sending waves of heat and desire through her.

"Hope," he said again, and drew her helpless hand to his face and buried his mouth in her cupped palm.

"No, Jude, no!" she whispered, because she was deeply terrified by the heat of passion that lashed through her, like a wild animal faced with a forest conflagration.

Now he stood up, his nakedness a primitive threat, his arousal overwhelming her, the dark, dark flame that flickered in the depths of his eyes melting her like wax. He took her hand and laid it inexorably on his male sex, and watched her face hungrily as her eyes fell shut and her neck became too weak to support her head. She moaned in a mixture of shock and desire.

Then she was wrapped in his arms, and he kissed her mouth with a ferocity of passion she had never dreamed existed. Her whole smouldering being went up in an explosion of flame, and she wrapped him in it, her arms going around his neck, her body pressed to his, her mouth open hungrily, devouring, being devoured.

His arms pressed her so tightly his bones met hers, but the pain was transmogrified into pleasure in her, as darkness seemed to envelop her in waves. When he tore his mouth from hers and bent to kiss her neck she felt starved. She moaned her hunger to the air, her hands pressing him, holding him, her head falling back to offer her throat, crying aloud with each thrill of his lips over her skin.

With urgent, possessive hands he dragged aside the collar

of her shirt and kissed the exposed skin of her upper breast, then, as her head fell weakly forward, back up to take possession of her mouth.

He was grunting, murmuring; words of passion and desire assailed her ears and burned their laser path through her already overheated system. "Hope, I want you; how I have wanted you."

"Jude!" she cried. "Jude!" Again his mouth came up to smother hers, his tongue licking over her lips with hungry fire as he held her head and tried to get enough of her.

She fell backwards, half onto the sofa, Jude on top of her. His aroused sex, marble hard, pressed against her body, and she moved upward against it, crying something, words she could not comprehend, into his ear.

He dropped onto the floor and dragged her down with him. Now she was on top of him, her legs spread, her sex forced against his sex, melting her, melting her, over and over again, in waves like the sea.

His hands pressed along her back, trying to eliminate the border between his flesh and hers, as if he could drag her inside his own body and so become one with her. She felt their hard, bruising pressure against her flesh, and her blood churned and pounded in answer, waves against the rock of his hard touch.

Their mouths clung, as she held his head and he pressed her body all along its length, into his. She felt his hands between her legs at last, sending shooting sparks of sensation through the clouds of desire that smothered her, then one hand dragged up the material of her shorts, and his fingers found their way to her centre and pulled aside the fabric that covered her. And then, with one long, urgent, uncontrolled thrust, his body pushed deep into hers.

They groaned into each other's mouth, and her head swam in the blackness of too much pleasure. He did not thrust into her again, but began to press her buttocks rhyth-

mically, moving her impaled body against his, so that she
was assaulted by sensation within and without.

She suddenly burst with the flower of pleasure, lifted her
mouth from his, arched her neck and cried over and over
as the waves of sweet, exquisite ecstasy coursed through
her, honey on her nerves and nectar in her blood.

"Jude, Jude, Jude!" It was her own voice, crying his
name. He pulled her tightly to him as the pleasure subsided
in her, then rolled over, taking her with him, so that he was
above her, supported on his arms, gazing hungrily down
into her eyes.

"You are so beautiful!" he cried hoarsely. "Hope, let
me see it in your face, let me see it again, come on, come
on…"

He thrust into her repeatedly as he spoke, long, sure
strokes that drove her blind with sensation and renewed
pleasure. She clung to him, writhing, spreading her legs as
wide as she could, as though only thus could she take in
the full size of him, hungrily pushing up against the thrust
to meet his body that much sooner.

She began to cry out again as the pleasure climbed to a
peak in her, and then stopped writhing to press up hard
against his thrusts as the blinding sensation hit her, a notch
higher this time, while she arched her neck, panting and
crying her surprise to the world.

He kissed her hungrily, ruthlessly. "I knew it would be
like this!" he said. "I knew we would drive each other
mad!"

He pulled out of her then, and she moaned, but it was
only to tear her clothes off and toss them aside. He knelt
between her legs, pressing her thighs apart with strong,
trembling hands, then muttered something and thrust into
her again.

She lost track of time. There was nothing but the madness of physical joy, of impaling herself and being impaled
on the instrument of her pleasure, in every posture, every

way that existed and then more, of him answering her body's wild cry of demand, over and over and over, in and in.

After endless time she had been stripped raw by pleasure, down to the very marrow of her bones. There was nothing left, only pleasure and the stars.

"Jude, no more," she gasped at last. "I can't take any more!"

"No more?" he growled, as if her words ignited yet another level of passion in him, and he thrust so powerfully she was driven along the floor underneath him. On his arms above her, he crawled after, and drove into her again, then wrapped a hand under her hips to stop her escaping him again, and held her there to take the force of his driving passion, like a battering ram against the stronghold of her soul. "No more, Hope? No more?"

Nothing anywhere had ever prepared her for what came next. The doors of her soul burst open, and a fountain of utterly unbearable excitement rocketed through her system and out to the very ends of the earth. She died, and was born, in the same moment, and her soul was naked and exposed to the dangerous embrace of the universe.

She wailed the cry of her transfiguration, and only then did his pleasure explode, burning her, and him, so that the rhythm of his pounding broke, and he heaved and writhed against her, crying her name, as the fire consumed him.

He raised his head to look into her eyes, then covered her mouth with his, and subsided against her.

They went to his apartment. What had happened was not enough, they both needed more. She was barely inside the door before he kissed her, pressing her up against the wall. He was aroused again.

"You're like fire in my blood." She knew it was true, because he was fire in hers, consuming her with almost unquenchable desire. She pressed against him, and his hands caught her buttocks and lifted her up so that her legs embraced him, and he carried her to his bedroom.

It was hot. The sun had been burning down from a cloudless sky all day. He flung open a window, but no wind stirred the heat in the room. They were sweating as they stripped off their clothes again and embraced again on the cotton sheets. The sweat made their bodies slide liquidly against each other, it soaked their hair and dripped into their eyes, they drank it from each other's lips and skin.

Darkness washed over her in waves, alternating with the streaming sunlight of the long, hot afternoon. Hope knew it was night only when he turned on the bedside lamp. It went on and on, the incredible, indescribable hunger of the flesh and the senses.

When he fell away from her for the tenth—or the hundredth—time, and she lay in a pool of their mingled sweat, her hair drenched on her scalp, her body drained of everything, she came to a momentary clarity and whispered, "My God, what *is* it?"

He replied, "I'm obsessed with you." And even then, *even then,* when she was utterly weak, worn out with pleasure she had never dreamed possible, these words had the power to stir her, and her womb clenched with anticipation.

Groggily, wearily, she struggled up. A clock beside the bed read twelve minutes past one in the morning, but it did not register. She looked down at him. He lay flat, one arm bent over his stomach, his head back against a twisted pillow. He was bathed in sweat, his dark hair made black, his skin glistening in the soft lampglow. He watched her from half-closed eyes.

"You're beautiful!" she breathed.

He reached up and clasped her neck, pulling her down to kiss him, and she subsided against his chest and fell asleep.

They awoke in the hot night and found each other in the darkness, and their mutual hunger was as deep as ever. In the morning the heat had not lifted, and again, sweating and groaning, they pushed and pulled at each other's body, seeking the solace of physical completion.

It was after noon before Hope staggered into the office. Her body felt bruised, weary, sore, and she had never been so physically exhausted. Every muscle was slack with overuse. Everything ached. And yet through her blood happiness sang a song that constantly pulled the corners of her lips into a smile.

Lena, her father's secretary, looked at her with one eyebrow raised, but there was no time for joking today. "Thank God you came in. I haven't had time to get to the mail yet, with all the problems at Concord House East. I didn't know how I was going to cope."

In any case, the mail was Hope's job. She picked up the pile from reception. "It's Jude on the line for you, Hope," said the unsuspecting receptionist. "He's down at the site."

She went into her father's office and closed the door before picking up the phone. "Hi."

"Hi," he returned, his voice stirring her so that her head drooped and fell against the high back of her chair. "How are you?" They had parted only an hour ago.

"Exhausted."

"Yeah," he agreed. "I'll see you tonight. If I'm late, wait for me." It was half plea, half command.

"Yes," she said, and put the phone down.

She worked, she never understood how, with thoughts and images of the night whirling through her head. Wherever she looked she saw Jude's eyes, or his urgent body; if she closed her eyes she felt desire and the memory of sated desire ribboning through her blood and bone.

She went home at seven, bathed and changed, packed a suitcase. She left a note for her father, saying she wouldn't be home for a few days, threw her bag into the car and drove to Jude's and let herself in with the keys he had given her.

The heat of the day was stifling, more uncomfortable indoors. Yesterday his apartment had been hot because he had not left the air conditioning on, but today the air conditioning did not have the power to cool the burning air by more than a few degrees.

She took another cooling shower in his bathroom and pulled a spaghetti-strap white cotton sundress over her still-damp, naked body, then sat down to phone Jude. His mobile phone did not answer. She knew he would be either at the Rose Library site or on his way home, and there might be a hundred different reasons why he didn't answer his phone. But still she wanted to go to him, and only the thought that she might pass him en route stopped her. She left her hand on the phone, feeling the pulse of potential connection with him.

Under her hand it rang. "You're there," he said. "Did you call a few minutes ago?"

"You didn't answer."

"I was up on top. I dropped my phone trying to answer it, and nearly followed it down."

She had a sudden vision of the little phone spiralling down and smashing itself to shards on concrete, and her stomach twisted. If he had fallen, too, would she have known it? Or would she have sat there, her hand on the phone, waiting for him...

She said, because nothing else could be expressed, "Are you coming home?"

"I'll be there in half an hour."

She turned on the radio and played music to pass the time. They were playing love songs from her teenage years, and she closed her eyes and remembered the years following the accident, when she had listened to these same songs with such desperate yearning—fearing, knowing, that it could never happen for her, and yet praying that someday it would.

We didn't wait to fall in love
We loved and then we met
No promises
No thought of time
And no room for regret...

How well she remembered the haunting ballad from those days after the accident. It had hit the charts when she was recovering, when she had nothing to do but lie in bed and mourn her mother, grieve for her lost future.

So wake me up to say goodbye
'Cause now it's over.

It had meant her life then. Her mother had not woken her up to say goodbye, and so much was over. Her sports, her dancing, her carefree life...and that future that had just been beginning, of boys and dates and watching her girl's body change into a woman's. Instead it had changed into something that would forever limit her. "Hope, I'm afraid the pain will never go away entirely," the doctor had said.

From then on, the slow understanding, revealed over the years, of just how much would be denied to her. Then this song, played over and over in those lonely moments that could never be expressed to anyone, had become a mantra of what she would never experience.

There seems to be so much to give
All through the night...

She would never have that, she had thought then. Even if passion visited her, it would never be wild, untroubled, spontaneous. Everything she did was painful. Any man who wanted her would have to be so patient, so controlled. But she was pretty sure it would never happen. Hope had written herself out of the romance sweepstakes early; her behaviour and attitude had been a constant signal to men that she knew she was unattractive, and was anyway unavailable.

Hearing the song for the first time in years, remembering that pain now against a background so bright it blinded her, she smiled and wept at the same time. Tears of joy. She thought, *I'll find someone who has the same problem I did, someone who can't afford the treatment, and send them to Raoul Spitzen for the miracle.*

Her passion for Jude, and his for her, was a miracle. The power of it was with her every second, even when she was thinking of something else. She had only to tune in to the signal, and there it was, blinding, deafening her.

Another song from her past—moody, sexy. The singer's voice touching her skin and reminding her of Jude's touch, the erotic lower notes making her think of Jude's cries and her own, when the pleasure was too much for them.

Her stomach was churning with anticipation when she heard the key in the lock at last, but she stayed where she was, the music playing, and waited for him.

The door closed, his keys and briefcase clanked on the hall table, and then his footsteps sounded down the hall, and Jude stood in the doorway looking at her.

He was in work clothes again, the dirt clinging to his shirt and pants and his sweating skin as if he were a bricklayer, emphasising the swell and hollow of hard muscle. Her stomach clenched, her body already melting into readiness for him. Behind her, a woman sang of love.

Her head tilted against the chair back, and she gazed at him from half-shut eyes, up and down his body, her lips parting to breathe. Jude came towards her wordlessly, bent, slipped an arm around her waist and drew her helplessly to her feet and against his body, locked her chin in his other hand and pillaged her already bruised mouth with a deep, insistent kiss. She felt grit against her skin, and her hand stroked his sweat-damp hair and pulled him closer.

Now she smelled the man smell of him, sensuous, heady, heightened by his day's hard labour, and shivered in delight. *"You're all I dreamed of..."* sang the woman.

His hands cupped her and dragged her lower body against his, pulling the skirt of her dress up in his urgency, reaching for the heat of her. She was wearing no underwear, and when his touch discovered it, he grunted and his body leapt painfully against her.

"What are you doing to me?" he whispered hoarsely, and then she realized he was dragging at his belt, at his zipper, and then he had lifted her and driven home so suddenly that she cried aloud.

"When I dreamed of love."

The weeks that followed were the most intense, and intensely lived, time of her life. Hope became a completely physical being; nothing had validity to her except as it affected the senses. She and Jude did not speak, except of their lovemaking, but it felt like full communication. She did not miss those other chats that a woman might have with her lover. The physical said it all. When he looked at her and breathed an expletive, when he involuntarily put out a hand and dragged her against him, it was for her, for him, a whole volume of expression.

When they were not making love, she painted him. In between, she went to the office, and did her work there in another plane, her brain working independently of her real self, which was only physical.

There was a heat wave in the city. It contributed to the overwhelming physicality of their existence. Air conditioning use had to be rationed, and in any case, no ordinary air conditioner could cope effectively with the constant soaring temperatures. The city drooped, while Hope, like a hothouse plant, blossomed. Her skin glowed, her eyes glowed, there was a new energy in her walk even when they had spent the night in lovemaking and slept no more than an hour or two. *Especially* when they had spent the night in lovemaking and slept no more than an hour or two.

The painting was of a stone lion brought to life by sexual craving. She had never painted anything so blatantly erotic in her life. She thought vaguely of those paintings she used to do, of human struggle against the elements—all that powerful tension was transmuted into the sexual in the painting of Jude, and she realized belatedly that it always had been sexual. She had disguised her own sexual tension in those paintings—as sexual tension must when there is no direct outlet, it had found another. Now it had an outlet, and it leapt straight out into the world, like the lion of Jude.

The exact geometric centre of the canvas was Jude's sex. She had done that entirely unconsciously, that first day, and only realized it later. That was the truth she had been seeking in the painting, that answered the question of her hostility towards him. If she had gone on in unconsciousness, she would have discovered the truth when the painting was finished: the source of her dislike of Jude had been powerful unexpressed desire. As it was, she painted him in that split second before he became hard, so that the painting quivered with becoming. She called it *Transfiguration*. But she showed it to no one.

When he was not there, when she was in the apartment waiting for him, she painted him from memory. She painted him standing, or lying in tangled sheets, she painted his face, his hands...sometimes, when he was too long, an empty chair by the sitting room window, or an empty bed.

When he came in, whatever time it was, they made love before anything else, wherever she happened to be, whatever their intentions to the contrary. He would come into the room where she was, and kiss her with a passion that needed no coaxing in either of them, a passion that was instantly at a peak, and then he would say, "Let me shower first," or she would say, "You must be starving, let's eat first," but they never did. The floor, the sofa, the table, the bed, even the nearest wall—whatever was handy became their bed.

Jude worked long, hard hours. The Rose Library was up, the scaffolding gone. They were doing the interior now—flooring, plastering. In the burning hot sun of that remarkable summer the automatic sunscreen that the glass manufacturers had developed specially for this project made the glass rose glow a deep pink on the outside. People marvelled at the singular beauty of this small, perfect building, and began to wonder why other buildings could not, like this one, give solace to the human spirit, rather than assault it.

The camps in the city were now wildly unequal in numbers—the architects who found Jude Daniels a threat, and a few journalists who thrived on their unpopular opinions, were the only ones now in the anti camp. The city of people loved the building, and the way it conquered the less approachable giants surrounding it by its endless reflection in their mirrored walls—making them invisible. Jude was suddenly everybody's favourite architect. Enquiries came into the office every day, far more than Thompson Daniels could ever hope to undertake.

Then, one burning hot Sunday afternoon, a bank of dark storm clouds arose from nowhere over the city, and within half an hour the temperature had dropped and everyone knew the heat wave was over.

More than the heat wave. As they lay in bed, listening to the sudden unseasonable, freak burst of hail against the windows and revelling in the first cool air for weeks, Hope and Jude were startled by the phone.

Jude picked it up, and Hope, who was lazily stroking his chest, watched all movement and all blood drain from his face until he was a wax mask. His eyes black, his voice hoarse, he croaked a question, and swung up to a sitting position on the edge of the bed, his head bent over.

Hope's heart filled with nameless fear, unable to imagine

anything that would cause such a response in Jude. She sat back motionless on the sheet, staring in silent, still dread at his back while Jude asked two more questions and then put the phone down.

He did not move. He sat motionless, staring at nothing. "Jude?" she whispered, terrified.

He turned and looked at her, his face drawn and blank.

"The glass in the Rose Library has exploded," he said hoarsely. "A passerby has been injured. The night watchman is dead."

Chapter 5

It was a scene from the empty, cold version of hell. A field of massive hunks of curved, broken glass interspersed with knee-deep mounds of shards stretched endlessly to the horizon, and above it, regular rows of trees whose curving, naked steel branches glittered with rain under the grey of lowering cloud.

She stood aghast, and it was only when she saw a distant flickering image of herself that her brain sorted out the reflected images from the real.

"Stay back," Jude ordered tersely, automatically pulling on the hard hat that was always in the car. "There will still be glass coming down."

His caution did not extend to his own safety. He strode across the glass-strewn forecourt towards the cedar stem of his dead rose without once looking up.

The ambulances had already gone. A police car sat at the side of the road, but Jude had ignored the occupants. They leapt out of their car now and shouted after him, and Hope crossed over to them.

"It's Jude Daniels," she said. "He's the architect."

The wailing *whup* of sirens distracted them all, and around the corner came the first of a fleet of police cars and fire trucks, and suddenly the street was full of men and women with walkie-talkies self-importantly trying to decide what to do.

Jude, meanwhile, disappeared inside the building.

Another civilian car screeched to a stop beside a police car, and Hope saw her father, white and shaken, leap from it, the engine still running. He pushed past the cluster of uniforms and ran towards the building, stopping in horror at the border where broken glass began. By that time Hope was at his side.

"Father!" she cried.

"My God!" he breathed. "No!"

She was frightened suddenly. He was so white, and he was trembling. He looked twenty years older. "Dad!" she cried, because he had not seen her; he had seen nothing but the wreckage. "Dad!"

He turned blind eyes towards her. "Jude," he said. "Where's Jude?"

"He's gone inside to examine the damage," she said stupidly, trying desperately to make her voice sound normal, because her father's face, his being, terrified her. Not even at her bedside, telling her her mother was dead, had he looked like this.

"That's right, he'll look after it," he muttered, and then, without warning, Hal Thompson clutched his chest, grunted like a shot animal, and fell to the ground at her feet.

Jude joined her at her father's bedside in the hospital in the early hours of the morning. He was exhausted, filthy, and had been cut on face and arms; his blood had been negligently wiped and dried on his shirt.

"How is he?" he asked. She had never seen Jude so drained, so unlike himself.

"He hasn't regained consciousness yet."

He wiped a hand over his face and muttered a curse.

The sound of her father's oxygen hissed rhythmically in the silence as they sat together, not speaking. After a while she said, "Jude, shouldn't you go home and get some sleep while you can?"

He shook his head. "I wouldn't be able to sleep. Can you?" She silently shook her head. They sat and watched through the night, but there was no change. Jude left at seven to go home and shower and change, but Hope stayed on, tired but with nerves too stretched to think of sleep.

Her father regained consciousness later that day, and the doctor assured her his prognosis was good. "Of course, it's a concern after the last one," he said. "He's going to have to take it a lot more carefully now."

"The last one? I think there's been a confusion," Hope said. "My father has never had a heart attack before."

"I'm afraid he has." He looked at her, and named the time she had been in the Maldives on the yacht. Hope closed her eyes with disbelief. "He had a heart attack? Why didn't he *tell* me? I would have come home!"

But of course the doctor couldn't answer that.

Things suddenly fell into place. She understood why her father had not told her about his illness—because loyalty and emotion would have demanded that she go back to architectural college, and by then her father had realized, if she had not, that architecture was not for her. She saw, too, why he had taken Jude into partnership.

Over the next few days he slowly recovered, came off the oxygen and could sit up. "I want you to call Barry Ingelow and get him down here," he told Hope. Barry Ingelow was his personal lawyer.

"Dad," she said, "I'm sure you shouldn't be worrying about legal affairs right now."

He didn't have breath for apologies. "Get Barry," he

said. So she got Barry, and she supposed her father signed a new will, though she didn't ask and no one told her.

Friends came and sat with him, so that Hope could go to the office and help with the carnage. Work on everything else stopped as they organized and supervised the cleanup. It was an appalling task, and the pressure was the greater because there was constant fear that there would be a wind before they had cleaned up, blowing glass dust over the city and into people's lungs. The site was soaked with special chemicals every day to prevent this, but every day new dust was created as workmen shifted the tons of glass fragments. In addition, the entire area had been cordoned off by police. Traffic was fouled, and people had to walk through long, hastily built wooden tunnels to get to work in the surrounding buildings.

Of course it was not long before people were publicly wondering what had gone wrong. Everybody accepted that extreme weather conditions had been the cause—but why had the building not been built to withstand extreme conditions?

Jude was looking for the cause. He spent long days poring over the design calculations, over the site, and over the broken glass—which now lay spread out on the floor of a giant warehouse where he was joined by officials whose job it also was to come to some conclusion.

One of Hope's tasks, meanwhile, was to locate the documentation that showed the manufacturer's test results and outlined the stress capabilities of the curvilinear glass, which wasn't in its proper place in the files. Hope and Lena and Sarah daily extended their search.

Between the hospital, the office and Jude's apartment, she was stretched to breaking point. Worst was the helplessness she felt. She could not find the documentation, and she could offer Jude little comfort, except to sleep beside him, and be there when he awoke in the night, restless and disturbed, to take solace in her body.

Then Toronto's afternoon newspaper called Jude to say they would be running a story in the next day's paper in which the glass manufacturer would declare he had warned Thompson Daniels in a letter weeks ago about unexpected late results in the testing of the glass, and advised him to modify the design to accommodate for extra thermal expansion; and did Jude want to comment?

After that everything happened too quickly to absorb. The Serious Crime Squad came and searched the office, and impounded certain files. Two days later the papers were full of a police leak: the police had found the missing test results, and a letter from Bill Bridges, the owner of Environmental Glass Systems, advising Jude that "form 31AA is on the safety borderline for thermal expansion and we recommend the use of a channel frame to enclose these pieces."

Jude Daniels was likely to be the subject of a criminal charge.

"Jude, I just don't understand where those results got to!" she pleaded.

They had gone to her father's house, where he was hoping to find a copy of the glass test results in her father's desk. Hal Thompson sometimes copied things he wanted to bring home to look at or work on. But not, apparently, the test results.

"Shall I ask my father about it?" she asked, after a futile search.

Jude shook his head. "It doesn't matter," he said. "There is no reason to distress your father." His doctor had forbidden him all newspapers and the television news. "They'll have to show them to us anyway if there's going to be a trial."

Trial. Hope felt tears burn her eyes and squeezed them shut.

"They can't!" she protested hoarsely. She meant, charge

him. "Surely they won't! You don't think they will, do you?"

He only shrugged, and she remembered his background. His mother had died in a political prison, and she knew that his expectations of justice from the state were not as high as her own.

"How did it happen?" she whispered. "How did it all happen so fast?"

"Don't, Hope," he said roughly, and she swallowed and controlled herself. He was under too much pressure for her to add to it. He couldn't afford to crack.

That night, as consciousness of their own mortality hovered over them, they turned to each other with a deep, hungry ferocity, as though sex and only sex could keep the demon at bay. She clung to him and wept, and he held her so tight and drove her so hard he left bruises. They reached the desperately sought peak together, and as it tore ruthlessly through their too-fragile flesh and spirit and they gasped and cried the powerful release, it almost seemed as if something must have changed in the world.

But nothing was changed. They came for him in the morning. Jude Daniels was arrested and charged with manslaughter. In spite of loud protests from his lawyers, bail was denied on the grounds that, as a Czech national, there was cause to fear that he would flee the jurisdiction.

That afternoon she got an emergency call from the hospital. Her father had had another heart attack. Though his doctor had forbidden all newspapers and television news, someone had ignorantly responded to his request for a paper and brought him one headlined Jude Daniels Charged With Manslaughter. When Hope arrived, he was unconscious.

Suddenly, after so much activity, there seemed to be nothing Hope could do. She sat helplessly by her father's bedside, reading the brief report of Jude's arrest over and over, waiting for nothing.

Late, late in the night, her father regained consciousness. He looked at her and she saw recognition in his eyes. "Hope," he said.

"Dad," she whispered. "How do—"

Her father smiled at her. "I'm glad I had time to sign the will, sweetheart. You'll be all right now."

"You're going to get well," she began, but he was frowning at something and seemed not to hear.

"He's lying about that letter," he said urgently.

She shot to her feet with astonishment. "Who?" she cried. "Who's lying?"

And then he seemed just to fade out. Her heart leaping, Hope pressed the panic button and held on, shouting, "Dad, Dad! Don't go!" until a nurse burst into the room. "My father spoke to me!" she cried. "He was looking right at me! And then—don't let him die!"

Within seconds, the room seemed full of people dragging instruments to his bedside, bending over the bed, pushing her out of the way and calling unintelligibly to each other.

At the end of half an hour, her father was in a coma. They warned her there was little hope of recovery.

There never seems to be any reason, Hope reflected, why some stories become big news and others fade away. The approaching trial of Jude Daniels for manslaughter became big news, a cause célèbre. A lot of influential people disliked Jude, mostly fellow architects whose feathers he had ruffled at some time in his career, and their friends; and letters and articles kept appearing in the press about individual artistic ego and whether an architect had the right at any time to put his vision above the common good.

"This is rich, coming from Richard Sawyer," Jude said appreciatively, reading the architect's personal manifesto that declared that the "end user's" needs always took priority, in the magazine that she had brought to the detention centre.

Richard Sawyer's biggest and most prestigious building had been the subject of one of Jude's more scathing reviews, condemned for inhospitable space inside and inadequate response to the environment outside: the building reflected blinding sunlight directly into the eyes of motorists on a busy street, and had been blamed for several accidents and near misses before an entire facade of mirrored glass had been replaced with something less brilliant.

Slowly the tide turned against Jude. Few journalists had what it took to stand up against the opinion of so many of the city's wealthy and influential citizens, especially in an area where expertise was not easily come by. You could not phone someone up and get the lowdown on the architectural questions involved as easily as in other areas.

Gradually it became the accepted wisdom that Jude Daniels had counted on the hope that the freak weather conditions that might cause the glass to break would never occur. Although there was no evidence to back up the idea, it came to be assumed that his reason for doing this was that the fabulous Rose Library design would have been spoiled if he had had to accommodate for such conditions.

"He should have modified his design, but artistic ego got in the way," people said wisely at dinner parties and in letters to the editor, shaking their own more level heads.

Hope hardly knew what to believe. Her year of architecture had not given her any insight into the mechanics of Jude's design. It was far too innovative and unusual for her to make any judgement based on knowledge of fact. She had only character information to go on. She did not believe that Jude, of all architects, would have refused to modify his design if he had known about the possibility of the failure of that glass.

Set against that was the manufacturer's clear statement to the contrary...and perhaps her own father's testimony.

He's lying about that letter. Which "he" had he meant? Jude, or Bill Bridges?

Between these worries, visits to the hospital, and trying to keep the office going, she was worn thin. Her hip began to ache with the shadow of that old pain, and the thought that stress would undo the results of her operations and months of therapy frightened her and added more stress to the load.

One place she did not often visit was the detention centre where Jude was held. The sight of her only reminded him of the madness of the system that surrounded him, and neither of them could bear to see each other and not touch. There was no reason why the Detention Centre, which was mostly peopled by those accused but as yet unconvicted of any crime, should be so much more restrictive than a true prison, which housed the convicted; it was only one of many irrational results of dysfunctional group human endeavour. But for Jude, it was additional evidence of the evil at the heart of human organization. Just like what had killed his mother.

In the end he told Hope not to come. Visits from his lawyers were all the contact with the outside world he could stomach.

She stayed away as long as she could. When she could not stay away any longer, she would stare helplessly at him through the glass that divided them, seeing the awful resignation in his eyes, the acceptance of pain that her visits brought, and hate herself for her weakness.

"How are you, Hope?" he would ask.

"Fine, I'm doing all right," she would say, "How… how…" And then, although she had sworn to herself she would not, she would be struggling against tears. "Jude, are you—is it horrible?"

"It's all right," he would say in a flat tone. "It's manageable, Hope, stop worrying so much. How's your father?"

But her father was still in a coma, alive only at the behest of machines that breathed for him.

There was nothing they could say. They had always communicated through the physical, and being deprived of that was like having their tongues cut out.

Soon she stopped going almost entirely. They would send each other messages through his lawyer, whom of course she was helping in every way she could.

He was allowed a certain number of phone calls, and at least they talked on the phone, even though it was only about the business.

"Johnny Winterhawk is sending one of his architects down from Vancouver to supervise the last stages," she told him, about the Concord House East project, and that was one load off his mind. But there were others that did not go away so easily.

Thompson Daniels had won two contracts in the weeks before the tragedy. Both clients were willing to put their projects on hold for the immediate future and await the outcome of the trial, but a decision like that could not be indefinite. The defence was agitating for an early trial date.

Eleanor, her father's office manager, had recovered, and a decision had to be made. She had the offer of a job elsewhere, but if Thompson Daniels needed her, she would return. It was clear that Hal Thompson would never recover now, and anyway, if something did not change soon, the entire office staff would be out of work. And yet, it seemed impossible just to let her go like that. It seemed to be going to meet the horror halfway.

Hope made one of her rare visits to Jude. These were now always about business, involving paperwork that he had to see. During these visits she would press the various sheets up against the bulletproof glass while he leaned forward to read.

This time, reading one long document, he leaned close, one hand on the glass, his other hand over his mouth, frowning as he read. Hope, taking the sheaf of papers down every few minutes to flip the pages, saw his hand there, and, putting the pages back up to the glass, as if absently, rested her own hand on the opposite side of the glass to where his lay.

Immediately the familiar psychic heat of him invaded her system through her hand, making her arm weak, her skin shiver down her back. Her breathing quickened, and she watched him covertly from half-lidded eyes.

Reading intently, he took his hand away from the glass and shook it, as if he had received a little electric shock, or it had gone to sleep. Then, suddenly aware of the sensation, he switched his black gaze from the written words to her hand helplessly pressed against the glass, and her face behind.

He was immediately flooded with passionate desire for her, and she knew it. "Hope, damn it!" he exploded.

"I'm sorry, Jude, I'm sorry!" she pleaded. Her body was melting now, as if his desire came off him in waves and invaded her, and the glass was no barrier.

He went back to his reading, but it was no good. Her head felt too heavy for her neck, she was suddenly aware of the thin T-shirt he wore, and the chest that rose and fell beneath it in time with his breathing as, again and again, his eyes returned to the same place in the document and she knew that he could not take anything in.

She was remembering how that rhythmic breathing felt under her cheek, under her hand, within the circle of her clinging arms, and she was nearly blind with the need to touch him again.

There was one way she could touch him. With words.

"Jude," she said, taking the document away, and with the resigned breath of a man who is going to suffer, he looked at her.

"Jude, we never said it, it never seemed necessary, but

now I wish we had. I wish *I* had," she amended. "I—I love you, Jude. I want you to know that…I always will."

His jaw clenched, and he looked away. "Jude?" she whispered.

Now when he looked at her his eyes were blazing with the light of anger. "What do you want me to say, Hope?" he demanded ruthlessly. "Do you want me to say I love you? What kind of a fool are you? How can I say to you *now* that I love you? Do you know what kind of weakness that would be? Binding you to me now when I have no future, nothing to offer you except ruin?"

"We're going to beat this," she said firmly.

"Fine, we're going to beat it!" he mimicked ironically. "What will be left? We have just had another postponement from the Crown Prosecutor! There will be nothing left of what I have built, Hope," he said slowly, as if for an idiot. "No clients, no offices, no reputation!"

"Jude, I love you!" she cried.

But he only shook his head, stood up, and signalled the keeper that he wanted to go back to the cells.

Chapter 6

Sometimes Hope was capable of understanding why he refused to say he loved her. Other times she could only believe that it was because he didn't. The shadow pains she was now experiencing in her hip brought back all the weight of the old sense of physical and sexual inadequacy she had lived with for so long.

Of course she *had* been carried away by the first passionate lovemaking she had experienced. Jude was an incredible lover, and in her relative inexperience she had taken that personally, had believed that it was something that had happened between the two of them. But maybe it hadn't been special for him at all. He might be used to women responding in that way with him. Perhaps he didn't even realize that with other men sex was significantly different.

She knew that he desired her, was aroused by her presence when she went to see him, but what she did not know was whether he would have been just as turned on by some other woman.

Maybe, while in the aftermath of their suspended passion *she* was discovering that what had underpinned it was love, *he* was merely suffering from sexual deprivation. After all, if he loved her, why hadn't he said so while they were lovers? There had been opportunity enough.

The summer turned into autumn, the nights getting longer and longer, nights during which Hope lay in her bed and yearned and hungered and ached for him. She imagined him lying on his bunk, in his cell, and tried to send her spirit to him, seeking and offering solace. Sometimes, in a half-dream, half-trance state, it was as if she did see him, and putting out her hands she would touch him and shiver over her whole body as if the contact were real.

Sometimes she could imagine him standing over her, large and strong, could feel him in the darkness, and she would put up her arms and, tasting his nearness, feel him lie down on her body, even the weight of him. Then the memory of the thick length of his sex entering her would boil in her, and her blood coursed through her with such deep excitement that she moaned aloud.

She did not give herself release. She tried once, but it was shallow, a lie that did not release the deep psychic need that consumed her. She remained instead within a cocoon of desire that burned and melted in her for days on end, her whole body on some other plane of existence. Her skin shivered inside her clothing, her thighs were hot with readiness for him, she was in a permanently aroused state, physically expectant, a woman whose lover has briefly broken off proceedings to take a sip of warm brandy which he is going to lick onto her already trembling body...

His signature at the bottom of a business letter when she opened a file was enough to make her visualize his hand, and if she visualized his hand, she felt it stroke her, and if his hand stroked her... Hope inhabited two realities. The one where she was always with him, and that other, the one people called the "real world," which seemed less and less important to her.

She hung her bedroom with her oils of him. On certain nights she awoke to find the moon highlighting one or the other of them, making the skin come alive. Then she would remember the days she had spent painting it, and the heat of those long summer afternoons would happen again in the room, so that she was sweating.

She painted him from memory. That was perhaps the highest sensual experience of all. Re-creating him under her brush, watching his body form as she stroked it, the slipperiness of the oils all that was between them…it was almost desperately erotic.

She painted him as an ancient ithyphallic god, his sex hugely enlarged; as hungry, painting it, as she had been when she kissed it and took it deep into her mouth.

She painted less and less figuratively after a while, expressing herself instead in wild colours and suggestive shapes, so that the canvas seemed on fire with physical and mental need. She painted fire, she painted flood, she painted scorching sun and burning heat, and storm and hurricane.

But always it was Jude she painted. Jude, who looked at her and said, "Don't come here, Hope."

"The police came and took a statement from me," she said, on one visit. "They're going to call me as a witness for the prosecution."

Jude stared at her. "You? Why?"

"That letter—that letter from Bill Bridges they found in the files. Warning you about the results."

"There was no letter from Bill Bridges warning me about results," Jude stated flatly.

"No," she said, licking her dry lips and dropping her head. God, if only she could hold him! The look in his eyes was so dark and angry, but if she could hold him…

"You saw a letter?" he demanded, as if realizing it was futile to shout denial at her. "They showed it to you?"

She nodded.

"Why? What's it got to do with you?"

"It's got my initials on it."

Jude's eyes narrowed and he swore violently under his breath. "That's impossible! You weren't even there! What did it say? What's the date on it?"

He made her nervous and she began to stammer.

"Hope, calm down and tell me. I've got to know."

"It's dated August first, Jude."

"*August first!* The whole damned thing was built by August first! I saw the test results months before that! Who the hell are they trying to kid?"

His voice crackled hoarsely in the intercom that connected them. His eyes were hollow, his face pale. She wanted so desperately to help him, and all she could do was bring him evil news. They had shown her the letter, and it was stamped with the Thompson Daniels Received stamp, and initialled with Hope's initials, but Hope could not remember having seen it before.

"Jude, the letter has my initials on it," she said baldly, not looking at him.

"Had you seen it before? Did you remember initialling it?"

"I couldn't remember. I can't say whether I've seen it or not. I didn't necessarily read everything I opened."

"For God's sake, you'd have remembered that! A letter telling me—what did it say?"

"It said that they'd now completed all the testing on the more extreme forms, and were enclosing the test results. They pointed out specifically that all but one of the forms were within the specifications of your design, but that one shape had showed unexpected expansion or flexibility, or some phrase like that. They suggested that you modify the secondary structure to allow for greater movement at those critical points.''

Jude was silent when she stopped speaking. There was a frown of concentration on his forehead. ''What the hell is Bill Bridges playing at?'' he asked himself after a moment. She made no response.

''And was it marked for enclosures?''

''Yes.''

''And you're supposed to have forgotten whether you saw it or not? Don't be ridiculous, Hope! Either you saw it or you didn't. It's not something you'd forget! If you saw it, you passed the test results and the letter on to me. Are you telling me you absent-mindedly filed such a thing without mentioning it?''

''No,'' she whispered.

''Well, if you'd passed it to me, believe me, I'd have remembered it! So if you didn't pass it to me, and you didn't file it, Hope—it never arrived!''

''But they're my initials, Jude!''

''Somebody has forged them. Forgery's the easiest art there is! Initials—anybody can make a squiggle!''

''Jude, the stamp was our stamp, and it was found in our files—what are you suggesting? That the police are party to a fraud of that magnitude?''

''It wouldn't be the first time.''

''Jude, this is Canada, not Czechoslovakia, and you are not a political prisoner.''

''Hope, you did not see that letter. It is impossible that you saw that letter. It did not exist. I saw the test results for every single form we used before the end of June. There was nothing to come, and if there had been a discovery of some kind of test error, Bill Bridges ought to have phoned me as a matter of absolute priority. I had a building going up! Now, make up your mind that if you had seen that letter you would remember it, Hope!''

He was right. Of course. Her mind seemed to clear suddenly of doubt. She had been so deeply involved with her sudden new relationship with Jude in early August, and she had begun to imagine, when the police took her statement, that she had initialled the letter and passed it on without taking in the importance of the contents.

"Yes, you're right," she said, smiling at him with a huge feeling of relief. "Of course I'd never seen the letter. I would remember, wouldn't I?"

Their eyes met, and it was only as their gaze locked that she realized how rarely they now allowed themselves to meet each other's eyes. The flame of deeply suppressed desire puffed into life between them. That was all it took, just his dark eyes fixed on her, and she felt his hands on her face, her breasts, her thighs. She could feel her own sex swell with the heat of blood, and moisten with the liquid of desire, making her ready for him. She knew, she was certain, that his flesh was hard, that he too was ready for her.

"Hope," he breathed, and involuntarily his hand came up to press the glass that separated them. Her own hand flattened against it of its own accord, and ached with the force of the current that passed from him to her. "Hope, I'm sorry I've been so hard—it's the only way to stay sane in here."

"I know," she whispered. "It's all right, Jude, I know. I won't come unless it's necessary."

"If I think about you I'll go mad."

"Don't think about me." She drew her hand down, breaking the connection. She could feel pain all along her arm and into her breast. "See you, my da—Jude."

She got up quickly and left.

The prosecution put on a methodical case. They called the investigators who had examined the site and the shards of broken glass, and heard that several pieces of one particular shape had probably started the disaster. The days of extreme heat and then the sudden cooling had been more than these shapes could withstand. They had shattered, abruptly altering the pressure inside the building, and hurling chunks of broken glass against neighbouring sheets of glass, also at their limit because of the freak conditions. The hot air in the building rushing out into the suddenly cold outside air had also made a contribution to the destabilizing of the whole. There had been a kind of explosion, such that for some time there had been some question in the examiners' minds whether it was due to a bomb or a gas leak. But they were now satisfied that it was down to a design fault, the glass being subjected to stress it could not withstand.

They called an officer from the Serious Crime Squad, who testified that several letters later to be used in evidence had been taken from the files of the offices of Thompson Daniels. A document from DeMarco Test Laboratories, each page of which was stamped with a Thompson Daniels Received stamp, detailing the test results, had been found misfiled in the dead files.

Bill Bridges, the president of Environmental Glass Systems, testified that the tests on all the various forms of the curvilinear glass—which had been specifically developed for the Rose Library—had been ongoing throughout June and July, that Jude Daniels was aware that they were ongoing, and that only one form had not proven to be equal to the stresses that might occur in situ. When those results had been complete he had called Jude Daniels to tell him, and had sent a cover letter with the full test results calling his attention to the particular results that put shape 31AA on the safety borderline. He had suggested that the structure as originally designed should be modified by the installation of a channel frame around those pieces, to allow for the greater thermal movement the one particular form proved to have. Jude Daniels had replied that channel frames around these pieces would spoil his design because, unlike the silicone glass-to-glass joint on all the other pieces, they would be visible. He had urged Jude Daniels to examine the test results carefully before making a final decision.

He identified the letter and the lab report as being those which he had sent through ordinary mail.

"On what date did you call Jude Daniels to tell him these test results were coming?" asked the defence on cross-examination.

"I don't remember exactly," said Bill Bridges. "Around the time of the date of the letter."

"How close to the date of the letter?"

"Within a day."

"By phone, or in person?"

"By phone."

"Where did you talk to him?"

"Over the phone."

"I mean, where did you call him? Where was Jude Daniels when you phoned?"

"I don't remember now whether I called him at the office or on his portable."

"Did you ever discuss the results with him after Jude Daniels had seen the tests?"

Bill Bridges pulled his ear. "Oh, ah…I don't think so."

"You mailed the results by ordinary mail?"

"I believe so."

"It didn't occur to you to send such a significant document by courier, or registered mail?"

"Not then, no. Now, of course, I wish I had thought of it."

"Why?"

Bill Bridges stared. "Why? Well, because…" He faded off.

"Go on, Mr. Bridges. I'd like to hear why you think things would have been different if you had sent the results by registered mail."

"Well, just to make sure."

"So there's some doubt in your mind whether Jude Daniels ever saw these test results. Ever heard of them."

"No...no, there's no doubt."

"We only have your word that the conversation you talk about ever took place. You can't remember where you called him, or when you spoke to him. Are you absolutely sure you remember talking to Jude Daniels at all?"

"I'm sure I talked to him," said the witness testily.

"But you've admitted that perhaps if you'd sent the results by a more certain method, this tragedy of the explosion of the glass your company manufactured might not have happened! Now what is the jury to take that to mean, except that you are afraid Jude Daniels never saw these results, never knew anything about them?"

"He knew. I told him myself."

"But you don't remember the date."

"It was close to August first."

"And you don't remember the time."

"No."

"And you don't remember whether when you called him he was at the work site or the office or in the bathtub or in bed."

"He wasn't in the bathtub and he wasn't in bed."

"If you called his portable, how do you know that?"

They called an engineer from DeMarco Test Laboratories, the independent lab, who testified that they had done the testing of the various glass shapes throughout June and July of that year and had delivered the final results already in evidence to Environmental Glass towards the end of July.

They called a weatherman who detailed the extremes of the weather during the weeks prior to the disaster, and outlined in formal terms just what atmospheric conditions had produced the sudden temperature drop and the hail.

Hope was in the courtroom for every minute, and each

time Nicholas Harvey got to his feet for the cross-examination she relaxed a little more. He was masterly, easygoing, but getting to the central weakness every time. And where there wasn't one, he made it look as though there was. They were going to win. She was sure of it.

"Call Corinne Lamont." The Crown Prosecutor looked towards the judge. "Your Honour, this is a hostile witness. We may need a certain latitude here."

As an almost beautiful blonde woman approached the witness box, Nicholas Harvey got to his feet.

"I see no reason why this witness should be hostile to the Prosecution's case, Your Honour. Quite the contrary," he said.

Hope sat forward curiously. Weird. Who was this woman?

"As she is the fiancée of the defendant..." the Crown Prosecutor began, and there was a roaring sound in Hope's ears as the world closed in. She fought the beckoning oblivion. She would not faint. She could not. It was a trick, a *trick*.

"...and never has been, and I move that my learned friend's comments be struck from the record and that the jury be instructed to ignore them!" Nicholas Harvey was saying indignantly.

The judge leaned forward on his elbows and addressed stern words to the Crown Prosecutor, and then spoke briefly to the jury, but all Hope could do was sit upright and pretend to be alive while Corinne Lamont smiled long and lovingly at Jude and knives tore at her heart and gut and the heat of her own spilled blood flooded her.

When she could hear again, the deep pink, perfect mouth was saying with a sweet smile, "I'm listed in the casting directory as actress/singer/dancer."

Oh, Jude.

"...with the defendant?"

"Well, *sort-of* fiancée, I guess you'd call it. We're not exactly engaged."

"Can you explain more clearly to the jury?"

She obediently turned to the jury. "I got offered work at the last minute on a cruise liner for the summer, as a performer. Our relationship was just at a point...well, the job came at kinda the wrong time, but I wanted to take it. And Jude said, maybe it wasn't such a bad idea, maybe we'd get a better feeling for what we both wanted if we separated for a while. So we sort of agreed that we'd take this as time to think, and then when I came back, if we still felt the same, we'd get permanent."

Hope's stomach was churning. The knives were cutting her apart. She was going to be sick. She had to get out before the tears spilled over, before she made a fool of herself...

"Under this agreement, did you feel free to look at other men?"

"No."

But she couldn't leave. She had to listen. She had to know.

"Was Jude Daniels free to look at other women?"

A flicker of a glance at Jude, and then away. "We didn't discuss it."

So she was a fool, a woman who didn't know the difference between a love that could never die and a summer fling. Hope could scarcely control her response to this final destruction of her world. There was bile in her throat.

"You didn't ask him, and he did not promise, not to get involved with anyone else?"

"Your Honour, may we know where all this is leading? This sounds like a fishing expedition and I'm curious as to what my learned friend is hoping to catch," said Nicholas Harvey before the witness could answer.

"May the jury be excused while we discuss this, Your Honour?"

There was an interminable delay while the judge so ordered and the twelve members of the jury struggled out of their seats and out the door. The witness departed too, and then there was a low-voiced argument between the two lawyers in front of the judge. Hope sat in sickening suspense through it all, and only when Corinne Lamont was getting back into the witness box did she think that it might be better not to hear this. But to get up *now* and struggle out in front of everyone was more than she could do.

"Now, Miss Lamont, if you remember, I was asking you whether you and the defendant had a mutual agreement and commitment to avoid other relationships during your own absence on a cruise ship in the summer."

"No, we didn't," Corinne Lamont said flatly, but with a tremble in her voice that made it clear she was lying.

"Why not? If this was a testing time, isn't part of such a test the discovery of whether each party can remain faithful during an absence?"

The actress shrugged with charming candour. "I knew that if Jude really loved me, it wouldn't matter who he saw while I was away. I mean, it's the bird in the cage, isn't it? You open the c-cage door to let it out, and if it's really yours, it'll come back to you. If it doesn't, it was never yours in the first place."

The witness blinked suddenly and looked down, her upper lip just caught between her teeth. There wasn't a member of the jury who didn't understand that Corinne Lamont was suddenly thinking of the cage door that she could not open for Jude Daniels.

"At any time during your absence did you have cause to believe that Jude Daniels had started seeing another woman?"

The actress swallowed, glanced at Jude and away. "Someone wrote and told me."

"Do you remember who?"

"No."

"It was not Jude Daniels himself?"

"No."

"Did it distress you?"

"No."

"Why not? I know I would be deeply distressed if my husband couldn't remain faithful during a few months' separation."

"But men's sex drive is less attached to their feelings, isn't it? I know it's not politically correct to say so, but men are different. Aren't they?" She sounded pathetically in need of reassurance.

"You came back to Toronto—when?"

"When the cruise was finished. Late September."

"What was the situation when you got back, Miss Lamont?"

"Jude was...under arrest."

"In prison?"

"In the detention centre. When they told me he hadn't got bail, I was just—"

"Just answer the question, please. Did you go and visit him there?"

The actress pressed her lips together. When emotion suffused her, Hope saw, she really was beautiful. Her eyes took on depth that seemed to reach all the way to her soul, her mouth became fuller, swollen with feeling, and the slight trembling of her chin made a dimple in her cheek come and go.

She lowered her head and nodded.

"I'm afraid I have to ask you to answer that verbally, Miss Lamont," said Ms. Holt. "For the record."

She cleared her throat, and it was a pathetic sound. "Yes, I went to visit him."

"Were you already aware at the time you visited who the other woman in his life was said to be?"

The pale blue eyes unerringly found Hope in the body

of the court. The jury followed her eyes. "Yes, I was aware."

"Did Jude Daniels confirm the rumour you had heard?"

"I think he said her name."

"And who was it?"

"Hope Thompson. The boss's daughter." The flick of contempt in the witness's tone cut her, but Hope didn't wince.

"Did Jude Daniels say anything to you at that time about his reasons for getting involved with Hope Thompson?"

"He had—he has a very strong sex drive," said the witness.

"Did he tell you that was his reason?"

The witness looked suddenly lost, as if she did not know which was the right way to answer this question. "Ummm..." She licked her lips.

"Please answer the question, Miss Lamont. Did Jude Daniels tell you that sex was his reason for getting involved with Hope Thompson?"

She made up her mind. "Yes, he did." It sounded like a lie.

"Did he give any other reason for having cheated on you?"

Her eyes fell. "No."

"He never suggested to you that he had a very particular reason for his relationship with Ms. Thompson?"

Corinne Lamont gazed at the Crown Prosecutor in dismay. "No!" she denied hotly. But she was not a good enough actress to cloak the lie. "He just said it wasn't important and he was sorry."

Sondra Holt looked down at a paper on her table. "Did you at any time after visiting Jude Daniels tell one of your friends that Jude Daniels had another very particular reason for this involvement with Hope Thompson?"

"Objection, Your Honour. What this witness told a friend has no bearing on my client."

"Sustained. Try to keep within the limits, Ms. Holt."

But the witness decided of her own accord to answer the question. "I told Marsha Goodfellow that he did it so she would testify on his side, but I was lying, and if Marsha told you about it, she's a liar and a cow!" she said in a hot rush of words.

Nicholas Harvey erupted in a volcano of indignation, and the defence moved for a mistrial, but the judge cited the jury's intelligence and the public purse and refused. The Crown was admonished, the witness rebuked, and the jury instructed to ignore her last remarks. In all this violence, Hope's heart was the still, small centre of the storm. Like a small animal afraid to move lest it discover that it is bleeding to death, her heart cowered in her.

Nicholas Harvey rose to his feet and approached the lawyer's lectern. He looked at the witness for a long appreciative moment and then raised both hands and applauded, the noise his hands made as they slapped together shockingly unexpected in the silence of the court.

Corinne Lamont stared at him in disbelief that slowly changed to fury.

"Excellent performance," said Nicholas Harvey in mocking admiration. "You really took us all with you, Miss Lamont, we were there every step of the way. What an actress!"

"What are you talking about?" she demanded, in a tight voice. Her eyes narrowed, but she opened them again in wide, innocent incomprehension.

"You even got my learned friend here, and believe me, she isn't just anybody's fool!" The defence lawyer gestured widely towards his opponent with a smile. "You really convinced her that Jude Daniels as good as told you that he was using Hope Thompson, pretending to love her so that she would testify—well, let's not wrap it up in clean linen!—so that she would *lie under oath* on his behalf. You might even have got one or two members of the jury to believe it! But you didn't get me, 'cause I know the truth! He never told you any such thing! Did he!"

"I didn't say he did!"

"No, you didn't!" he said admiringly. "Instead you said he *didn't* tell you that. Nobody'll ever get you for perjury, will they? Because that is the truth! He didn't tell you any such thing." He was grasping the lectern with both hands, leaning over it towards her, pushing his head aggressively towards her as he spoke. Then he stood back and watched her as she very obviously struggled for what to answer.

"You don't have an agreement with Jude Daniels, do you? There's no half engagement and there never was. He was glad when you got that job offer, wasn't he, though he was polite enough to let you think he wasn't."

"He wasn't glad! But I really wanted to take it!"

"Why? A job on a cruise ship?"

"It was a career opportunity! Anyone might have seen me—producers…"

"Come on! Producers? On a cruise ship? Was there any passenger on the whole list who wasn't over sixty-five?"

"Producers can be over sixty-five," she said triumphantly.

"As I'll bet you know! But not even over-sixty-five producers turn up on a cruise like that, do they? It's for retired couples taking that trip they've saved all their lives for at last, isn't it?"

The witness did not answer.

"So, if it wasn't for the sake of your career you took such a dead-end job, what was it, Corinne?"

"I like to keep in work."

"You knew it wasn't going anywhere with my client before you accepted that job, didn't you? It was a relief when you got that offer because it was your chance to make it look as though you were the one in control."

"That is not true! It was a time to think."

"And did it make you happy that Jude Daniels was prepared to let you go off for five or six months to think about whether you loved him or not? While he thought about whether he loved you?"

"We both wanted it. We wanted to get our feelings sorted out."

"Let me tell you a secret, Miss Lamont, that you might find useful in future. A man who is willing to let a woman go off on a Mediterranean cruise for six months without nailing her down to a firm commitment beforehand already has his feelings well sorted out."

She glared at him.

"But you already knew that, didn't you? As long as you could cover up the fact that he wasn't seriously interested in you, and make your friends think it was your own choice, you could let him go. So you talked about 'thinking it over,' and when you came back you intended to let everybody know you'd just lost interest. But Jude Daniels made a mistake, didn't he? He fell publicly and deeply in love with another woman while you were away, and everybody thought you'd been jilted. Isn't that about what happened?"

"He didn't fall in love with her!"

"Didn't he? Later on, a witness will get up where you are now and testify that Jude Daniels was so besotted with Hope Thompson he nearly fell off a hundred-foot-high scaffolding grabbing at his portable phone when it rang, because he knew it was her! Did your correspondent tell you that Jude Daniels was besotted? Is that what got your pride? The fact that he never felt like that for you?"

"I don't know what you're talking about."

The lawyer walked back to his desk and casually eyed some papers. "Did you sort out your relationship with him during your visit to the detention centre?"

"No. He refused to discuss it. He said he might not have a future and I should consider myself free."

The lawyer grinned.

"But I told him that I loved him and I'd wait for him however long it was."

It went on and on, Nicholas Harvey hammering away at every brick in the edifice of her testimony.

"Did Jude write you while you were away?"

"We agreed not to write, to really give ourselves space."

"He never wrote you one letter? The truth, Miss Lamont!"

"I said, we agreed not to write."

"Did you strike up any liaisons while you were on this extended tour of all the high spots of the Mediterranean?"

"Nothing serious."

He nodded. "Was there sex involved?"

"I object, Your Honour. This witness's sex life is of no relevance to the case."

"Oh, I beg to differ! She has testified that she did not feel free to engage with other men, and that she considered herself all but engaged to the defendant. We have a right...."

For Hope it was slow torture. She was beyond knowing what to believe, almost beyond understanding what she heard. She was tormented alternately by hope and despair. There was nothing to cling to, except her ability to sit there inside her stone envelope, showing nothing.

"You're a professional actress."

"That's right."

"Ever see that old Marlene Dietrich film, *Witness for the Prosecution?*" he asked conversationally.

The witness admitted that she had.

"The plot hinges, I think," the defence lawyer said, "on the defendant's wife pretending to hate her husband in order to make the jury dismiss the damaging testimony she gives, is that right?"

"I wouldn't know."

"Have you ever played the Marlene Dietrich role in that play, Miss Lamont?"

She blinked. "Only in a high school production."

"How long ago was that?"

"Five—six years."

"When did it occur to you that you could play a real-life reprise of that role today by pretending to this jury that you're in love with my client when in fact you are furious with him for letting the world know that he prefers another woman to you?"

The witness gasped. "That's not true!" she stormed.

"You would be very pleased if Jude Daniels were convicted of this crime. It would be his punishment for the humiliation you foolishly set yourself up for, wouldn't it?"

The witness hotly denied it.

"And clever and manipulative as you are, you are not really intelligent enough to understand," Nicholas Harvey went on in a ringing voice, "that to promote a miscarriage of justice of this magnitude for your own personal, vindictive ends is a betrayal not only of what you term love, but of truth itself and of one of our country's most cherished institutions. From a position of complete self-absorption and ignorance you have set out to pervert the course of this trial and of justice for your own petty ends. Isn't that so?"

"No!"

"Your Honour, I ob—"

"I have no more questions of this witness, Your Honour," Nicholas Harvey said in disgusted dismissal.

Chapter 7

They broke for lunch.

After lunch they called Hope's father's personal doctor. He detailed the number of years that he had been Hal Thompson's physician, described the heart attack that he had had two years ago, and said that it was as a direct result of this that, on his advice, Hal Thompson had gone into partnership with Jude Daniels. He described his two more recent heart attacks and said that, given the stimulus, it was no surprise that they had occurred. He agreed that Hal Thompson was now in a persistent vegetative state and unable to testify.

Thereafter they called a nurse from the hospital where Hal Thompson was currently in an intensive care bed. She had been present on the night following the day of his second heart attack, which had no doubt been caused by reading the newspaper story about Jude Daniels' arrest that had been unwittingly given him by a hospital volunteer.

"And from the moment he had the second attack, has he been in a coma?" asked the Crown.

"Except for that one moment he regained consciousness and spoke. It was after that he sank into the coma."

"He spoke? What did he say?"

Hope blinked with surprise. She hadn't mentioned it to anyone. How could the nurse know? She herself had been alone in the room when her father spoke.

"I never heard what he said. I was told that he'd spoken just before he slipped into the coma."

"Who told you?"

"His daughter. Hope Thompson. It was to her he spoke."

It was in a daze, feeling battered from all directions, that she heard the Crown Prosecutor say, "Your Honour, we expect the next witness to be hostile."

The judge nodded. "All right, Ms. Holt. Proceed."

"Call Hope Thompson," said Ms. Holt.

In a maze of fear and confusion, Hope took the stand and was sworn. As if knowing that her brain was reeling, the Crown Prosecutor moved quickly to establish her identity for the jury, while, blinking, Hope looked into the body of the court and at Jude's face. He was smiling slightly.

"Now, Ms. Thompson," said the cool blonde woman before her, and Hope was afraid of her piercing gaze and determined mouth. "You have just heard the testimony of Rachel Clarke, who nursed your father at the time of his heart attack. Will you tell us, if you please, what were the last words your father said to you before going into a coma?"

Nicholas Harvey was on his feet. "Your Honour," he said smoothly, "may we know to what this pertains? Is my learned friend expecting to show that Hal Thompson..."

The Crown Prosecutor turned towards him, and, released from that gaze, Hope began to breathe. Suddenly she realized that that was the purpose of Nicholas Harvey's interruption—to give her time to collect her scattered thoughts. She tried to call on relaxation techniques, tried to breathe slowly, but her heart did not slow, and no matter how slowly she tried to draw air in, it came in little uncontrollable pants.

"I think the witness may answer the question," the judge said finally, and there was that slightly smiling, dangerous face again.

"Ms. Thompson? Will you tell us what were, effectively, your father's last words?"

I swear to tell the truth...

"I—he said, um...something like, 'I'm glad I got the new will signed. You'll be safe now.' I can't remember his exact words. And then—"

Sondra Holt nodded. "Do you know what he was referring to?"

"Yes, he'd—after his first heart attack, he asked me to call his personal lawyer, Barry Ingelow, to the hospital. I assumed then that he wanted to change his will."

"Did Barry Ingelow come to the hospital?"

"Yes, he did." Hope began to relax. She had not deliberately omitted anything, but if the Crown's own questions led her away from it...

"And to your knowledge, was a new will signed?"

"I never thought about it again."

"But your father's words indicated that that was what he had done?"

"That was what I thought he meant."

"Do you know what is in the new will?"

"No."

"You say your father said something to the effect that, 'you'll be safe now.' Those words sound as though your father felt he was facing death, would you agree?"

"Oh, I object, Your Honour. This witness is hardly an expert on deathbed words. How many of us, outside of those in the medical profession, can pretend to know whether another person believes he is facing death when he speaks?"

Grateful for the momentary break, Hope straightened her spine and breathed more calmly. When the brief battle, which Nicholas Harvey again technically lost, was over, she replied to the Crown's prompting, "I suppose at the time I thought…he felt he wouldn't be there to look after me anymore."

"And we've already heard that your father did indeed immediately slip into a coma from which he is not expected to recover. So anything else your father said at that time would have the effect of a deathbed communication," Sondra Holt said comfortably, and as quickly as that, Hope was looking into the void.

"*Did* your father say anything else?"

"I—" Unwisely, uncontrollably, she glanced at Jude, and then at Nicholas Harvey. Oh, what a fool she was! Why hadn't she told that capable man about this?

"Would you like the question repeated, Ms. Thompson?"

"No, no, I heard it." She licked her lips. It could have meant anything. Why should she have to repeat something that would sound so damning but could have meant anything at all? And yet, if she didn't—did they have another witness who had overheard?

…*the whole truth*…

"He said, 'He's lying about that letter,'" said Hope softly, her voice cracking.

"I'm sorry, I don't think the members of the jury heard you. Would you repeat that, please?"

"'He's lying about that letter.'"

There was a brief pause, while Sondra Holt stood with slightly opened mouth and raised eyebrows to take it in. She nodded with the utmost interest. "'He's lying about that letter,'" she repeated carefully. "And Ms. Thompson, were those the last words that your father spoke to you, effectively on his deathbed? The last words, so far as you know, that he ever spoke?"

She risked one glance at Jude. He looked poleaxed. Nicholas Harvey was leaning casually back in his chair, surreptitiously looking at his watch with a bored eye, and then back at Hope, stifling a yawn, as if her testimony were a tedious but uninteresting ritual that had to be got through.

"Yes." Hope coughed to clear her stricken throat. "Yes. But he didn't say who—" she began urgently.

Sondra Holt simply ran over her verbally, as if not even noticing the attempt at a rider. "Did you tell anyone about this, Ms. Thompson?"

"No."

"No one at all?"

"No."

"You didn't tell the police when they talked to you, for example?"

"No."

"Did you tell Jude Daniels?"

"No."

"He didn't advise you to suppress this evidence?"

"No. He didn't know about it."

"You would agree, wouldn't you, that the words might have a deeply significant bearing on this case?"

She simply could not gather her wits. She had been dealt too much of a blow. Hope lifted her hand to her head and frowned. "Um...well, I thought—I didn't know who he meant."

"Do you believe the jury has a right to hear those words and make up their own minds as to what he might have meant?"

"Yes, I guess so. Yes, if they—"

"But you independently decided to keep the jury from hearing them."

"I object, Your Honour. The witness has made no attempt to conceal any facts from the jury."

"The witness by her own admission did not tell the police about a deathbed communication from her father, who was in perhaps a better position to know the facts than anyone else save Jude Daniels. I think that fact speaks for itself, Your Honour.''

"Then it ought to be allowed to speak for itself, Your Honour, and my learned friend should refrain from putting words in the witness's mouth,'' said Nicholas Harvey dryly.

Sondra Holt dropped it. "Now, Ms. Thompson, during the period in question, that is, during the final stages of construction on the Rose Library, did you have any connection with the firm of Thompson Daniels?''

"Yes, I was working as my father's temporary office manager.''

"And how did that come about?''

"I had just got back from Europe and his office manager broke her leg. He asked me to fill in for her.''

They established the exact dates of her tenure.

"Now, can you tell us about the way mail is treated in the firm?''

"There's so much important mail coming into the office that it's never left to anyone junior, like the receptionist. My father's office manager always opened the mail, and in her absence, his secretary.''

"And did that continue while you were substituting for the office manager?''

"Yes, it did.''

"Was opening the mail one of the duties that you undertook?''

"Yes, it was.''

"Will you tell us, please, exactly what the process was?''

"I opened the envelopes, stamped each page of any enclosure with the date stamp, and initialled the top page.''

"I see. Why was this procedure so rigorous?''

"There were invitations to tender and things like that, and you never knew when it might be important to know exactly when something had been received.''

"I see. Thank you. When you had stamped the mail, what did you do with it?"

"If it was important, I passed it on to whoever it was addressed to, usually my father or Jude Daniels. If it wasn't important, or I could act on it myself, I afterwards filed it."

"Now, I show you two sample letters which the police have taken at random from the Thompson Daniels office files, that were received during the period of this year when you have told us you were working as the office manager. Are these letters stamped in the way you have described?"

"Yes, they both have my date stamp."

"And what is this squiggle here in the lower right hand corner of the stamp impression?"

"Those are my initials."

Sondra Holt smiled as she gazed down at the mark. "This mark represents your initials?" she drawled, glinting a grin at her. The courtroom tittered with friendly laughter, and suddenly Hope felt she wasn't so dangerous after all.

"Well, it's my scrawl," she said, smiling.

"Is there any attempt to form an *H* and a *T*?" The Crown Prosecutor was still amiable.

"It's more just a kind of *H*," Hope admitted.

The two letters were passed to the jury.

"Now, Ms. Thompson, I show you another letter—" Hope unconsciously tensed "—taken from the files of Thompson Daniels, also with a date stamp, this time of August fifth this year." She handed Hope the letter and stood beside her looking down at it. Hope breathed again. Not yet. "Now, the first thing I notice about this is that the date stamp is slightly different from the previous one we saw. The capital *R* on the word Received is different. Would you agree with that assessment?"

"Yes, this is the date stamp from Lena's desk."

"Who is Lena?"

"Lena Thorpe-Mason. She's my father's secretary."

"And here the initials are quite plain, aren't they? A printed *LTM*."

"That's right."

"Why would this letter have the date stamp and initials of your father's secretary rather than your own?"

"Well, either I was busy and Lena was doing the mail, or I was off sick that day."

The Prosecutor was back at her table, casually glancing down, her hands in her pants pockets, speaking as if absently. "Can you remember which it was?"

"No. But the office records would show whether I was there or not."

"I see. I now show you a letter that we have previously heard was sent by Mr. Bill Bridges to the defendant's office. It is date-stamped August sixth of this year, and it also has a squiggle in the lower right hand corner of the stamp."

Sondra Holt took her hands out of the pockets of the grey suit trousers she wore under her legal robes and accepted another sheet of paper from her junior. She approached the stand again and offered the paper to Hope. This time she stood not at her side but facing her, confrontational. Her face had lost its smile. The sudden change of attitude unnerved Hope.

"I ask if you have ever seen this letter before."

Hope looked at it. "Yes, the police showed it to me."

"When was that?"

"A few weeks ago, when they talked to me."

"The police interviewed you about this case and showed you the letter at that time?"

"Yes."

"Had you seen it before that?"

...and nothing but the truth...

Hope tilted her head. "Um...no, that was the first time I saw it."

Sondra Holt flicked her a look. "Ms. Thompson, are you

sure you understood the question? I asked whether you had ever seen the letter before the police—''

"Oh, Your Honour," said Nicholas Harvey lazily, only half-standing from his position at his table, "I think this witness is intelligent enough to understand even my learned friend's piercing style of questioning."

"Sorry, Your Honour," said Sondra Holt, as someone in the courtroom tittered. "Ms. Thompson, I draw your attention to the lower right hand corner of the date stamp on this letter. Can you identify the initials there?"

"No," she said stiffly.

"Ms. Thompson, forgive me, but to an untrained eye, I have to say that the squiggle on this letter looks remarkably similar to the squiggles on the two previous letters which you identified as your own."

Jude's face was a blank, everything shut inside as he watched her. He was a stranger, completely detached. She thought of him saying, *And you're supposed to have forgotten whether you saw it or not? Don't be ridiculous, Hope! It's not something you'd forget!* He had convinced her then. What did she believe now?

"It's not mine. It can't be mine."

Sondra Holt heaved a determined but unhappy sigh, turned back to her table and lifted a sheaf of papers from the top of a stack of documents. Her junior approached and handed one to Hope, and one to the judge.

"Ms. Thompson, I draw your attention to the transcript of your conversation with the police on October fourth of this year. Do you remember that conversation?"

Hope stared down at the stapled-together sheaf of papers. *Don't forget they will ask you about your earlier conversation with police,* Nicholas Harvey had said. *If there's a discrepancy, you'll be asked to clarify.* Why hadn't she got the message?

"Yes," she said.

"If you will turn to page four of this transcript, you'll

find the record of your answers when these questions were put to you by officers of the Serious Crime Squad on that date. Have you found the place?''

Listlessly, her brain almost lifeless, Hope turned the pages. "Yes, I've found it."

"Now, just above halfway down the page is a question from the officer, which I'll read: 'Have you seen this letter before?' Now, would you be so good as to read your answer when that question was put to you six weeks ago?''

"'I can't remember. I guess so,'" Hope read.

"Good, and then the officer said, didn't he, 'Is this initial yours?' And what did you reply?''

"'It looks like mine. I suppose it must be.'"

"Thank you. And the officer went on, 'So you received this letter at the offices of Thompson Daniels and stamped and initialled it on August sixth?' and what is your reply to that?''

"'I don't remember, but I suppose I must have.'"

"Thank you. Now, Ms. Thompson, on October fourth this year, you were prepared to say that the initial on this letter was your own and that you 'must' have received, date-stamped and initialled it at the offices of Thompson Daniels on August sixth. Today you've testified under oath, and your story is different. Could the court reporter read the questions and answers out to the court, please?''

The court reporter lifted the paper coming out of her machine, found the place, and recited in a monotone, "'I draw your attention to the lower right hand corner of the date stamp on this letter. Can you identify the initials there?' Witness, 'No.' Ms. Holt, 'Ms. Thompson, forgive me, but to an untrained eye, I have to say that the squiggle on this letter looks remarkably similar to the squiggles on the two previous letters which you identified as your own.' Witness, 'It's not mine. It can't be mine.'"

"Thank you," said Hope's tormentor. "Now, Ms. Thompson, will you let us in on what happened to make you change your mind between the moment on October fourth when you were interviewed by the officer and admitted the squiggle 'must be' your own, and today, when you say that it 'can't be'?''

"Nothing *happened*. I just realized it couldn't be mine. I'd have remembered such an important letter."

"You just thought about it and came to a different conclusion?"

"Yes."

"Did you discuss it with anyone between those two dates?"

Hope's heart thudded in heavy, doom-laden beats. She swallowed and stared at the deadly, experienced woman who was her adversary, and understood that she had been led around by her nose through all of this. There was not a moment when Sondra Holt had lost sight of her goal or the way to it. Not a moment, from the time when Corinne Lamont had taken the stand, that Hope had not been ruthlessly manipulated.

She opened her mouth to tell them about the conversation with Jude, but the Crown Prosecutor was too sharp to allow her to admit it freely after having been given the gift of that terrible, significant pause.

"Ms. Thompson," she jumped in accusingly, as if Hope had denied it, "I have here the visiting records of the Toronto Central Detention Centre, where Jude Daniels has been held without bail pending this trial. It shows that you visited Jude Daniels on the seventh of October this year. Do you remember that visit?"

"Yes," Hope said firmly, getting control of herself at last. "We—"

Sondra Holt cut her off. "Ms. Thompson, did you and Mr. Daniels discuss your interview with the police at that meeting?"

"Yes, we did."

"Did you tell him that you had virtually identified the

letter from Environmental Glass Systems as being one which you received and stamped?"

"I told him they had showed me a letter with what I thought were my initials on it."

"And did he tell you that you were mistaken in thinking so?"

"Oh, please," said Nicholas Harvey. "No leading questions are needed, Your Honour. The witness has been perfectly forthright and open throughout her testimony. My friend can ask without leading and expect an honest answer. No need to put words in the witness's mouth."

"I withdraw the question, Your Honour. What was Mr. Daniels' response to what you told him, Ms. Thompson?"

"He said that it was ridiculous to think I would have forgotten a letter of such importance and that if I'd seen it I'd remember."

"And that convinced you?"

"It made me think about it, and I realized that the letter *was* too important for me to have overlooked."

"But it was Mr. Daniels' attitude that made you re-think the situation?"

"Yes." Suddenly, involuntarily, she was thinking of Corinne Lamont saying, *I told Marsha Goodfellow that he did it so she would testify on his side,* and she could not prevent her gaze sliding doubtfully to Jude.

"Up until that moment you were satisfied that you had received the letter and stamped it and that the initials were yours?"

"I couldn't remember it, but I thought that must be what had happened. Now I realize..." But did she realize? Or had he convinced her?

"Thank you," said the Crown after a moment's pause to let her hesitation sink in. "Ms. Thompson, what is your connection with Mr. Daniels?"

"My connection? He's my father's partner."

"Do you have a personal relationship with him?"

"Yes. We—we're..." She faltered, not wanting to use the bald word 'lovers' but not knowing how else to put it.

"Have you ever had a sexually intimate relationship with him?"

"Yes. I do now. I mean, we did until—"

"When did you first meet Mr. Daniels?"

"In June, when I came back from Europe."

"And when did the relationship develop into something personal?"

"In late July."

"I see. So just around the time that we have heard from Mr. Bridges that he telephoned Jude Daniels with the results of the lab tests on the glass, you and Mr. Daniels were developing a romantic relationship?"

But Hope was learning. She looked at the Crown Prosecutor. "I don't know whether Bill Bridges phoned, or when, or what the timing would have been relative to my relationship with Mr. Daniels."

Sondra Holt smiled. "Are you in love with Jude Daniels, Hope?"

Her gaze locked with the brightly questioning gaze of her tormentor.

"Oh, Your Honour, this is an unwarr—" began Nicholas Harvey.

"I withdraw the question. Thank you, no further questions."

Nicholas Harvey leaned lazily over to glance at a piece of paper his junior had thrust under his nose and waved it away with blithe unconcern. Then he got to his feet. He was a big, lionesque man, with an extremely imposing presence. He looked completely unruffled by what had just passed, and Hope immediately began to feel that her testimony had not been nearly so damaging as she feared. She smiled involuntarily in response to his own easy smile.

"Hope," he began in a slow, friendly way. "When your father said those words to you—those 'deeply significant' words as my learned friend terms it—did you know who he was referring to?"

"No, I didn't." She almost wept with the relief of being allowed to explain herself. "I jumped up to ask him *who,* but he—just lost consciousness."

He looked at her carefully, pausing, and she got the message: *Don't volunteer anything I don't ask for.*

"So for all you know, he might not have been referring to this particular letter at all, or any letter relevant to this case."

"That's right."

"Or it might have been Bill Bridges he was accusing of lying about the letter."

"Yes."

"Was your father fully conscious when he spoke, Hope?"

"I don't know."

"He might have been delirious, wandering?"

"Yes, he might."

The lawyer nodded as though it all made sense.

"Is that why you didn't tell anyone about it?"

"Yes."

"Was there any intention in your mind at any time to pervert the course of justice by not discussing your last moments with your dying father with the world?"

"No, never. I didn't think of it that way."

"Now, I ask you to look at these letters again, which have been chosen by the police from among the many thousands of letters, I imagine, that are in the Thompson Daniels offices. I notice that on the two letters actually initialled by you, one is in what looks like blue ballpoint, and the other in what appears to be black felt tip ink. Is this pretty representative of how you initialled the mail that came in?"

"No, it's not. I almost never used a ballpoint. I use felt tips."

"Why is that?" he asked curiously.

"Well—it probably sounds silly. But I don't like the feel of a ballpoint, it's just too hard. A felt tip is smoother, more like a paintbrush."

"You're an artist, I believe you said."

"That's right."

He smiled. "What do you work in? Oils? Acrylic?"

She made a face. "Oils!"

She could feel herself relaxing with each question and answer, though without understanding that his purpose was to make her relax and let the jury understand her better, sympathize with her as a person.

"Why not acrylic?"

"They don't feel right on the brush, and they don't look right on the canvas. Too harsh, in colour and texture."

"So you have a sensitive touch."

"I guess so."

"And you'd know instantly whether you were using a ballpoint or felt tip pen?"

"Yes. Doesn't everyone?"

"So this letter with the initial in ballpoint is what—one in ten of the number you initialled? One in twenty-five?"

"Not nearly that high."

He nodded, taking his time, reminding her to take hers.

"Can you remember how it happens that you used a ballpoint on this particular letter from...ah, Winterhawk Associates in Vancouver?"

"I don't remember specifically. But the date is June 25th, and that wasn't long after I started in the office. I remember I kept mislaying my own felt tip, people would borrow it and not bring it back, so after a week or so I just bought myself a supply and put them in my desk so I always had another one."

"So the police must have had quite a search to find this one letter signed in ballpoint."

"That's a letter about the Concord House East project,

and there must have been at least a dozen in that file received after that one in June.''

''There was a heavy correspondence going back and forth?''

''Yes.''

''And how would those dozen later letters have been initialled?''

''With a black felt tip.''

''So we might almost imagine that the police went on a deliberate search to find a letter initialled by you with blue ballpoint?''

''Your Honour, this witness is hardly competent to comment on police methods,'' protested Sondra Holt.

''Sustained.''

''Now, turning to the letter that's caused so much... excitement. I notice that this one seems to be initialled in blue ballpoint. Do you agree with that perception?''

He was standing beside her, putting the letter in her hand, waiting for her response, treating her like an authority.

''Yes, that's what it looks like to me.''

''Now, will you tell the jury whether it's likely that you were using a blue ballpoint in the office on August sixth?''

She looked up. ''Very, very unlikely.''

''Is there anything else that's unusual about this letter?''

''Yes, it's got my father's secretary's date stamp on it, and not mine.''

''How unusual is that? I remember we have already seen a letter with this date stamp on it.''

''Yes, but that one has Lena's initials, which is what you'd expect. This doesn't. If this is supposed to be my initials, why is it Lena's date stamp?''

''Let me sum up. You're saying that the normal thing is for a letter to bear either Lena Thorpe-Mason's date stamp and her initials, or your date stamp and your initials, but not a mixture of the two?''

"Yes."

"In terms of office geography, assuming these were your initials on this letter with Lena's date stamp, what would it mean?"

"It would mean I was opening mail in my office, and when I got to this letter I got up and went into Lena's office, took her date stamp, stamped it, took a ballpoint pen from somewhere, initialled it, and then—" Hope shrugged.

"Would that be an unusual occurrence?"

"It's almost beyond possibility. I can't think of any reason why I would do a thing like that."

"Would you remember it if you had done it?"

"Yes, because it would be so unusual. It would have stuck in my mind."

"And do you in fact have any recollection of performing this complicated ritual?"

"No."

"Now, Hope, we've heard about your interview with the officers of the Serious Crime Squad on October fourth. You did tell them, I believe, that 'it must be' your initials on this letter. Was that the first time you were aware of the letter's existence?"

"Yes."

"Were you surprised by it?"

"I was just astonished. I couldn't remember it at all."

"When you said, 'it must be,' did you accept that you had seen the letter and initialled it and then forgotten it entirely?"

"Just in that moment, with the officer pushing it at me, he convinced me." She looked at the jury. "I just felt very surprised and confused, and that's why I said that."

"How many officers were in the room when you were interviewed?"

"Four."

"Men or women?"

"Men."

"So you had four big policemen insisting that you had initialled this letter?"

The Crown Prosecutor got halfway to her feet. "If the Court please, I don't think we've heard testimony as to the size of the officers. We're not even sure they have flat feet," she said, as if the defence lawyer's tactics amused her but she really couldn't allow him to get away with manipulating the jury's minds.

"Sustained."

"I understand that you have more experience of architecture than a few weeks as your father's office manager."

"Yes, I did a year of architectural college. I was at one time planning to become my father's partner."

"So this letter, which might be gibberish to some, would have been easily comprehensible to you?"

"That's right."

"What would your response have been had you seen it?"

"I'd have rung all the alarm bells."

"What in particular would you have noted about this letter?"

"The building was almost complete and the letter is advising modifications to the framing. That's sort of like saying 'You'd better put some sugar in' when the cake's already in the oven."

He paused to let that sink in.

"Now, forgive me for casting doubts on your own efficiency, but is it possible that you received and filed this letter and the documents that we are told were attached to it without yourself reading it, and without passing it on to Jude Daniels?"

She sighed. "Well, maybe. But it would be so unusual. The whole thing seems impossible."

"Have you got any explanation of how something that looks so like your own initial got onto this letter if you never saw it?"

She shrugged. "Unless somebody did it deliberately, I just can't imagine."

"Hope, did Jude Daniels attempt to influence you in regard to your testimony in any way?"

"No."

"Has he said anything at any time about how you should testify in this court?"

"Never."

"Thank you. No more questions."

Hope felt the tension building up again as the Crown Prosecutor got to her feet again.

"Do you like your father's secretary, Ms. Thompson?"

"Yes."

"Ever gossip with her, joke with her?"

"Yes."

"Ever go into her office for a little chat during the day?"

"Sometimes."

"If you were in her office joking, and you happened to need a date stamp for something that had just arrived, would you borrow hers?"

"I don't think that ever happened."

"Ms. Thompson, did you read every word of every letter that you opened each day?"

"No, of course not."

"Were you always one hundred per cent operational in the morning?"

"No."

"So is it possible that there might have been a very important letter that you never read fully, but just in an automatic way date-stamped and passed on to Jude Daniels without really being aware of the contents?"

"It's very unlikely, given that it was attached to a—"

"Just answer the question. Were there times when you passed on important letters without being fully aware of their contents?"

"There may have been."

"And would you then perhaps not remember having seen such a letter before, but recognize that you had seen it only by the fact of your initials on it?"

"Well, but—"

"Thank you. No more questions."

"You may step down, Ms. Thompson."

Hope glanced over the courtroom as she came out of the witness box, at Nicholas Harvey, who was stifling a yawn, and then at Jude in the defendant's box.

She would never have known it from the lawyer's demeanour. It was Jude's face that told her that her testimony had been a major blow to the defence case.

Chapter 8

Then it was the turn of the defence.

Jude made a good impression on the stand. He spoke clearly, concisely, he explained arcane facts to the jury without condescension, and he gave every appearance of integrity.

"Let's just get this absolutely clear for the jury," said Nicholas Harvey. "First the factory produced what you would call a typical shape from among the various moulded shapes that the design called for, and that typical shape was tested."

"That's right."

"Who carried out those initial tests?"

"Environmental Glass."

"And then what?"

"Then when we saw what the general capability of the glass was, I completed the design within those specifications. Then I sent Environmental Glass the final design drawings and they produced the actual profiles of the various shapes required."

"Those shapes hadn't been tested yet."

"No, each of the profiles was to be subjected to all necessary tests before the factory went into full production."

"I'm going to show you a contract for some glass and I ask you whether this is the contract you entered into in January this year for the glass to be used in the Rose Library."

They went over the contract with a fine-tooth comb.

"Under this contract, who was obliged to see that those tests were carried out, and pay for them?"

"Environmental Glass Systems."

"And the prices in this contract were based on estimates made by Environmental Glass taking into account the testing that would be required?"

"Yes, they were."

"Is it an expensive process?"

"It can be."

"So if Environmental Glass Systems billed you for expensive tests that they never carried out, they stood to make a substantial financial gain."

"I suppose so."

"Did Environmental Glass Systems, to your knowledge, have those tests carried out?"

"To the best of my knowledge and belief, all the necessary tests were completed and the results sent to me before the primary structure was complete."

"What did Environmental Glass show you that made you believe those tests had been carried out?"

"They sent me a report of test results on every shape of glass to be produced for the design."

"What date was that?"

"Approximately early June."

"So while you built the structure that would hold the glass in the Rose Library, it was with the exact knowledge of how much stress each differently-shaped form of that glass would bear."

"It's less a question of stress than the amount of what's called thermal movement. The glass contracts and expands in varying weather conditions. The structure that holds the glass must accommodate that movement."

"Now, did you have particular reason in this case to be rigorous about the test results?"

"Yes, I did."

"Would you tell the jury about that?"

He didn't smile, but nor did he seem forbidding as he turned to the twelve just and true citizens. "The building was partly surrounded by mirrored glass in the walls of two neighbouring buildings. This meant, of course, that the Rose Library would be reflected in them. It also meant that sunlight would be reflected off the mirror at several points during the day, from various directions, and that in addition to direct sunlight, reflected sunlight would hit the Rose Library. That meant the glass had to be tested for thermal movement at substantially higher temperatures than would have been the case if it were surrounded by concrete. I was concerned that the glass should undergo tests that took into account not only the direct but also the reflected heat of the sun."

He didn't look her way once. He kept his eyes on the defence lawyer, or on the jury. It was as if Hope didn't exist. She didn't know what that meant. All she knew was that she wanted him to look at her, to exchange one glance, something that would tell her...

"Now, you say you saw the test results that this contract obliged Environmental Glass to supply to you early in June?"

"I did."

"What did the results that you were given at that time show?"

"They showed some variation in the amount of thermal movement between the shapes, but there were no surprises.

They all fell within a certain range that could almost have been predicted from the original test.''

''Who produced those test results?''

The results Jude had seen had been on the letterhead of Environmental Glass Systems, but as far as he knew an independent lab had done it all.

''To your knowledge, do Environmental Glass Systems have their own testing laboratory?''

''Yes, they do.''

''But the testing was not to be carried out in their own laboratory?''

''No. It was a new glass developed particularly for the project and I wanted the testing to be independent and extremely rigorous.''

''And as far as you knew, that was what you got—the results of independent and extremely rigorous testing.''

''That was what I believed.''

Nicholas Harvey walked back to his table, pausing to let that sink in.

''What happened to those test results that you saw? I mean, the actual pages of Environmental Glass letterhead that it was all typed up on?''

''I don't know. We haven't been able to find it.''

Nicholas Harvey looked interested. ''You looked for it and couldn't find it?''

''I had the entire office staff looking for it from the moment the glass exploded. It should have been in the files. It wasn't.''

''The police searched your offices, too, I think.''

''Yes, they did.''

''Did they find these test results?''

''They haven't said so.''

''Is that an unusual occurrence, that such a document should disappear from the files?''

''It's unprecedented in my experience.''

They went over every detail of the letter and the lab results from DeMarco.

"These are not the results you were shown by Environmental Glass before proceeding with the building?"

"Absolutely not."

"Were the results similar?"

"Except for the particular results of shape 31AA, the shape that exploded, the original results I saw were, as far as I remember, very similar to these."

"Now, Hope Thompson was acting as your office manager during July and August."

"Yes, she was."

Still he did not glance her way. Yet she knew that he knew she was there. She had been in the same seat every day. His back had been to the body of the crowded courtroom until he took the stand, and he had not glanced her way once, but still she was sure that he knew where she was.

"...and filed it?"

"Hope sometimes made mistakes. She hadn't been in the office very long." The whole courtroom drew one breath, waiting to hear how he would pass the blame. "But she never made an *important* mistake. She would automatically have passed a letter of such significance—especially if, as the letter says, it was attached to the test figures—to me. She would probably even have drawn my attention to it. She had an instinct for what was important and what was not."

"But she didn't pass it to you."

"No. Therefore this letter never arrived at the Thompson Daniels offices."

"Yet we've heard from the police that it was found in the files."

"Well, it did not get there through the normal methods," Jude said dryly.

He had more faith in her than she had in herself. Hope

blinked back the burning tears that suddenly pricked her eyes.

"Now, we've heard Bill Bridges say that these new results meant that you would have been required to enclose all the pieces of glass shape 31AA in channel frames. Is that the case?"

"No. I would have expanded the silicone glass-to-glass joint on all 31AA pieces by three millimetres."

"So a channel frame would not have been necessary."

"It would not have been necessary, but if it had been necessary I would not have ignored safety considerations for the sake of my design."

Nicholas Harvey made sure the jury got the impact of Jude's testimony. At last he said, "Let me just recap for the benefit of the jury: you would have been within your rights as architect to halt construction and redesign the building in accordance with these new test results, and Environmental Glass would have been responsible for the huge cost overrun which that entailed."

"That's right."

"Now, Mr. Daniels, your private life has been made an issue here." Nicholas Harvey paused, looking down at his table, then looked up.

"Are you going to marry Corinne Lamont?"

"No."

"Is this a recent decision, or a long-standing one?"

"There has never been any question of our marrying at any time."

Harvey raised an eyebrow. "From your point of view there was never a time, such as Miss Lamont described, when you were both going to think it over?"

"There was a time when Corinne said something like that as a way of avoiding the direct admission that we were splitting up. But we both knew it was over before she took that job on the cruise ship."

Jude came across as not only expert at his work, but a

man of integrity. He was unshakable on cross-examination, and Sondra Holt did not make the mistake of challenging him for long.

The general contractor had long experience of building for Jude. He testified as to Jude's perfectionism in all matters of construction and pointed out that the safety record on a Daniels site was always very high. Jude Daniels did not cut corners in matters of quality or safety. He was sometimes difficult to work for but at least you always knew what was wanted. The best.

The glazing contractor discussed in minute detail Jude's concern over the glass-to-glass joints which held the glass. He was sure that Jude had consulted the test figures on many occasions before August first, by which date the installation was nearly complete.

He also testified to the fact that everyone on the site had known and freely discussed Jude's sudden love affair with Hope Thompson. The glazing contractor had even saved Jude's life when the architect lost his footing on the scaffolding one day when he grabbed for his phone when Hope was calling.

"Did you ever get the impression that Jude Daniels' affair with Hope Thompson was making him lose concentration, on the job in hand?" he was asked on cross-examination.

"Nope," said the man laconically.

She backed off that. "Did he ever show you the papers with the test results?"

"Probably. Maybe. I can't remember."

"So you have no recollection of what lab had done the results or any date on the document you say Jude Daniels was working from?"

"Nope."

"No recollection at all?"

"Nope."

"Is that unusual?"

"Nope. The lab's not my business. The building is."

Hope had been going to be called by the defence. Nicholas Harvey had planned to show her the DeMarco test results and question her as to the date stamp, and the fact that there was no initial on the top page. She would have said that that simply could not have happened, that as well as the cover letter, she would have initialled the top page of any document attached. That, in her opinion, someone not entirely familiar with the procedure must have got hold of a Thompson Daniels stamp, stamped the document and misfiled it. But it had never been received in the mail at Thompson Daniels.

But he did not call her. Hope was sure that it was because he did not want the jury reminded of her dismal performance as a witness for the prosecution.

Nevertheless, he put on a good case. Hope relaxed more with each successive witness who testified to Jude's integrity and attention to detail. She was sure her own testimony had been long forgotten under the weight of what had come since. By any standards there was reasonable doubt, and that was all Nicholas Harvey had to prove.

Between the prosecution and the defence summing up, there was almost nothing to choose. Both were masterly performances, but Nicholas Harvey had the advantage of addressing the jury after the Crown Prosecutor. It was clear to almost everyone that he had won the case.

And then came the judge's address. "You may think that the defendant's previous history shows a man of integrity who would not have stooped to put the public at risk for any reason. But we have the testimony of two women who have been badly treated…I would ask you to consider whether it is appropriate to place too much emphasis on the testimony of a witness who is being browbeaten as Ms. Lamont clearly was…. Then we come to the witness who could testify only from a distance. The man who said, *He's lying about the letter.* Now, you may ask yourselves why this man's daughter, the defendant's mistress, who as we all saw had no idea of the existence of the defendant's fiancée, kept that final deathbed accusation quiet if she believed her father was referring to Bill Bridges...

"You have heard Mr. Bridges suggest that something called a channel frame would have been needed to accommodate the shape called 31AA, and you have heard Mr. Daniels say that a simple increase in the width of the already existing joint would have sufficed. You may like to ask yourselves whether Mr. Daniels thought of that innovative solution *at the time* or only later, and whether he did in fact fear that his design would be spoiled...

"You may ask yourselves whether the defence has provided you with an alternative hypothesis that is reasonable, that a reasonable person would accept. Is he suggesting that someone broke into the offices of Thompson Daniels to plant that important letter? You may like to ask yourselves whether in the absence of any evidence of a break-in that seems feasible...."

And so the judge tore down the structure that Nicholas Harvey had built up, and painted a picture of a man who was honourable only so long as he was not threatened, a man who used women for his own ends, who had interfered with the testimony of a significant witness, using the fact that she loved him to make her submit to his demands to change her testimony....

The verdict was guilty. The sentence, four years. Jude did not once look her way, not even as they handcuffed him and led him out.

She went to the medium security prison to visit him a few days after he was taken there. It was only then that Hope understood, at last, what the future held for her.

The ritual of metal bars, clanging gates and sneering guards was something she thought she had got used to at the detention centre, but at least there she had believed that these things were temporary. She thought of what Jude's feelings must have been as he had entered this place. For her the gates would open again in an hour. For him, probably not in under a year.

She sat in a room with twenty other women, waiting for her name to be called, for another locked door to open, and then she passed through into the prison visiting room, the only place, for prisoners, where the prison connected to the outside world.

He was standing waiting for her on the other side of the void.

"Jude!" she'd whispered, seeing him for the first time since that moment when they had handcuffed him in court and led him away. Close to him, with nothing between them, for the first time since his arrest, long months before. Other couples around them in the visiting room were embracing, and she instinctively, hungrily moved close and half lifted her arms before his face stopped her cold.

"Don't touch me, Hope," he said, as he had said once before. But though the words were the same, now he spoke a completely different language. Then his voice had been ragged with erupting passion, now it was blank, a coating of ice over a face of granite where no living thing could get a foothold. She flinched as the cold of absolute zero burned her.

"Jude," she said again, uncertainly, wanting to comfort him but not knowing how to reach him if she could not touch him.

"I don't know why you've come here," he said.

"You—" She stared and swallowed. He didn't know why she'd come? Had he imagined that she would *abandon* him? Hope smiled tremblingly, frightened for what had happened to him. "But I—"

"And I don't care," he overrode her ruthlessly. "I am seeing you now because I want to make it clear that I do not want you to come again."

Fear was cold. She felt it creep down to the roots of her soul. Frantically her spirit moved to ward off understanding. "Jude, what *is* it?" she begged, but he had not finished.

"I am not interested in seeing you now or ever."

"*Why?*" she whispered finally. She understood nothing. The world was on its head. Nothing was as it should be. He did not blame her, he *could* not blame her.

He laughed a sound that was entirely without mirth.

"I'm sorry," she tried to say, through her tears. "Is it because—?"

"Get out of here," he interrupted. "Get out of my life."

She stood stock-still then, all the blood leaving her head as she finally faced the truth. "*Nooo!*" she sobbed. "*Jude!*"

People looked at them, but she did not see anything but Jude's back as he turned from her and walked away towards the door that led back into the prison.

Tears streaming from her eyes, she ran after him. The door opened for him as she reached him. "Jude!" she cried again, but without one glance back, he passed through.

A uniformed guard stood in her path as she tried to follow. Stunned, blinded by tears, she pushed at him. "No!" she said. "Let me go! I have to—"

"Stand back, please!" said a cold voice, with a tone of threatening authority that cut through the fog in her brain at last.

"Oh, *God!*" she cried. Beyond the guard, Jude, his back to her, stood waiting in front of another metal gate.

That was the last view she had of him.

Chapter 9

"**Y**ou *found* something?"

Jude's voice expressed contemptuous disbelief. The passion he had once felt for her had lost none of its intensity, but was now transmuted into hostility. Instead of his object of desire, she was the enemy.

Hope felt it coming from him in waves. She shivered. "Can we sit down?"

Jude's eyes narrowed in suspicion. His hand shot out and grasped her upper arm as she half turned to look for empty chairs in the inhospitable room. In the centre of one wall was the glassed-in enclosure where the guards sat watch. Around them a disturbing scene was forming as men and women collected coffee from a machine and sat down over low tables to engage in domestic discussion, as if the Saturday breakfast tables of the nation were under the watchful eye of Big Brother. "Jerry's teacher is saying..." she caught on one side, and on another, "What does Dad think about it?"

"Who told you to come here?"

"What?"

He was silent, his gaze compelling.

"Nobody *told* me to come here! Who would want me to, and why?"

"That's what I'm wondering."

She still wanted him. Whatever he had changed into during the months he had been here, whatever had changed him, there had been no change in the essence that mingled with hers and caused that overwhelming, inexplicable physical and mental reaction in her. Feeling it, she closed her eyes and looked away. She had hoped to find it dead.

When she faced him again, his smile told her that he saw that movement not for what it was, but as an admission of guilt.

"Jude," she said. "No one even knows I'm here. I came because I found something. Your appeal is still ongoing, isn't it?"

He crossed bulging arms over his chest, and she thought that he must have gained twenty pounds, all of it muscle. He was wearing a cheaply cut beige shirt, the sleeves rolled up over muscled forearms, and green gabardine prison pants. His thighs and buttocks were different from what she remembered, too. There, too, he had added muscular bulk. She wondered if pumping iron was a release for his anger.

"Now, why would that be of interest to you?"

"Because your conviction was a miscarriage of justice and I contributed to it, and I would like to help put it right," she said furiously. "How dare you imagine otherwise?"

"Hope," he said softly, dangerous. "Don't say *how dare you* to me."

"Jude—"

"The only thing within your power to put right is coming here today. You can do that by leaving."

He was a mountain of iron. But Hope was stronger than she had been a year ago. She, too, had been tempered by the flame she had passed through.

"All right, I'll do that. When I'm gone, suppose you have a look at this. If you don't find it interesting, maybe your lawyer will. He can call me anytime."

She was wearing a simple sheath dress in soft corduroy, with two hip pockets. She pulled a paper out of one pocket, unfolded it, and thrust it into his hand. Jude involuntarily took it. Their gazes locked, but she stood her ground, saying nothing, and after a moment he glanced at the typed front, then at the blank reverse, flipped it back and began to read.

It was a *curriculum vitae* of one George Henry Young. She watched Jude's eyes flick along the lines outlining the personal details, the education, and reach the section titled *Career History*. Suddenly all the tension left the muscles around his eyes, and he read something twice. She knew what line he had reached without looking.

1991—present: Environmental Glass Systems
                      Woodstock, Ontario

Jude looked at her. "Well?" he demanded.

"You probably don't remember him. He was only with us for two weeks. We called him Gig."

His whole body became intent. "We hired him? He was working in the office?"

She nodded.

"When?"

"Dad took him on in early July last year. He left before the end of the month. I don't know what reason he gave. Someone else was hired to replace him."

"Where did you find this?"

"At home. I've been…cleaning out Dad's study." Her voice cracked.

"I'm sorry about Hal." He said it unwillingly, she could hear from his tone. He had no real sympathy for her, it was just a social ritual whose promptings he could not resist.

"You got my letter?" she asked woodenly.

Dear Jude, I'm writing to tell you that Dad died last
night...I know you were almost as close to him as I
was...he never regained consciousness. They had kept
his body alive, but I knew he had left it a long time
ago...

"Yes. In any case, his—uh—" he flicked her an unreadable look "—his lawyers got in touch."

He had sent no reply, no acknowledgement of her letter.
That was as hard to forgive as anything else. That he could
blame her for cracking on the stand, that he could refuse
to see her, was one thing. But he had pretended to love her
father, and he had let his death pass without a word.

"Yes, it was completely unnecessary for me to write
you," she said coldly. "Of course Barry Ingelow had to
tell you about the will. But I hadn't read the will when I
wrote, so I didn't know."

When the will was read, she had learned what her father
had meant by those last words—*You'll be safe now.* Hal
Thompson had left his daughter and Jude Daniels half
shares in everything he had possessed.

So that was the mystery solved, of who he meant by
"he" when he said, *He's lying about that letter.* Not Jude
Daniels. Her father was not the man to think his daughter
would be safe with a man who lied. Hal Thompson had
had full faith in Jude Daniels, right to the last conscious
breath he took.

Hope had asked Barry Ingelow what had been in the
previous will. "He had left his share of Thompson Daniels
to Jude and everything else to you," the lawyer had said.
That made it conclusive: her father had believed and hoped
their involvement would be permanent, and had done his
bit to see that at the very least they would be deeply en-
tangled financially.

It did not endear her father to her. Safe, he had called it, but she didn't feel safe. Every move she made, whether to sell off some of her father's effects or close down the office, had to be approved by Jude's lawyers. She was tied hand and foot to a man who wouldn't even talk to her directly, and who, seeing her now for the first time in months, still had nothing for her but anger and contempt. He had not even begun to try to find understanding or forgiveness.

Jude turned and nodded her to a table, and they sat. He set the paper on the low table between them and leaned forward, elbows on his knees, frowning at it in concentration. "Where are the office records?" he asked.

"Still there."

At this he looked up. "Still where? Hasn't the office been shut down?"

"Yes, but—we haven't been able to sub-lease the space, so what was the point of paying more money to store everything? I just left it all there and locked the door. When we find someone to take over the space I'll put everything in storage."

With neither her father nor Jude to run the place, Thompson Daniels was nothing. No new commissions would come in, and all the company value had been in the skills and talents of the partners.

He came to some decision. "Has Nicholas Harvey's office got a key?"

"I don't think so."

"Do you mind sending one over to him?"

She shrugged. "I don't mind, but why?"

"I want him to get someone over there and search through those files. I need—"

Hope took a breath. "Forgive me for interfering, but do you have any idea how much you already owe Nicholas Harvey?"

Jude looked at her.

"He's been putting in a lot of hours on your appeal, Jude, and I think you're running up a pretty big bill."

"You know that, do you?" His eyes were flat as he looked at her, without emotion, coldly assessing.

She was involuntarily remembering the first night they had met. Then, too, he had assessed her, but that had been very, very different. She had thought him hostile then, but she hadn't known what hostile was. Then he had been a furnace compared to this. Well, she wanted no more from him. She had stopped wanting anything from Jude on the day she had stood in this room, her life in pieces around her, and he had delivered the death stroke with merciless cruelty. *Get out of my life.*

"I have to talk to your lawyers practically every week," she said flatly, because if he didn't know this, it was wilful ignorance. "The firm is looking after your share of the estate. Who do you think I deal with every time I want to lift a finger regarding my father's effects?"

He took that with a slow blink. "What's your point?"

"The point is, you have run out of money. I have run out of money. I'm sure Nicholas Harvey has told you that my father's estate wasn't what he imagined it would be because there was no one managing his stocks portfolio, and by the time we looked at it..." She faded off. Jude must know as well as she by now. Hal Thompson had always managed his own investments. Hope hadn't thought once about them until he died, and by then most of his wealth had disappeared. "The house we own outright, but if we have to raise a mortgage on it, it may not be so easy to pay off when we're already stretched paying the office lease."

"I thought we were selling off the art collection."

"It's hardly a collection. We have sold the Picasso. Your half of that paid for the trial."

It had broken her heart to part with it. It was one of the first that her father had acquired, and she had always loved it. As a child she had stood in front of it for hours, just gazing. Once her father had found her standing on a desk with her ear pressed to the canvas. "I'm listening," she had gravely explained. Hope could not remember the moment, but her father had never tired of telling the story.

Without doubt it was the most valuable piece he owned, and she had allowed it to go—to a rich man who had only wanted "a Picasso" to hang on his wall.

Jude nodded and stared at her from burning black eyes.

"If Bill Bridges planted an employee on us, I need the proof," he said. "And if that proof is in the office records, someone has got to go and search for them."

"Fine. Tell me what I should look for. I'll do the search. It won't take me half as long to find what you want as it would take one of your lawyer's assistants."

He still looked at her. "Sell another painting," he said flatly.

She closed her eyes against the fury that arose in her and looked away. "I remind you that the majority of what Dad had was new artists whose work hasn't appreciated much yet." Her father had enjoyed risk in art as much as in the financial markets.

"We don't need—"

"Jude," she interrupted. "The woman who was injured in the explosion is suing. The city is considering whether to sue for the cleanup and policing costs after the accident. The widow of the night watchman is suing. It's just barely possible we're going to end up underinsured and be liable for some of the costs. If we sold every single thing Dad left it wouldn't scratch the surface of a bill like that."

Jude gazed at her for a long, assessing moment, then gestured with the paper he held. "Why did you bring me this?"

"Because it points to your innocence, Jude," she said, with slow, angry emphasis.

He dropped his eyes to the paper. "My word didn't convince you, but this piece of paper did?"

She did not reply, and his eyes lifted to hers again. "You never gave me your word and I never asked for it," she said.

Behind his eyes a thousand angry thoughts flashed. "And now, too late, you've got a guilty conscience."

"Call it what you like, Jude. So why don't you tell me what you want to look at, and I'll bring you those files?"

As Hope boarded the train taking her away from Jude again she remembered the first time she had made this trip.

If she had read it written in the sky she would not have believed that love could turn to hate like that, without making any diversion in her, as though at a certain point in its course a rushing river simply began to turn red. On the day that Jude had spurned her, Hope had climbed on the train in Kingston dissolved in tears, but she got off it in Toronto with a heart of stone.

She had no explanation for what he had done. The manipulation she had been subjected to on the witness stand was so clear in her own mind, so obvious, that she could make no allowances for Jude's not understanding it. Hope was a novice, the woman prosecutor who had faced her was an expert. Yet under the laws of the country, Hope had been forced to fence with her for a man's freedom. It was as stupid a system as sending Christians against lions, and served about as much purpose in society, Hope thought bitterly.

Jude had stood up against the same prosecutor, a voice whispered. Was it so unreasonable that he had expected her to be able to do likewise?

But Jude had not had his entire inner certainty dismantled in the moments leading up to his testimony, she answered the voice angrily. Jude had not been faced with a woman of whose existence he had known nothing, claiming to be his almost fiancée. Jude had not had his fragile belief in himself as a person who was loved shattered...why could he not understand?

She was sorry, desperately sorry that it had happened. She hated herself for the weakness that had let that woman get to her. But he had no right to hate her. He might have warned her about Corinne Lamont. He had chosen not to. Why?

The only reason Hope could see was—that Corinne Lamont could not be explained away. In that case, his anger was understandable. He had manipulated Hope's feelings just as Corinne suggested, and the gamble had not paid off. He blamed Hope, and he had never loved her anyway, so why should he go on pretending? Simple.

The alternative was inexplicable. If he loved her, if Corinne Lamont had been lying...why had he not understood?

But if Jude blamed Hope and only Hope for his conviction, he was wrong. People had been shocked by the verdict. A reporter had written an article describing the judge who had presided over the case as a "women's judge," notorious in legal circles for the ease with which he could be manipulated by breasts and sobs. He suggested that the judge had been too much swayed by Corinne Lamont's "masterly portrayal of the injured woman" and outlined certain errors in his summing up to the jury...it was not *all* Hope's fault.

She had written Jude. She begged him not to judge her so harshly, tried to explain how her mind had simply refused to work under the pressure of being on the stand...but he never answered. She had no way of knowing if the letter even reached him, but she did not write again.

Then she began to think of the day when she had asked him to say he loved her, and he had refused. Had she been a fool, then, to believe what he would not say? Why hadn't he told her? Why hadn't he given her that to cling to in those terrible days leading up to his trial? Her father dying, himself facing trial...why hadn't he comforted her with his love, if he had felt any?

He did not feel any, said the voice of hurt inside her. And little by little, the river turned redder and redder, until it ran with blood.

She never knew how she coped with the loss, the loneliness, the huge burden of responsibility that fell on her...or the terrible, burning longing for Jude that, in spite of the flame of cold anger that now burned in her, tortured her night and day in those first weeks after his conviction.

We shared a moment out of time
But now it's over...

She had played her music, but it did not comfort her. It flailed her with remembering. Vividly did she remember that day when she had sat in his apartment waiting for him, listening to this song. She could remember every detail of how he looked when he had finally come in—the sweat streaks on his face and arms, the dust of construction...the bruising hardness of his body. How he had lifted her and taken her just where they were... "Jude," she would cry softly, despairing, when she remembered. "Oh, Jude, was it *all* a lie?" Then, weakly, she would weep.

She could hate him, but the physical yearning she could not suppress, and it was unbearable. She ached in every cell of her body. She bled from every vein, every artery, every part of her ripped open and unable to heal.

It had been a long, terrible time. Her father's body was kept alive by the life-support machine; the law did not allow it to be unplugged. Hope went and sat daily by his bed, knowing that her father was no longer there. He had been released from the bulk of flesh, even if the huge machine still forced it to take oxygen in and out, still cleaned the blood, still delivered nutrition. She told herself it was no different from visiting a grave—perhaps his spirit hovered there, perhaps he would find a way to send her comfort.

But it *was* different. It was an added torture, because there was no finality, and no true grieving could happen till there was.

Her day-to-day life, as well as her inner life, had changed out of recognition overnight. Her social life had died anyway when she had started with Jude; with him gone, and her father gone, she was alone. She had to let the housekeeper go, and she hated being alone in the big house, but although she thought of taking in a boarder, and the money would have helped, somehow she never did it. She took a computer training course and then got work, and fortunately they demanded long hours.

Everyone at Thompson Daniels had turned to her for the answers to unanswerable questions, and slowly she picked a path through unknown terrain to dismantle the firm that her father had spent a lifetime building up. She wrote references, she begged people she knew for jobs for ex-employees…she did what she could, but she could not protect everyone.

Old friends had rallied around, or tried to. Her father's friends, in particular, tried to help in the first few months, but Hope was too wounded to be able to face their affectionate concern. Caring made her weep. The only way she could be strong was to stand alone.

When her father's body finally gave up, it had been a relief. That was perhaps the worst blow, that she should greet death as a friend. She thought, *Well, at least now maybe I can grieve.* But she was wrong. Her heart had been stone for too long. She stood and watched the coffin lowered into the cold, cold ground and her eyes felt scraped dry. She had lost the person who had meant most to her in the world, but mourning was denied her.

She had written Jude to tell him, wondering if he would ask for day release to attend the funeral. He did not even answer. Maybe his love for her father, too, had been invented, dissembled for a purpose. She no longer cared.

Her father's will was simply one more blow of life's sword against the stone of her heart. There was a spark, but it flickered once and was gone.

After a while, she picked up her paints again. She made a studio for herself in the attic and hid away there for hours on end. Everything she painted was sterile, but what did it matter? She could forget sometimes, forget who she was, forget she had ever thought she loved.

Now all that's left is how to end
How to begin.

Finally, the yearning had stopped, too. But there had been no new beginning for Hope. There were only endings. Shutting up the office. Burying her father. And then, clearing out the things in his desk.

When she returned to the prison visiting room a week later, her briefcase bulging with every working drawing Gig Young had executed, the office records that should pin down the exact time of his tenure and the area of his operations, as well as other random files Hope did not understand the significance of, the visiting room guard would not allow her to take them in to him.

"Why not?" she demanded.

"Because we can't allow it," said the woman flatly.

Hope had never before met that voice of petty authority, but it was instantly recognizable. She stuffed the briefcase into a locker as instructed, and went in empty-handed.

Jude swore when she told him what had happened, a string of profanity that shocked her. "Maybe I could come back on a day when that woman's not on duty," she offered quietly.

"They don't give us advance notice of the guards' work

schedule.'' They sat staring at each other, Jude's eyes burning into hers. "I have got to get out of here," he said. His voice was all the more terrible for being quiet. The tension in him was electric.

"Jude," she cautioned softly, frightened.

"There's nothing they won't do to stop me proving I'm innocent," he said. "I'll never get that information while I'm in here."

"But your parole hearing is coming up. There's a good chance you'll get parole, isn't there?"

"Do you think so?" Jude asked dryly. He sounded as if he were certain there was not.

"Why shouldn't there be? It's based on behaviour, isn't it?" She looked into his eyes and wondered whether his anger at the injustice of his conviction ever expressed itself in self-defeating violence.

"It's based on three things. Good behaviour, community support, and a proper display of remorse. One out of three is not an overwhelming score."

"What's community support?"

"It means a stable environment to return to. Something that might keep a man on the straight and narrow," he told her, with a dry sarcasm in his voice that she did not understand the significance of.

"Jude, if there's anything I can do—there must be something." She supposed she owed him that much, however he had hurt her. If she could undo some of the damage she had done, by helping him get early parole, of course she must. She did not love him anymore, but that did not blind her to justice.

He leaned across the table and grasped her wrist. "You can help me," he whispered.

"What do you want me to do?" The message of his touch, carried by blood and nerves, travelled to all the usual destinations within her, but she fought down her response.

"If I—" The intensity in him was catching. Her own

heart was suddenly beating in hard heavy thumps. "For what I'm planning I need a safe house. If I turn up on the doorstep, will you let me in, and not ask any questions? I won't stay."

She gasped, a hollow, hoarse noise like a death rattle. "Jude!" she whispered. "What are you talking about?"

"Never mind what I'm talking about. I won't stay long. I'll need a change of clothing and some money, as much as you can spare. Will you do it?"

"Jude, but then you'd have the police after you! How can you prove anything if you're on the run? Wouldn't it be better to—"

"Never mind your advice. I want out of here, and I'm going to do whatever it takes, with you or without you. If I'm free I can prove my innocence, and then it won't matter how I got out. Now, give me your answer."

She thought of what Corinne Lamont had said on the witness stand. Had he used her? Was he using her now? Who was he? She really did not know him, had never known him. Even less now than before. What was in his heart?

"Jude…"

"Hope, I'm innocent. It's wrong that I'm here. It's a mistake. If I get out, I'll find the proof."

She was stirred by unnameable emotions. "Exactly what would you want me to do?"

"I told you, money and clothes. You would have to start making small withdrawals now. If they see that you've made a big cash withdrawal, they'll suspect you immediately. Can you get me some clothes?"

"Your stuff's all in Dad's bedroom."

He frowned in anger. "*What?* What's it doing there?"

"When you gave up your apartment we put the furniture into storage, but there was no knowing when you might need…well, anyway, that's where it is."

"Who did you arrange this with?" he demanded furiously. "Not Nick Harvey?"

"His secretary was given the job of seeing to your place. She...asked for my help."

He swore.

She fired up suddenly. "Jude, it's half your house! She had the right to ask and I did not have the right to refuse! You have no other home now—if you do make parole, where are you going to go?"

"Into a halfway house, of course. What did you imagine—that they would let a dangerous criminal like me straight out onto the street?"

This deflated her anger. "Oh. Well, I didn't know that."

"Now you do," he said dismissively, and returned to the main point. "I'll also need those files you've collected, and keys to the office. That's all I need. That, and you keeping your mouth shut when they come to ask you questions."

His eyes fixed her, dark, intent, full of more messages than she could ever hope to disentangle. She swallowed convulsively, torn beyond imagining, opened her mouth and closed it.

"Come on, Hope, make up your mind."

Again she dropped her eyes. "Jude, it's wrong. I'm so sure that this is the wrong way to go about it. Why don't you—I mean, if your parole date is next *month*, why don't you just concentrate on that? You've put up with it this long, you can wait another month, can't you?"

A muscle in his jaw tightened. "I could wait a month if I thought I'd get it. But I won't get it."

"Why not?"

"I told you. I'll be showing no remorse for the crime."

"But you're innocent."

"And if I tell them I'm innocent, that my conviction was justice set on its ear, to the parole board that's lack of remorse."

Her head still bent, she looked up at him. "Can't you fake the remorse, Jude? For the sake of your freedom?"

"I am not going to lie to those bastards about having killed a man." He spoke with calm, cold fury and she knew he was unshakeable.

"Well, Jude, a lot of people are saying now—you didn't do it. Somebody was writing in the paper about unsafe convictions just the other day and used you as a prime example. The parole board must know that. Are you sure they won't listen if you tell them you're innocent?"

He looked at her.

"Jude, this is not Czechoslovakia under a repressive regime. This is not the Stalin show trials. This is Canada."

"People are the same all over the world. Why do you think that woman wouldn't let you bring in those papers today?"

She looked at him levelly. "Because she is a petty official with petty power over others and she likes to exercise it. If you're thinking she had instructions from above, all I can say is, I doubt it very much. The other guard would have let me bring them in. I could see that in his eyes."

He looked at her as if unsure whether to believe her.

"Now, what do you mean about not having community support? You have friends."

"But I don't have the love of a good woman, Hope," he said dryly.

"I can't believe that's the only thing they look for."

"No, but it's the most convincing. They figure that's what'll keep a man on the straight and narrow. How little they know, eh?"

She ignored that. "What would we have to do to convince them that you—" she swallowed "—had the love of a good woman?"

His dark intent gaze was fully arrested as he stared at

her. ''The most certain thing would be marriage,'' he said with slow precision; and then, as if he knew her answer, he drawled, ''So, Hope, which would you rather do to put right what you put wrong—marry me, or just give me some money and turn a blind eye?''

Chapter 10

"That's blackmail!"

"Is it?"

"You're as good as saying it's one or the other!" she choked.

He shook his head, unimpressed by her panic. "You offered to help. If you don't want to help, you are capable of seeing the alternatives without me outlining them for you."

"You're saying if I don't marry you you'll—" She broke off, aware that her anxious voice might alert the guards, who had microphone access to each table.

"And what's that to you, Hope?" Jude asked coldly.

What it was to her was that he had made it her business now, by telling her. Nothing more. "If I know about it beforehand—"

"Call the police," he advised. "Tell them what I'm planning. Then your ass is covered."

"How dare you! You know damned well I won't do that!"

"Won't you?" Jude shrugged as if he didn't believe her,

but didn't care. "Then don't. If you don't tell them I told you, believe me, I won't."

"And if I refuse to help you, what will you do?"

His eyes narrowed. "I'll get by without you," he promised flatly. "I don't *need* you, Hope, now or ever."

"I hate you!" The words involuntarily erupted from her.

He laughed. "Why? Because I'm not still panting with need for you? Is that what you wanted to see?"

"No, it is not!"

"Sorry to disappoint you, but the scales fell from my eyes when you looked at me from the witness stand and it was there in your face for anybody to read that you thought I'd set you up."

Her eyes widened. "I didn't!" she protested.

"No, and they didn't say *guilty,* either," Jude said with angry irony. "The whole of this past year has been a hallucination! We're still in bed drinking each other's sweat and trying to pound ourselves into oblivion as the only escape from obsession with our own pleasure!"

Sensation rippled through her at the unexpected assault of his words. She grunted.

"Shut up!" he whispered fiercely. "*This* is the reality." His finger hammered the table. "The hallucination was then, me inside you and thinking I'd reached bloody nirvana. Thinking you had, too. Wasn't it!"

He was beating her with words. She shivered, half with fear, half with need. But she had the strength to say, "No."

"No? It wasn't a hallucination? I push into you and you moan as if my sex is a torch and your body is gasoline, and that's real? You felt it? You can remember it?"

"Jude," she begged. Sensation leapt up and down her body now with no path or order: here, there and everywhere she puffed into agonizing need and life. "Don't! Not here!"

"I want to know whether you remember it," he said, his

voice rough and hard. "On the floor, the table, up against the door, Hope. You were there?"

"What are you trying to do?" she croaked.

"I'm trying to find out who was there with me. I want to know where you were then, when I couldn't get inside you far enough...you were painting once, remember that day?"

"Yes," she said, knowing which of the many days on which she had painted he was referring to. "Please. Don't."

"You put your brush down and came over to me, and you took me in your mouth as if I were water in a desert. You remember that?" he rasped. She said nothing. "That look in your eyes, I thought I'd never forget it. I've never been so moved in my life." He cursed, as if trying to destroy the grip of the memory he had unleashed. "All it was was my sex in your mouth, but it was as if you had my heart in your hand, squeezing...I wept. Remember that? I cried as if you'd torn my chest open and ripped out my heart. Have you forgotten that?"

"No." The memory beat upon her. Her eyes burned.

"No. But you forgot it that day on the stand, didn't you? That day when you wondered if Corinne was telling the truth and everything I'd done had been a trick to fool you into perjuring yourself for me."

His eyes were black, his gaze so cold it seared her.

"Jude, I'm sorry, I'm sorry, I'm *sorry*." She could no longer hold back the tears. They spilled over onto her cheeks, burning her like acid. "Please!" she begged. She reached out a hand and stretched it across the table to where his own hands were linked between his knees.

"I told you once before, don't touch me, Hope," he said between his teeth. But it wasn't once, it was twice. She lifted her head, looking into his eyes, remembering the first time when he had said those words, so long ago, so far away and then she remembered the second time.

She withdrew her hand. The terrible rejection in him gave her strength somehow. She sat straight and looked into his eyes. "All right, Jude, what do you want from me?" she said, ignoring the tears on her face. "What do you want me to do?"

She felt she hated him more than ever now, not only for what he demanded of her, but for the yearning he had released in her with the shock of his words. She had been stone, but now a core of lava erupted in her. She could no longer hide from, or control, the burning physical longing for him.

It was because he had admitted it had meant something to him. For the first time he had told her, in words, what those days and nights had meant to him. Hope only half believed him, but even that half was enough to undermine her. She had learned to cope during the past months through convincing herself it had been a lie, and if she gave that up, what defence did she have against his repudiation of her?

She began to remember, without any control, the minute details of their weeks of passion. Her body came to life, and she could not prevent it. The yearning suffocated her, more terrible now because of the possibility that he also felt it.

With wooden determination she filled out the marriage licence application and went to interviews with Jude's "prison counsellor," and talked to parole board members to convince them of his community support, smiling determinedly, playing the part of the good woman who would make sure her man kept to the straight and narrow after this, without, of course, actually admitting that he had ever gone off it.

She knew, somewhere in her, that she was setting up torment for herself. To agree to this madness when she hated Jude and felt nothing for him was bad enough. To do it when the old torrent of desire had been uncovered in her, not dead, merely bricked over, must be an act of madness.

Yet she was driven to go through with it. She told herself she was getting Jude out of one prison by putting herself into another, and yet she went blindly on with it.

Her painting was no longer sterile. It was bleak, tormented, angry and yearning, but at least it was alive. Abruptly, one day, she tired of the half-world of ignorance. She had not shown anyone any of her work since Cannes, fearing as much to be told that she did not have talent as to be told that she did.

Suddenly, she had the strength to know. She thought, *If I'm going to marry Jude like this, I have to know who I am first.*

The man from whom her father had bought most of his collection was an art dealer who owned two galleries. It was Daniel who had sold the Picasso for her when they had needed the money, and it was natural to turn to him now.

Girding her loins to face the truth, because she trusted Daniel's opinion and because he would be honest with her, Hope asked him to look at some of her work and tell her whether it was worth going on.

"Well, Hope," he said, when he had gazed mostly in silence for so long she had convinced herself that he was looking for gentle ways to tell her she was a gifted amateur. "I can't say I'm surprised, because your father used to show me work you had done in high school." He nodded. "I'm grateful that you came to me. It'll give me personal as well as professional pleasure to launch you."

Hope stood blinking at him as he reached into his jacket pocket and pulled out a little diary. Silence fell as he pondered its pages. "I think—how many finished canvases have you got now? I think about twenty-five, yes? I'm sorry

I haven't got a more immediate date, because you're virtually ready now, but gallery calendars don't allow for spontaneous combustion. I'd like to put you in the Village Gallery, but the first date I have is a year from next January. Just under eighteen months. How does that suit you?''

She stared at him. The Village Gallery was every new artist's dream. "What, a show of my own?" she gasped.

"I might be able to slip an introductory few paintings into a joint show earlier than that, but I'll want to think about that. It might be better to introduce you with your own show. Now, if you can give me another half dozen canvases..."

She swallowed, and said, "I can't show all of these. Not the...ones of Jude. They're—can we leave those out?"

"More than half of what you've got are of Jude."

"Yes. They're—private."

He stared at her, as if hearing a language he had once studied and was trying to remember. After a minute he seemed to have deciphered it. "Right. Well, in that case, I'll need more than another half dozen. I'll need at least thirty I can choose freely from, Hope, so—" he smiled "—so you'd better get down to work. Eighteen months always seems longer looking forward than looking back, and do I understand that you have a demanding day job?"

"Yes. I need it."

"Get down to work when you can, then. I'll check back with you in a few months to see how you're progressing. If there's not enough time for you we'll push the date back then."

One summer morning Hope Thompson passed through a series of clanging prison gates and for the first and last time entered the prison yard, where a little chapel stood in the centre of a plot of grass. Jude stood waiting with a prison officer. He moved towards her when he saw her, meeting her halfway.

"Darling," he said, loud enough for the official to hear. One hand came up to grip her upper arm and simultaneously drew her closer and kept her at that distance, and his mouth pressed against hers. Hope had not been expecting it, not yet. Her guard was down, and his nearness ignited her. She opened her mouth under his in raw hunger, and her hand clutched his shoulder. Jude drew away from her, lifted his head, and stared at her.

"Don't mistake what I do," he advised her softly, and the ice in his eyes froze the heat in her blood. She knew he meant *Don't imagine that this is passion, or even lust.*

"Just making it look good," she hissed at him. "Or would you prefer it if they thought I was frigid?"

"You *are* frigid," he breathed. "Where it counts—in the heart."

"Just so long as you understand that," she returned coldly. She would not give him the satisfaction of knowing he hurt her. That was all she had left now.

Jude turned and led her back to the prison officer. Hope had met him before. "Hi, Grant," she said smilingly, trying to look like a happy bride instead of a woman taking part in a bitter travesty.

"Hi, Hope. All ready for the big day?" He was trying to be jovial, trying to pretend for them that this was an ordinary marriage, not something taking place in a prison yard with a groom who was a convict. His words fell flat, but she pretended to believe him.

"Too late now if I'm not," she smiled.

"That's right," said Jude. He was smiling, too, but between them the words had meaning that Grant did not see. "Too late now."

Hope shivered, though the sunlight was bright.

She was wearing a cream-coloured trouser suit with a plain cream silk bodice underneath that left her neck and upper chest bare, plain beige low-heeled shoes. Her red hair was drawn back and held in a floppy cream silk ribbon that flowered behind her head.

And that was enough fakery. She carried no flowers, wore no hat or veil. Which was just as well, because compared to Jude she was already overdressed. He wore a black short-sleeved shirt, open at the neck, and black suit trousers. The jacket of his old suit no longer fitted him.

He was dark, and darkly tanned. She was as pale as the cream silk she wore, her hair and eyes the only splash of colour about her.

"Beauty and the Beast, eh?" Grant said with another attempt at joviality, standing back to look at them. "Ah, here's the Rev." He left them to go and meet the prison chaplain, who now stood waiting for a guard to push the control that would open the massive metal gate giving access to the yard.

Jude cast a glance sideways at Hope. "Beauty," was all he said, but his voice was so full of ironic contempt that she felt sick.

"Beast!" she returned, in a half-whisper.

His eyebrows went up. "Believe it," he warned her, and for long seconds the air between them was filled with the deafening silence of unspoken accusations, unvoiced fury.

"Right!" enthused Grant, rubbing his hands as he approached them again with the minister. "Well, I think we're ready now!"

It was not a nightmare, just one of those dreams that leaves you feeling slightly sick and apprehensive for no reason that you can remember. Hope smiled and was introduced to the minister and listened without taking in more than one word in five to the brief discussion that followed.

"Now, I have the civil...but it's...and if there's no reason...so if you've both been baptized I'll be quite happy..."

"I was born in Soviet Czechoslovakia. I was not baptized," she heard Jude say.

"Ah, I see. But if you…"

"Oh, yes," said Jude. His voice intruded on her blankness. She could not shut him out. "You'd prefer that, wouldn't you, darling?" he was saying, and only she knew, and he knew, that he had devised some additional torture for her this day. She did not know what, but she would find out soon enough.

"Is that what you'd like, Hope?" The minister was smiling approvingly at her, and she smiled brightly back.

"Oh, yes, of course," she said.

"Now, if we can just have the other witness…"

A guard was summoned from somewhere, and his ill-fitting beige uniform and the deliberately emphasized jangle of keys and handcuffs at his waist put the finishing touches to the ugly unreality of the scene as they all stepped inside the little chapel.

The minister arranged them in front of the altar, Hope at Jude's left, Grant beside her, the guard on Jude's right. The guard was snapping his fingers impatiently, whistling soundlessly, rocking on his leg so that the faint jangling of those handcuffs continued. One of the breed of guards who hated all inmates, she saw, determined to rob the romantic scene of its meaning as far as it lay in his power.

It was not a romantic scene, it was already as coldly cynical as a marriage service could get, but nevertheless the sheer villainy of the man got to Hope. Jude was in his power, he was telling her silently. *Your fiancé isn't even a man. He's my prisoner, he can't protect you from anything I do without suffering for it later.*

Instinct told her that she, also, was powerless to confront him. Even if she only asked him to be quiet, Jude might have to pay for that. As the minister found his place in his book, Hope bent slightly forward around Jude and smiled at the guard.

"Did you come by bus, or did you bring your own lunch?" she asked.

"What?" Everything seized in him, his body ceasing to move as his brain involuntarily began to grapple with the irrational. "What?" he repeated, staring at her.

Still smiling, she opened her eyes at him, then turned back to the minister.

"Dearly Beloved, we are gathered here in the sight of God and the presence of these witnesses to join together this man and this woman in holy matrimony," she heard. Her mouth opened and her eyes closed and she only barely managed to hold back the instinctive protest that formed in her throat. He had chosen the religious ceremony. That was what he had done.

She looked up at Jude. He was looking at her, his mouth half smiling, a glint of pure enmity in his eyes; this was his deliberately chosen added torment for her. A dark mockery to underline the utter travesty of this marriage. And his eyes told her that he did not care if she cracked and halted the ceremony. He might even welcome it.

She faced the minister again, but now she could not keep the comparison from the forefront of her mind. The might-have-been. If the Rose Library had not exploded, she could not prevent herself thinking, she might well have stood in another church somewhere with Jude beside her...it might have happened. Even on this exact day. This ceremony now was the negative image of that other that had once been possible. Then the church would have been filled to overflowing, her father would have been beside her...and there would have been love in her heart and in Jude's.

"Jude Miloš Daniels, do you take this woman..."

She did not look at him. She could only fix her gaze on the minister and pray that she could get through this without screaming at him to stop.

"...in sickness and in health..."

"I do," said Jude, and the vibration of his deep voice

trembled down her spine. Oh, if only they could go back to that other life, if it could be real...

"I, Jude Miloš Daniels, take thee, Hope Antonia Russell Thompson..."

She looked up into that rock-hard face and with a thrill of fear the thought came to her...*He really means it. He takes me, to have and to hold. But not to love and to cherish. He wants me close so that he can punish me.*

They had timed the ceremony to give them an hour in the visiting room afterwards, not because either of them wanted it, but because Jude's counsellor had taken it for granted that they did. But instead of leading them back towards the prison block, he began shepherding them down the length of the prison yard.

After a few moments, their destination became obvious, to Jude if not to Hope. He was leading them to a small trailer that sat in isolation near the high prison wall.

Jude's step faltered, and he glanced at the man beside him. "What's this?" he asked softly.

"A little surprise from me," said Grant. "Consider it the prison's wedding gift to you."

"What is it?" whispered Hope, and with a broad grin Grant turned to her and explained: as a special surprise he had arranged for them to have a few hours alone in the "conjugal visits house." Jude had not applied for the privilege, it was a special favour from the prison officer himself, he told her as he led the way to the little house. A last-minute surprise for them both.

Hope was filled with such disquiet and dismay she could scarcely conceal it. She gasped in a breath and her eyes flew to Jude's wooden countenance. "Oh, but—" she began.

But there was nothing to say. She stared at the ground as they walked, and resolutely smiled. She knew she should put her hand on Jude's arm, should hang on him, but it was beyond her to touch him. Grant unlocked the door, and stood aside to let Hope enter, then Jude. He followed them in. They stepped inside a conventional motorhome kitchen/lounge, done in pink and cream.

"Mostly the wives bring in groceries when they come for a weekend visit," Grant told Hope. "But of course you and Jude didn't know about this. The guys took up a collection and asked me to get you a few things."

On the counter there was a jar of instant coffee, a loaf of bread, a packet of cookies. Grant opened the fridge and indicated a half magnum of champagne with a gesture like a conjuror. "That stuff's illegal in here, so I never saw it," he said with a grin.

"It's very, very kind of everyone," Hope said in a stifled voice. "Will you tell all the—everyone that we're just overwhelmed?"

"You bet. Now I'm going to make myself scarce," Grant promised with a grin. He was putting her awkwardness down to bridal jitters. Not every bride wanted to spend her wedding afternoon in a trailer that was the focus of several hundred men's thoughts, however politely and resolutely they all averted their eyes. "You don't want to spend any more time with me. Bathroom's there...bedroom...well, you know."

He solemnly handed Jude the key to the door. "Three o'clock, Jude. I'll be back then." The door closed behind him.

Silence settled on them like a new fall of thick snow. Hope looked at the floor, the window, the wall, anywhere but at Jude. He was standing where Grant had left him, a statue in black basalt.

"Shall I just go?" she asked after an intolerable time. She glanced at him then, to discover that he was looking at her, and her voice faltered.

Released from some spell, he moved. "No," he said. He sounded trapped. "No, you have to stay. Damn it to hell!"

"Four hours," she said faintly. "What are we going to do?"

He moved towards her, and reached out an arm, and for one moment she believed that this was his answer to her question. And that was all it took. With terrifying abruptness her heart leapt into her throat, and the wind of desire stormed through her.

Almost a year since she had been alone with him.

"Jude."

As his hand continued past her to the fridge door her breath caught on his name. A cold black flame spurted into life in his eyes as they fixed on her face.

"What are we going to do with the next four hours? Is that what you asked?" he asked in a flat, hard voice. She swallowed and made no answer. Jude jerked the fridge open, bent and reached inside to grab the bottle of champagne. "Let me start by telling you what we are not going to do. We are not going to do what's in your eyes right now."

He slammed the fridge door, and stood looking at her, the bottle in his hand. Her body was on fire, her brain a maelstrom of anger and desire.

"There's nothing in my eyes," she lied furiously. "I wouldn't touch you with a bargepole!"

"Good."

He busied himself opening the champagne. The muscles of his arms and chest bulged like a bodybuilder's. He was a man she had been more intimate with than anyone else in her life. She knew what gave him pleasure, he knew every secret of her body. Yet he was at the same time a bitter, hard, angry stranger whom she did not recognize. Only her body's involuntary, uncontrollable physical response to him was the same.

"Why are you opening that bottle?" she demanded, because otherwise she might have said something else.

He smiled grimly at her over his shoulder. "So that we can drink to our marriage."

"You've got to be kidding!"

The cork popped under his hand and he turned to her, holding the bottle as foam billowed out of the neck. It was a symbol so phallic she had to press her lips together to keep from crying out. What she was feeling was insane. How could she still feel like this for him after all that had passed?

"Kidding? Why?" He turned back to the counter and filled two cheap water glasses with the foaming liquid. "The guys spent money on this, do you expect me to pour it away? I haven't had a decent drink for a year." He handed her one glass and picked up the other. "To success," he said, lifting his glass mockingly. He watched her over the rim as he drank. She did not move.

"Drink to the success of our marriage, Hope," he commanded softly. There was foam on his upper lip. She flicked her eyes away from the sight.

"Wipe your mouth," she said stonily.

He wiped his lip with one broad thumb, then briefly sucked his thumb. Was he doing these things deliberately to provoke her? "Drink to our marriage," he said.

She hated him. "To this marriage." She lifted the glass and drank. "But I hope you aren't planning on indulging in any of the other little rituals of marriage, now or at any time," she said, with cold precision. "Because this marriage has zero meaning as far as any conjugal rights are concerned."

His hard face hardened even more. "Never think it," he said. "Never again. If I made love to you now it would not be to you, but to a *woman*. After months in here any woman would do. But I will never make love to you again."

"If you made love to me now, I'd scream, and then with

any luck you'd be thrown in—what do they call solitary?—the hole!''

His cold smile glinted at her. He shook his head contemptuously. ''No,'' he said.

''No? They wouldn't put you in the hole if your wife screamed?''

''If I made love to you you would not scream.''

Sensation rocketed through her. So he knew. She closed her eyes.

''You're sure about that?'' she tried. Whatever he thought he knew, as long as she did not admit it, she was safe.

''Moan, you would moan, I would hear you moan, yes? But you would not scream.''

It was unbearable, that deep, grating repetition of the word *moan*, stroking every nerve ending in her. Hope's head fell forward on a neck that was suddenly too weak to hold it up. She lifted her glass and tossed back more of the champagne. It went straight to her head; she had not eaten this morning.

''You're wrong. I would scream.'' She would scream, her heart told her ruthlessly, but with pent-up passion. Something in her snapped as she admitted it to herself. She pressed her eyes, feeling as if she were going mad, and suddenly she grunted as if she had been struck.

''I don't understand how I can hate you, can be so angry with you, and yet still my body wants you like thirst in the desert. Why won't it go *away*?'' she exploded.

Shaking, she set down her glass on the nearest surface and put both hands up to cover her face. She began to whimper with the fierce pain of wanting him. ''Oh, God!'' she cried. Her hands pressed to her mouth, she looked at Jude in torment.

''How did you do it? How did you stop wanting me? How does it work, Jude? I don't want to want you, I don't want to feel like this! What can I do to stop wanting you?''

There was a sound of breaking as he smashed the glass he was holding into the sink, and then Jude turned, and she was in the grip of hard, bruising hands.

"Understand this!" he said with barely controlled ferocity. "Before you try a trick like this again, understand one thing, my wife!" His eyes were hard black bits of glass in the unmoving musculature of his face. "Your power over me is gone. I would rather kill you than have sex with you. If I waited ten years without a woman, I would still not want *you* to take the edge from my hunger!"

She whimpered his name, but he was unmoved.

"I have spent months of my life in a place where no man, guilty or innocent, should spend a day. I have spent every day of that time pushing out of my mind the image of your face as you sent me here. I see it in my sleep, the face of the woman to whom I gave my soul and who gave nothing, not even simple trust, in return."

She was silenced. The tears dried in her eyes, so that they burned as she stared at him.

"Do you understand now, Hope?"

"Yes," she whispered. It was true. She had not understood before.

"Good. Because I do not want to watch you degrade yourself with attempts to entice me. So never tell me again that you desire me, Hope. I do not care."

"No, I won't do that," she said lifelessly.

Later, she knew, she would understand what she had lost. But she would not think of it now. She couldn't let herself think of it now.

Chapter 11

"It is not within the mandate of the Parole Board to put right possible miscarriages of justice," said the parole officer, delivering the decision of the board. "That is a matter for the courts."

Jude looked at him without speaking, then flicked his eyes round the other faces. A muscle in his jaw clenched.

"It is very rare for prisoners to be granted parole at their first hearing, Jude, as I'm sure you know, and granting you parole now may well give ammunition to those who will suggest that this is the Parole Board making a statement about the justice of your conviction, which we are not entitled to do."

Still he said nothing.

"So we want to make it absolutely clear to you that there is no intention on the part of the Parole Board to subvert the normal course of justice, and that no judgement as to the safety or otherwise of your conviction is meant. We leave all such decisions to the Court of Appeal. Do you understand?"

Jude's eyes narrowed and he frowned at the officer. "No," he said shortly.

The man cleared his throat and tried again. "The Parole Board has taken the decision to grant you unusually early parole entirely and solely on the basis of your exemplary conduct in prison and the fact of your solid community support, as well as our belief that you have a valuable contribution to make to society and should be allowed to get on with it. This decision is not by any means to be taken as a comment on the justice of your case before the Court of Appeal by you or anyone else. Is that clear now?"

He sat still as a statue while the earth heaved and shifted around him, only his eyes moving to flick to each pair of eyes around the table. They were all smiling at him. When the world had reformed itself, and was solid under his feet, Jude opened dry lips and breathed between them.

"Yes, that's clear," he said hoarsely. Then, "Thank you."

"Good luck, Jude," came a chorus from around the table.

"Thank you," he said again.

"Oh, thank God, thank God, oh, thank you, God!" Hope breathed the litany of gratitude and felt the unbearable weight lift from her heart. "Oh, Jude, I'm so glad!"

They were alone in the visiting room. This was not regular visiting hours, but it was common practice for the prison to allow a brief visit after a parole hearing, whatever the outcome. He had come straight from the hearing room to her. They had agreed upon it as a necessary part of the deception of their marriage, but he had had no expectation of a successful hearing. He found that he was glad she was there, if only to reflect back to him the news, and make it real and comprehensible to him.

"Yes," he said.

"What's the matter?" Hope smiled. "Didn't you expect it?"

"No," he said. "Nobody gets parole so early without political connections. They didn't even ask me about remorse, just about you and my plans for when I got out."

"So our marriage was worth it?" she asked quietly.

"If I understood what they said, all they needed was something…a reasonable hook to hang the decision on."

She bowed her head. "Jude, I'm very glad about that."

He looked into the distance, as if her emotion had no meaning for him. "You may be a little less glad when you hear my parole conditions."

She looked at him.

"A week in the halfway house, then one night every week I have to report back. The rest of the time I'm expected to reside in Toronto at the house I own with my wife."

Of course, they had known that it would come to that eventually; it was part of his "community support" that he had a home to go to. Knowing it would arrive some day and facing it as an imminent future, however, were two very different things. And looking into Jude's face now, Hope knew that dealing with it as a reality would be something else again. Something else very difficult.

Most parole restrictions were much more severe than this. He might have been allowed no more than one night a week in Toronto for several months.

"Why are they being so lenient?" she asked.

"They said they understood that I needed to be in Toronto, where the office is, in order to repair my career."

Hope swallowed and was silent.

"I'll be coming home to live with *my wife* in just over two weeks," Jude said, as though that would be the beginning of another prison sentence.

It was a clear, perfect summer day when Jude walked down the path of the halfway house to where Hope waited for him, leaning against the sexy, low-slung red car which had been her father's last gift to her, her arms crossed over her chest.

"Good morning."

"Good morning."

They stood looking at each other, but there didn't seem to be anything to say. Hope lifted one hand and dangled the keys. "Want to drive?"

His eyes raked her, and then the car, and she knew she had done the right thing. For most of a year he had needed permission for every action. Driving, he would know he was free at last.

"Thank you." He took the keys in a firm fist.

After that, they did not speak. On the highway he put his foot down and growled over into the fast lane. Hope wondered whether speeding was considered a breach of parole, but said nothing. After a few minutes of insane speed, he lifted his foot and eased down to eighty.

"You've been able to keep up payments on the car?" he said then.

"I didn't have to. Dad's—there was automatic insurance cover on the leasing agreement. It took over the payments when he fell ill, and paid the outstanding amount outright when he died. Otherwise the car would have had to go."

He grunted. He had the window open on the crystal-clear day, and there was little traffic. The air of freedom smelled like holy perfume to his starved palate.

"There was no insurance on the office lease," he said, after another few miles.

"No."

"And no life insurance."

Her father had not believed in life insurance. But no doubt he had not envisioned leaving Hope a share of a cleanup bill that would impoverish her for years.

"No."

"But you've managed to keep up the rent?"

"We're two months in arrears."

"How did you manage to keep it up so long?"

"Can we leave this discussion till later?"

"How?" he repeated grimly.

Hope took an angry breath. "There were fees coming in till Christmas with the projects that were still completing. We didn't close down finally till January. George and Janine—" she named Thompson and Daniels' two assistant architects "—didn't leave till the last project was completed."

"That still leaves several months' rent."

"I've been paying it partly with my wages and partly with my share of the Picasso," she admitted at last.

Jude glanced over with a frown. "Your wages?"

"I have a job, Jude," she said, irritated by his evident surprise.

"Doing what?"

"Computer graphic design. I took a Quark course."

"Well, we'll have to find some other solution. There's no reason for you to be working to pay the rent for Thompson Daniels."

Hope gritted her teeth at the implication. "Contrary to your understanding of my character, I am actually quite used to hard work. And do I have to remind you that my father left half of his share of the company to me?"

"It was not his intention to leave you a share of a massive liability."

"Well, you win some, you lose some. It was my responsibility. Now that you're ho—here, maybe some different decisions can be made. Have you got any idea yet what you mean to do?"

He swung into the centre lane to let a car scream past.

"I'm going to open the office again. But I don't fool myself we'll have the kind of business we were getting before, not for a long time. Maybe never. What I have to

do is cut down overheads by sub-leasing some of the space
to one or two small firms. That shouldn't be as difficult as
you found trying to get rid of the whole space.''

She digested that in silence, but there was nothing to say.
Either he would get commissions or he wouldn't, and there
was only one way to find out.

''Have you talked to Nicholas Harvey since you got
out?''

''Only briefly. We agreed to save it until I was in Toronto and could go to his office.''

''What are your plans for your appeal?''

He glanced over at her, his eyes hard points of light. But
it was not Hope whom he saw. ''I am going to clear my
name,'' Jude promised.

''I've put you in Dad's bedroom,'' Hope said two hours
later, leading him up the stairs in the house they would be
forced to share for months and maybe years to come. ''It's
the biggest room, and his study has a communicating door,
so I thought you'd like it.''

She opened the door to her father's room as she spoke,
and stepped inside. It was the master bedroom, a large airy
room with windows on two sides, a king-size bed and a
fireplace. Jude stopped on the threshold as if he had walked
into a glass wall, looked around and took a deep breath.

''What is it?'' she asked in concern. ''If you'd prefer
another room—''

Jude shook his head and stepped into the room after her.
''No, this is fine,'' he said. But she was sure there was
something.

''Please tell me. There are other rooms you could use.''

''This is fine. It's a big room, that's all.''

''What?''

''And there are no bars on the windows, Hope! That's
all it is, I'm just not used to space or freedom!'' he said

impatiently. He did not like expressing his feelings to her. It made him feel vulnerable.

She stood in silence, hating what had been done to him but knowing it would be futile to say so.

"His—your study is through here." She crossed the room and opened another door. "I guess you've been in here before."

She had removed her father's personal effects, but had left his books and the paintings on the wall. Even without signs of occupation, it was a comfortable, warm room, and this space brought her father back to her more than any other. Hope had spent many evenings with him in here after her mother's death, doing her homework while her father worked or read. This room had become their shelter against loneliness. Here they had had each other.

Even now she was not sure why she had given it to Jude. Perhaps to prevent herself making a shrine out of it.

On the desk were piled all the papers and drawings that she had culled from the office files. Jude crossed to the desk and slowly riffled a pile of papers. "Right," he said, more to himself than to her.

"Do you want some lunch? I promised to go into the office this afternoon," she said.

He had involuntarily picked up a sheaf of papers and was reading. He looked up. "What?" he asked absently. "Oh—no, I'm not hungry. Thanks," he added, as an afterthought.

When she got home that night he had cooked dinner. Ham, corn and scalloped potatoes. "This is a luxury!" she said.

It was no lie. Some of her loneliest moments in the past year had been at mealtimes. Mostly she had eaten in the kitchen, often on her feet, not liking to be reminded of her father's absence by sitting alone in the dining room. Jude had set the table there, and it was a funny kind of inner relief to sit at the table with him, sharing a meal.

It was a long time since Jude had cooked a meal for her. In that other life, when she had been practically living at his apartment, he had prepared meals, but that was a fact that she had almost forgotten. She had lost so many things.

"I'd forgotten you used to cook," she said, to fill the silence.

"So had I. I'd forgotten how enjoyable it is," he said.

"Where did you learn to cook?"

"From watching my father. But whether he learned to cook only after my mother was killed, or always did, I'm not sure. He was a good cook later on, anyway. Did your father cook?"

She shook her head. "My mother could cook. I guess I learned some things from her. But after she died, Dad hired a cook housekeeper. I don't mind cooking, but I don't usually cook when I'm on my own."

"You don't? What do you eat?"

"Oh—bread and cheese, or a salad. In winter I heat up soup. I don't need much food to keep going. If I ate like this every night I'd get fat."

What was weird was the absolute ordinariness of the scene, of the conversation. When they had finished the main course, Hope put her chin in her hand and looked at him.

"Do you know we never, ever talked like this?"

"Like what?"

"Just—plain, everyday stuff. Who you are, who I am. What we like and don't like. We never talked about things like that."

"We didn't?" He looked remote.

"No." She shook her head. "Don't you remember? We sort of grunted at each other, we were always touching instead of talking. Sex seemed to say it all. We never found out who we were."

"We found that out later," he said deliberately, and that

shut her up, because the look of absolute mistrust was back in his eyes again, and she knew she couldn't fight that.

One area might be safe. When they sat over dessert and coffee, she asked, "Jude, what do you think happened?"

"Bill Bridges perjured himself at my trial. That much I know."

"Why, do you think?"

His face was grim as death. "Because he had something to hide. He lied to protect himself. If I find what he was trying to hide, I have the whole answer."

"I'd like to help. What are you—"

He interrupted. "There is no reason for you to concern yourself, Hope. It has nothing to do with you."

The injustice of it ignited a spurt of anger in her blood. "Do I have to remind you that we are married?" she demanded harshly.

One eyebrow went insolently up. "No."

Her liver curled at the tone of his voice as he spoke the word. But she stood her ground. "Well, then."

"Is it relevant to anything, this marriage?"

Never had any marriage been so contemptuously dismissed. Hope plonked her elbows on the table and leaned forward furiously. "Is it relevant? Is it relevant? How long does your parole have to run, Jude?"

"You know it. Three years."

She nodded. "Three years in which you are expected to reside with your wife and maintain this house as your address. Do you imagine that I'm enjoying this charade, Jude? Do you think I'm looking forward to spending three years with a man who blames me for the destruction of his life with every glance?"

"We can get divorced any time. We can divorce now."

"Oh sure, *after* your parole officer has conducted a little enquiry into our reasons and granted his permission! Thanks but no thanks! I'm not going to discuss invented marital problems with a...with a...and anyway, which one of us would get to stay in the house? You have no income, have you forgotten?"

The heat of her fury had arrived at the kindling point of his. "What is your point?" he asked, struggling to keep his voice level.

"My *point*, Jude, is simple. You know perfectly well that you can't afford to divorce me now, on several grounds. I understand that, and I'm willing to put up with this situation for as long as it takes. But not one minute longer. I do want a divorce, Jude." She stared at him. "In the paranoid fantasy you're creating about what I'm getting out of this, try and remember that you forced me into this marriage and I want out of it as soon as possible!"

"You made a choice. I did not force you."

"Oh yeah, I made a choice!" She began counting on her fingers. "I had the choice of doing nothing until I was arrested as accessory to your escape attempt, *grassing* on you—that's what they call it, isn't it?—or marrying you. If that's your idea of a free choice, it isn't mine!"

"What do you want?" He was losing the struggle with his temper.

"I want you to recognize common sense! There are two of us in this, and it's stupid not to work together. It's stupid and self-defeating if you don't let me help."

"So, *now,* you want to help. You must forgive my surprise."

Hope lost it. She scrambled to her feet, meaning to leave the room, but instead, suddenly, she was shouting at him. "I *always* wanted to help and you know it! How *dare* you accuse me! You were so cool on the stand—why can't you understand what they did to me? They put your girlfriend on the stand and told everyone she was your fiancée five minutes before me—I felt like such a fool!"

Jude shouted back. "Why had you no faith in me? How could you believe this stupid woman with her stupid story?"

"Why didn't you tell me she existed if she was so unimportant? That's what I kept thinking. Why didn't you warn me?"

He got to his feet opposite her. "Do you know how much I had on my mind? She was completely unimportant to me! Why should I think of her, why should I tell you about a woman I stopped seeing before I *met* you?"

"She came to visit you!"

"I had no control over who came to that place, Hope! I couldn't go to the *toilet* without permission, I couldn't see the sky except one hour a day! I was told to go to the visiting room and I went, expecting maybe to see you, or Nicholas! And instead Corinne with her games. I thought, well, she has now an exciting part to play with her friends! *My boyfriend is accused of a dreadful crime, darlings, it's simply too awful!*" he mimicked brutally.

"You should have told me it was coming!"

"*Yes!*" he agreed violently. "Yes, we didn't think of this! I told Nicholas there was nothing anymore between us, and he said he would deal with her on the stand. Neither of us thought of what use they might put her to—but if we had thought of it, how could I have dreamed that it would work on you! If I had known how deep your trust of me went—as deep as your pretty skin!—maybe I would have thought to warn you. *There is a woman who will tell lies about who it is I love. Don't believe her.* Should I have said those words to you? Should I have had to tell you that, after what we had?"

She did not understand her anger's sudden transmogrification. All she knew was that she was trembling with sobs that seemed to come from nowhere.

"I wish you had," she sobbed. "Oh, Jude, if only you had!"

But with equal suddenness his anger had retreated behind the wall of ice. He gazed impassively at her, his lips compressed into a thin line. Then he turned and left the room.

* * *

Although nothing was ever said, after that moment Jude accepted her into partnership in his attempts to find the truth.

"I think the original testing on the glass was flawed, but Bridges didn't find out about it till the glass was already manufactured and on site," he explained to her a day or two later. They were sitting over coffee in her father's study, Jude behind the desk where her father always used to sit, Hope in the big leather chair that had always been hers. "He was faced with a dilemma. If he told me the truth, it would cost money to fix. Maybe a lot of money—if I had to redesign the whole primary structure, all the glass already manufactured might be useless. But there might never be a problem, or not in our lifetimes."

"But he had to cover himself in case there was one in the future."

"Yes."

"So he planted someone in our office to steal the original test results and plant the other set."

Jude nodded.

"But then why did he have the glass re-tested? Why didn't he just *fake* the figures in the new document? If a disaster happened ten years down the road, who could prove anything?"

"I don't have the answers to that yet."

"And you think it was Gig Young's job to steal the original test documents and plant the new ones?"

Jude shrugged. "But there's a problem with that, too: his last day was July twenty-second, and the letter attached to the new figures was dated August first. So it would be easy enough to take the original document, but how did he plant the other?"

"I wonder if he ever came back?" Hope said softly, as the idea came to her. "I wonder if he just dropped in one day to say hello or pick up an umbrella he'd left behind…"

"Do you remember anything like that?"

"No, maybe I was absent, or late, or at lunch…but somebody would remember if he had. The receptionist or Lena. He wouldn't have been able just to walk in, he'd have had to talk to someone."

"It may be that he stole the office keys. Who had the office keys?" Jude asked.

"You and Dad and Lena each had a set. Eleanor did too, but I didn't bother to get them from her. I never went in before Dad in the mornings, so I didn't need keys."

"If anyone came to the office after hours, they had to sign in with security downstairs. I'll check that out. But the important thing is to find Gig Young and ask him some questions."

"He's not at the phone number listed on his résumé. The man who answered said they'd had the number about six months."

"Did you ask Directory Enquiries for a new listing?"

Hope sipped her coffee. "Young is too common a name. Without an address I had no luck."

"There might be another way to find out where he is now. I'll check that tomorrow. Will you check with the old employees to ask them about your theory? I'll take a look through last year's security sign-in book when I'm at the office."

It was curious how well they worked together in this, Hope thought the next day, as she spent her lunch hour phoning her father's old employees at their new jobs to ask if anyone remembered Gig Young turning up again a week or two after he'd left, to pick something up or say hello. Every other area of their mutual lives seemed full of pitfalls and dangers, but once Jude had accepted her involvement in this, they had had no trouble.

No one could remember Gig Young returning to the office. While she had Lena on the phone, Hope asked her about her keys.

"Hope, if you're asking if anyone could have got the keys from my bag and copied them and put them back without my noticing, I have to say it's nearly impossible. Don't forget how paranoid everybody is about computer chip thieves. Your father was absolutely rigorous. I carried the keys in my bag and I locked my bag in my desk drawer."

"Good afternoon, Environmental Glass Systems, Lucinda speaking. How may I help you?"

"I would like to check on the references of a former employee of yours."

"Thank you, I'll put you through to Human Resources."

"Good afternoon, Human Resources. Jennifer speaking, how may I help you?"

"Jennifer," said Jude. "I want to check on a former employee of yours. What can you tell me about Gig Young?"

"Oh!" A note of surprise threaded Jennifer's voice. "Just a moment, I'll get his file. I'm afraid everybody's at lunch and I'm…but just a moment, please."

Jude was happy to wait. It was exactly in the hope that something like this would happen that he had called at just after one. He waited through several minutes of a bland melody, before an apologetic Jennifer returned.

"I'm sorry it's taken so long! But his records just aren't in the file, and I can't find him on the computer either. It's really weird! But I'm a clerk, my supervisor is at lunch. Maybe she could help you, if you'll phone back in an hour."

"But you know that he did once work for you?" Jude pressed, unwilling to let his advantage go.

"Oh, yes, I remember doing his termination documents,

I really don't understand why he's not on file. Gosh, I hope it wasn't anything I did!"

"I'm sure you're too efficient for that. Do you remember the date he left?"

"Well, not exactly," she said apologetically. "I guess it was—two weeks ago, maybe? Maybe only one?"

Jude blinked in stunned silence for a moment, and then forced his brain to recover. He cleared his throat. "Right. And he says on his résumé that he was there from 1991. Would you agree with that?"

"I know it was quite a few years; he was here before I started. Probably if you phone back Isabel will be able to tell you exactly. Or Mr. Bridges, maybe."

"Thank you."

"I'm really surprised he's looking for another job. He left so suddenly—I'm sure someone said he'd had an accident."

"That's right," said Jude quickly. "We're his insurers, he has applied for temporary disability benefit. We're just checking his history."

"It must have been that article in the paper!" Hope exclaimed jubilantly. The *Globe* had run a tiny item mentioning Jude's release. *Jude Daniels has consistently maintained his innocence, and is said to be determined to clear his name,* it had said. "You've got him spooked!"

"It might have served our purpose better if he were not spooked," said Jude. "How the hell are we going to find him on the run? He might be anywhere in the world now."

"He's bound to have left a trail. You can't just disappear anymore, can you?"

"A trail a professional could follow."

"Can't you go to the police? I bet they could find him."

He looked at her. "Do you imagine that the police are eager to find the evidence that would prove they had run a slipshod investigation and got the wrong man convicted?"

"No, you're right," admitted Hope.

Jude laughed. "What? I expected a comeback that *this is Canada, Jude!* What's happened to your faith, Hope?"

"I'm not Pollyanna, Jude. There's a big difference between individual police officers trying to cover their incompetence and the entire system conspiring to injustice. And you have to admit I was more right than you were about your parole."

He was silenced. "Yes, you were," he admitted at last. With the words he felt the earth move under his feet. He had never admitted it before, had never allowed the reality of his release from prison and the probable reasons for it to enter his soul. This simple acceptance that the whole world was not against him shook him, frightened him, as though something in him knew that the entire structure of his worldview was now at risk.

Chapter 12

Nicholas Harvey leaned back in his chair. "There's no doubt in my mind that we'll win the appeal, Jude. The judge was wrong in failing to declare a mistrial after Corinne Lamont's extremely prejudicial testimony, and also wrong on several points in his address to the jury. So you can put your mind at rest. The conviction will not stand."

Jude looked at him. "Win, how?"

"Good question. The Court of Appeal will have two choices." He held up two fingers. "It can declare a mistrial and order a new trial, or it can quash the conviction and give a directed verdict of acquittal. Now, in the first case, since you've already served your sentence, the order for a new trial would be a technicality, and the court would seek the agreement of the Crown Prosecutor's office not to proceed to a new trial. In those circumstances, it would be as if the case had never come to trial."

"So I was accused but the charges were dropped."

"Technically that would be the position. In the second case, of course, the decision would have the force of an acquittal. In both cases, your record would be wiped clean. You would no longer be on parole or subject to parole conditions. You will be, in effect, a free man without a blot on his record.''

Jude shook his head. ''No. Not without a blot. People will always doubt, always wonder.''

''Jude. It's not very likely that the police will proceed with the case even if you get a directed verdict of acquittal. It's old news, it's not hot. If you want the whole world to know you are absolutely innocent, you would have to find the guilty party yourself.''

''Yes,'' said Jude. ''I know. I intend to.''

Nicholas Harvey raised his eyebrows as he took it in. ''Now, why doesn't that surprise me?'' he asked rhetorically. ''Bill Bridges?''

''Bill Bridges.''

Nicholas Harvey nodded. ''Well, good luck. If there's anything I can do to help, let me know.''

''I want the name of a very good, a top private investigator. Someone with brains, Nick.''

The detective examined the tiny photo-booth photograph. ''How old is this?''

''Just about a year,'' Hope supplied. She had pulled it from the Thompson Daniels employment files. ''It makes him look a bit swarthy, but otherwise, I remember, it was a pretty good likeness.''

''And he absconded when?''

''Within the past couple of weeks.''

He nodded and wrote. He was an ex-policeman, a fact that was only apparent when he made a note. Otherwise he looked like someone who might work on an oil rig.

''Right. Well, he could be anywhere, but you don't need me to tell you that. I can maybe get a lead from the old phone number and address, and I can check the airlines in Toronto, but if he drove to Montreal airport or down to the

States…'' He shook his head. "And even if we got a line on where he went, there's no guarantee he stayed there. You understand that?''

"I understand," said Jude.

"The place to start would be his last employers," the detective said. "That's the first place I'd normally go. But if the employer is his partner in the crime, it'll be very difficult to ask any questions at all without arousing his suspicions, and then who knows where he'll go? Or his partner might even kill the man to protect himself.''

Hope shivered.

"My instinct," Roger Beatty went on, "is to try other avenues and see whether there's any lead, and judge our approach to Bridges accordingly. If we could get a tap on his phone, then it would be worth spooking him, see if he calls the guy. That kind of thing.''

Jude nodded.

"All right." He got to his feet. "I'll give a shot at a couple things and report back." He addressed Hope. "You say you thought Gig Young used his wife's illness as an excuse for leaving.''

"I'm not certain. It's a very vague memory.''

"That's all right. He's an amateur. If he did use his wife, he probably has one. And if he's got kids, too, it won't be so easy for him to disappear. Man can do a runner on his wife, but he misses the kids. I'll check for a phone listing in his wife's name.''

"How will you find out her name?''

Roger winked. "That's how I train my staff in detail work. I send them to the public records office. If he got married in Ontario we'll find the record. If not, I've got reciprocal arrangements with agencies in nine provinces and two territories.''

"We never sleep," Hope joked.

"Believe it." He put out his hand to shake first Jude's and then Hope's hand. "Be talking to you," he said.

* * *

Daniel Johnson turned away from the last painting and Hope, Jude and the art dealer all returned to their seats in the sitting room. "Your father originally bought a number of these works from my gallery," he said. "He had a good eye. I don't think he ever made a bad choice."

"But?" said Jude.

"But they haven't had time to appreciate. They are all the work of artists still painting. If I put them into an auction for you, you'll be disappointed with what they bring in."

"We may have to do it anyway," said Jude.

"If you give me more time, there is an alternative way to dispose of them. It entails my calling various clients and offering them individual works that I feel might interest them. I'm sure you can appreciate that this will not produce results overnight. But you will realize more from the sales. Something much closer to the real current value of the works."

Jude drank his whisky. "Either way, it's clear this is not the immediate way to raise money."

Daniel Johnson picked up his glass and looked at Hope over the rim for a moment. "I imagine Hope has told you about her show next year, Jude."

Hope jerked upright. "Oh! Well, no, not yet!" she said guiltily, as Jude repeated, "Show?"

"I'm sorry if I've spoiled a surprise," he said, but Hope shook her head. "Hope's work is going to be shown at my smaller gallery in about sixteen months' time. She should be working hard towards it now, as a matter of fact."

Jude glanced at her. "This is very good news." His voice was wooden. She found it impossible to read him.

Daniel smiled and set down his glass. "As it happens, Hope, I was on the point of calling you when you called me. I'd like to put a proposition to you."

Hope nodded, her eyes fixed on him. Daniel had been a

friend of her father for almost twenty years, and her father had trusted him.

Now, he said, "I've just learned that an artist I have booked for a show next month isn't in a shape to show. That leaves me with two weeks to fill at the Village Gallery. I expect you know that Hope's got a large number of finished canvases done over the past year, Jude. But because many of them are nude and other portraits of you, she was reluctant to show them." He turned to Hope. "I'd like you to fill that slot next month, Hope. If you were to change your mind about the portraits, we would have enough for a very respectable show."

There was a long silence while Jude and Hope looked at each other and remembered.

"Do you want to show them, Hope?" Jude asked at last.

The artist in her did, of course; the woman did not. Hidden deep inside Hope was a woman who wanted to keep the precious memory of the discovery of love as her still centre in the driving storm that life had become. The thought of those portraits hanging on anyone's wall but her own seemed irreligious to her.

And yet this might be a way to ease the immediate financial pressure.

"It won't raise very much money, will it?" She turned desperately to Daniel. "We might sell only two or three."

He looked at her bemusedly. "New artists at the Village tend to do better than that," he said gently. "And I expect you to be very well received." The Village Gallery was a very prestigious gallery, and Johnson had a wide clientele. It was said to be the best launch a new artist could have, because Johnson had a reputation for discovering the best new talent. "In addition, you two have got a high curiosity value at the moment, if this is not the wrong thing to say. There's a buzz around you. That will add interest even for those who are capable of appreciating the merit of your work."

"Where are your paintings, Hope?" Jude asked.

Her breathing quickened with nerves. "In—upstairs."

"Shall we look at them?"

"You want to see them?" she repeated stupidly. Her skin was twitching with nervousness: she did not want to look at those paintings with Jude.

"Why don't we do that?" Daniel said comfortably, getting to his feet. "I'd like to see them again myself."

So Hope mutely led the way to the attic room which she had converted to a studio. Once it had been her bedroom, but it was the logical room to convert into a studio.

She had taken up the carpet and laid down plain grey linoleum. A wooden trestle table carried jars of brushes and tubes of paint and rags; her paintings were stacked against the walls. Her easel stood under the north skylight.

On the easel was a painting she had just varnished, neither fully realistic nor truly abstract. The shape of a bed was suggested within bursts and blotches of blood red, black and grey. One side pristine, the other a tangle of sheets, this was a bed in which one person slept alone, and did not sleep well. The view from what might be the window was of ruin. It was a painting of the bleakest loneliness. She knew that Jude understood when she heard the intake of his breath.

Daniel Johnson stood silently in front of it. Then he nodded and said, "Mmm," flicking a glance at Hope. "I like this, Hope. I like the focus you're getting."

"Thank you."

"Does it have a title?"

She did not look at Jude. *"Empty Bed,"* she said.

Daniel nodded again, then moved over to where a stack of three or four paintings leaned against a wall. "May I?"

She nodded.

It was like a dream she had dreamed before, but couldn't remember the ending of. Jude with his burning dark eyes, and her pictures of him...a bad dream from which there was no escape. Daniel Johnson lifted the first painting and set it against the leg of the table. Then he began putting the others out in a semi-circle around him.

One by one the hot, sultry days of August and their passionate obsession returned as Jude and Hope gazed at the paintings she had made. Jude sitting on the floor, his knees drawn up, his arms folded across them, staring out of the canvas with a look in his eyes she would never see again. Jude prone on the tangled bed with the newspaper. Jude lying on his back in complete sexual fatigue, and in his eyes the information that he still wanted her, that he was exhausted physically but not sated mentally.

Jude the Lion. Transfiguration.

When that canvas appeared, the first she had done of him, she could not resist the compulsion to glance at Jude. He was looking at her, and a thousand memories danced on the air between them. *Don't touch me, Hope!* he had said then, and later, *I knew it would be like this!*

He looked away.

More reminders of those long, hot days and nights when the world was confined to each other's body. Another empty bed, this time with tangled sheets that held the promise of return. A window open on a world that was bland, uninteresting, because all the life was within the room...

Then Jude's face from memory, Jude as the ghost that haunted her bed, painted after his arrest, paintings full of desperate yearning...

Then, as the art dealer moved around her studio, gathering and spreading the paintings, he came to those she had painted after Jude's conviction, after his rejection of her. Jude's face scritched and scratched by black lines reminiscent of barbed wire, and blank walls, pain, and bleak, angry sterility.

When they were all displayed, Daniel Johnson stood looking at each painting in turn, mostly in silence. Sometimes he paused and looked back to a previous painting.

"Did you do that one before this?" he asked once, and Hope nodded.

"And that set there—before or after these?"

"Before," she said.

"There's actually quite a pronounced chronological cycle," Daniel observed.

Hope agreed.

Jude said nothing. His face was a mask. Leaning against one wall, his arms crossed over his chest, he looked at every painting, turned away from none, lingered on none. She could not tell whether this was a form of penance or simple lack of real response.

After a while a shift occurred, without any verbal acknowledgement—it was now understood that Hope would have the show, and that Daniel Johnson would take his free choice of her work to hang on his gallery walls.

"I think we won't hang these of the harbour," he said. "We'll concentrate on the cycle."

Hope nodded, and Daniel removed several early paintings of boats and stacked them against the wall.

"Are you thinking of rounding out the cycle now?" he asked, returning to look again at the group.

"Oh!" Hope stammered. "Oh, well—I haven't thought much about it."

"Give it some thought. If I may make the suggestion, I'd say it needs one or two more to bring it full circle."

"I do see what you mean," Hope said reluctantly. There was only one sort of picture that would round out the cycle, and that was another portrait of Jude, which was impossible. "I'll think about it."

"Good!" he said, as if they had come to the agreement that she would produce another painting in time for the show. "Now, how many have we got here? Twenty-eight," he said, counting. "Excellent. I'll take these now, we'll want to frame them, and time's short."

She glanced at Jude, but he made no move, gave no sign.

Without his clear rejection of the idea, Hope lacked the strength to stop the momentum Daniel Johnson had built up. "All right," she said.

When they had ferried the canvases down to his station wagon, and slipped them inside the insulated bags in the rack especially designed for holding canvases, Daniel climbed into the driver's seat, then spoke out the window. "Another portrait of Jude?" He sat looking up at her a moment. "Is that the direction you're thinking of?"

"Uh—" Hope coughed to clear her throat. "Yes, maybe, I'm not sure."

"Get her nose down to the grindstone," he advised Jude with a friendly grin, nodded and leaned forward to start the car. Then with a wave he was gone.

Jude did not like the churning mix of emotions that he felt. For the past year he had held down all feeling. He had believed that he had closed the door on emotion and locked it, and that it would not be unlocked unless he chose.

In prison things were brutally simple: talk tough, walk tough, be tough. He had quickly learned never to show weakness, never to relax his guard. The only emotion called for had been anger, and that had been easy enough. He had plenty of that.

He had spent the months since his conviction secure in the belief that all feeling for Hope had been killed in him. That she would never have power over him again. He had feared nothing, marrying her, except the tediousness of day-to-day living with someone for whom he felt no more than coldness and a lingering anger.

His mother had been betrayed, too, by those close to her. Her husband, deep in the throes of his loss, bitterly angry at the system and at the friend who had sold out to it, had made sure his son knew it. He had taught Jude that his mother's death was a warning to him to be wary of trusting.

He had forgotten the lesson. He had trusted Hope because she had stripped him raw, down to his essential self. She had made him naked. There had been no alternative to trust except death. But he had been so sure of her. He would have trusted her with his life, with whatever meant most to him. It was she herself who had meant most to him; he had known it almost from their first meeting, and had proved it later. Nothing in life had ever meant as much to him as Hope had.

His father had been right; he ought to have been more careful. She would still have betrayed him, nothing would have changed that, but if he had trusted her less it would have hurt less. If he had trusted her less, he would not have died in that courtroom and risen from his own ashes transformed into a man without a heart.

For his father the issues had been clear-cut. His wife was gone, and her betrayer, the one who had named her name to the secret police, had done it. For Jude, it was more complex, confusing, because Hope was gone, but she herself was the one to blame. He hated her because she had created the situation in which she was lost to him.

The first clue that he had had that he was not as emotionally dead as he wished and believed was the day when he had torn at her in prison. He was so sure that he had nothing to say to her, that there was no feeling left, that even blame was irrelevant. But when she was near his anger seemed to be born all over again, anger and hurt and other unnameable feelings assailing him when he most wanted to be in control.

He wanted nothing to do with her. If they could live like strangers in the house he could be comfortable inside his self-imposed emotional prison, and the bars would hold. He was not tempted by her physically—or at least, not as Hope. Of course the year of sexual deprivation meant that the smell of woman sometimes caught at him, or the sight of her soft flesh stirred him. That was only to be expected. It did not trouble him because he could control it. And he knew that as soon as he found a woman and the edge was taken off his appetite the desire he sometimes felt in Hope's presence would stop. It was not Hope he wanted, but Woman.

What was more difficult was the storm of emotion that raged in him at unpredictable moments. When she demanded that he allow her to help him in his mission to clear his name, common sense had forced him to submit. But cooperation with her, no matter how he fought his feelings, made him so sharply aware of what he had lost that he had to exert the extremes of control not to stand shouting at her.

He was not a violent man. What he had seen in prison had revolted him, appalled him, even though he understood the reasons for it. He had never been tempted to raise his hand to a woman in his life, and rarely to a man.

Yet there were times when it seemed the desire to hit Hope assailed him like an incoming tide. He wanted to lay hands on her, shake her, shout at her, till he was weak. Prison had changed him in some fundamental way, he thought, he had been transformed into an animal. And he hated her all the more because of what he had become.

His father would have despised him for it. He had taught Jude to respect women, almost to worship them. He had never raised even his voice to Jude's mother: Jude had childhood memories of his mother sometimes being angry, but not his father. His father had always weathered the storm.

"Women are just like nature, Jude," his father had told him, when the child, troubled by his mother's rage, had asked for an explanation. "When a storm comes, we don't go out and shout at the wind and the rain and the lightning, do we? We hide indoors. And when the sun is shining again, and you go out, what do you find? The wind has blown the dead leaves out of the trees, and the rain has watered the plants, and the world is clean again. If there were not storms, the world would never be washed. It's the same with your mother. When she storms, she washes her soul and mine.''

At five years old, Jude had been comforted. But the formula did not work for him now, because the anger was his own. His father's explanation had left out of the reckoning the male storm.

The maelstrom. That was what he felt, that he was in the grip of emotions that battered him unmercifully and drew him down to a place inside himself that he did not want to go.

When he saw her paintings of him, of that time when he had loved her and known that there would never be anyone else for him, his rage had almost consumed him. He looked at what she had painted in his eyes and knew that she had painted the truth. He had looked at her like that, with the need to possess her tearing at him even when he was too weak from lovemaking to move. He had had tunnel vision then, he had seen nothing but her. When he sat and she painted him, he could have told her afterwards every move, every brushstroke. When paint had spattered onto her fingers he had been jealous of its nearness to her. He had been jealous of the brush she held.

In prison, once, they had offered him potter's clay to work with. He had put his hands on it, a pound of clay, had begun to knead it as instructed, and he had thought of her, of Hope, of how his hands had moulded her, how his eyes had caressed her…he had lifted his hands from the clay then, and never touched it again.

The paintings reminded him that his first response to her, when they had met, had been hostility. Long before they met he had thought her a little rich girl who had jerked her father around, frivolous, who knew nothing about what was of value in life. On that first night he had taken a kind of perverse pleasure in the sight of her tanned skin, her expensive hair, the air of pampered kitten, because it had proven what he believed. He had enjoyed the thought that he would teach her a lesson one day.

But his hostility had not lasted. Long before that day he had gone to sit for her he had understood what the roots of hostility were. She became a physical and mental torment to him. He had waited for her to understand the truth, and with every sharp verbal exchange, he had fought the urge to say to her—*I could show you what the root of this is, I could set you on fire and we would never stop burning.* But he had not been sure of the ground. He had warned himself that it might be dislike all the way to the root in her, and steeled himself for her rejection when the day came—as he knew it would—that he could wait no longer.

Not until he had seen her face as she stared at his aroused flesh had he known for sure. He remembered the exultation, the exaltation, when he had known it, when he had put her hand on him and she had cried out with the first surprise of passion....

The pictures that came after, those he knew by looking had been painted when he was locked away from her, had reminded him of his own longing—before, when he was in the detention centre, when he had still trusted her and the not being able to touch her had been brutality. He had seen the hurt in her eyes when he asked her not to come there, but it had been impossible to explain that he could bear what he was going through as long as he was not reminded of it. An hour with her tore at him, made his life unbearable for twenty-four hours, till he had deadened himself again and could forget there was any life other than the one he led.

The paintings told him that she had suffered too, though for long months past he had told himself that she had not. That what he had experienced with her had been a fiction from beginning to end. That she was heartless and always had been.

He was sorry for her suffering, but it didn't change anything. Time would not run back. He could not love her again.

"Jude, do you mind?" she asked him.

He stared at her. "Mind what?"

"The show. Everybody seeing those paintings of you. People buying them and having them on their walls."

He smiled grimly at her. "Hope," he said, almost gently, "they are not paintings of me."

She only looked at him, round-eyed, like a frightened cat.

"The man you painted then is dead. I don't care who looks at a dead man, or hangs his picture on their walls. I'm grateful that your artistic talent is going to bring in some money—it's more than I can do."

Hope bowed her head. "Yes, I see. How stupid of me to think that you would care. Of course it all means nothing to you now. Just like the song—'we shared a moment out of time, but now it's over.'"

"Just like that," he said. "I'm glad you understand."

When she looked up at him now, her eyes were blank, her thoughts hidden from him. "Then perhaps you won't object to my 'rounding out the cycle' as Daniel put it. Will you sit for me again?"

He shrugged. "Why not? I don't suppose you'll need me nude this time, will you? You've already stripped me down past my skin." His voice was harsh. He did not know why he said it. He did not care about this one way or the other. If he did nothing but sit for her for a year it would change nothing. "No need to go repeat yourself."

"That's right," she said levelly. "Clothes will be an interesting novelty."

Chapter 13

"If you're interested and you have the time to take it on, I'd expect to give you a free hand with the design. You'll be down as our associate architect; it will be a Whalley and Sutton project. And as I said, we can execute the working drawings for you. But you'll have full approval. We'll share fees, of course."

Jude, wearing a new business suit, sat still in the plushly comfortable visitor's chair and stared out the wall of windows behind Rex Sutton's head. It was a luxurious corner office giving a fabulous view over the lake on one side and another high-rise on the other.

Rex Sutton could pick up and put down associate architects like pocket change. He did not need Jude Daniels.

Jude's eyes left the sparkling water of the lake and focused on the man who had never liked him. "Why are you doing this, Rex?" he asked quietly.

The architect frowned and looked down at his desk. "Well, I would have thought that was obvious."

"Not to me."

"Jude—" The older man scratched his eyebrow and snorted irritably. His suit, shirt and shoes were custom made. He breathed wealth. "Hal Thompson, maverick that he was, was one of my oldest friends. We were in the same class at architectural college. You are now married to his daughter, whom I have watched grow up. Hope was close to my own daughters before she went off to Europe a few years ago. And quite apart from all that, disliking a young man because he's abrasive and doesn't know enough to keep disagreements with his fellow architects within the profession is a very different matter from being happy to watch such a promising career take a nosedive for all the wrong reasons. And that's different again from standing back and doing nothing while an injustice is perpetrated by the courts of the land. Now, I didn't want to have to say all that, and I'd prefer it if you forgot I did. Will you accept the commission?"

Jude felt an unfamiliar mixture of shame and humility. Shame because he would not have believed Rex Sutton capable of such generosity. Humility because he had to scrape to the bottom of his soul for the answering generosity that would allow him to accept it.

"Yes, I accept it," he said. He looked at Hal Thompson's friend again. "Thank you, Rex."

When they had discussed the details, Rex said, "My wife tells me we've received an invitation to Hope's preview at the Village Gallery next month."

"That's right."

"Well, that's very good news. We'll be there, of course. Perhaps you remember Linda collects in a small way. She's very much looking forward to it. She says she hasn't seen anything Hope's painted since high school. No doubt she'll find one or two that she likes."

"We'll be very glad to see you," said Jude.

* * *

"When did you last see Rex Sutton?" he asked Hope that evening over the dinner table.

"At Dad's funeral. Why?"

"You haven't talked to him or his wife lately?"

"I sent them an invitation to the show and Linda called to congratulate me. She's always been kind to me and thought of herself as my substitute mother. Why?"

He told her about his meeting with Rex Sutton that day. Hope exclaimed with jubilant excitement.

"Oh, isn't that good of him! I'm so glad he didn't just offer you a job in his office! You wouldn't have liked that, would you?"

"Not very much. So you were expecting something like this?"

"No, not really. I mean, I figured they'd keep an eye out for us...but I certainly didn't expect anything so dramatic as this. I thought maybe a word in people's ears, something like that."

"Did you ask for his help?"

Hope shook her head emphatically. "But Linda asked how we were doing and I suppose she had a chat with Rex afterwards. I told her you would be opening the office again and were trying to sublet some of the space—you know, just in case they knew of someone."

"Rex has agreed that Whalley and Sutton will do the working drawings. That means I don't have to put out money hiring draughtsmen."

She could not read him. His voice was level, revealing no emotion. "It really is great news," she tried. "It must be a huge relief to get back into it all with a project like this." She knew that he had feared a future limited to office renovations and home extensions. But this immediately put him back into his own league. A small but important building was just Jude's thing. And to be Associate Architect on a Whalley and Sutton project would be a very loud message in the highly political world of architecture.

Jude was watching her. "Rex as good as told me that Linda is going to buy one of your paintings, though she hasn't seen anything you've done since high school."

Hope jumped happily in her chair. "Is she? Oh, that's nice of her! Well, they have *always* been very kind to me. I shouldn't really be surprised by all this. They did call a lot after Dad died, but I just cut off from everyone."

Jude looked curiously at her. "This wouldn't offend you, Hope?"

"*Offend* me? What is there to offend me?"

"That she is going to buy a painting not on its merits but because she is your friend, to help you out."

Silence fell between them as she looked at Jude and understood. As though she had just crested a hill, the outlines of his character and personality were laid out before her for the first time. Hope propped her chin on her hands, still watching him.

"Jude, what a lonely life you must have led," she said softly.

He returned her gaze impassively.

"Friends are friends, Jude. They don't wait around for you to prove yourself. If you need help, they give it. And it doesn't mean you're less of a person. Or less of an artist, or architect. It just means they care about you and they're helping."

"I had to accept," he said. "It would have been an act of madness to turn it down."

"Yes, I agree."

"But this is a handout from the architectural establishment that I have always challenged."

She understood his dilemma perhaps more clearly than he did. One of the things that Jude had always challenged in the architectural establishment was the way it closed ranks to protect its members. Most of the architects who disliked him, Rex included, disliked him primarily on the grounds that Jude went public with his disagreements. He attacked other architects' buildings in the press. Now—just at the moment when he was most vulnerable, when they could have moved in and finished him off, or simply left him to go under—at the hands of one of the most respected and successful architects in the city, that establishment had instead chosen to close ranks around Jude himself.

So, she understood, he was suffering on two fronts. First, he was experiencing the psychic confusion of someone whose worldview has been toppled in a sudden, dramatic moment. And second, he feared that accepting Rex Sutton's gesture would rob him of his teeth. Would he now become a tame member of the profession out of gratitude? Was this the end of Jude Daniels, the man?

"You know, my father always disagreed with Rex about you. Dad said that any profession like architecture only kept fresh if someone like you happened along now and then to stir things. He said the profession should be grateful that nature occasionally threw up a maverick.

"If Rex is helping you now, it's not an attempt to clip your wings, Jude. He didn't have to do that, did he? You were already pretty effectively clipped. All he had to do was leave you alone."

She saw the truth of what she said sink in.

"So my guess is that this is Rex's nod to my father." Hope blinked as unbidden tears came to her eyes. "He's helping you back to your feet because Dad believed that you were a necessary phenomenon, and he's going to let Dad have that. Rex knows that once you're on your feet you'll start swinging again."

He digested that. "So you wouldn't expect me to change because I accepted help from your father's friend?"

She laughed. "To be honest, if it were me, I'd put a moratorium on slashing up Rex himself in print for a couple of years. But it would still be no holds barred on everybody else. But I'm a woman, and I suppose men would look at it from a completely different perspective. Maybe you have to get at Rex on his very next building just to prove you're still independent.''

His face subtly softened, as if some part of him were relaxing for the first time. ''No,'' he said, ''I don't think I have to go to such an extreme. In any case, I have never criticized Rex very much. He's a good architect.''

This was the kind of discussion they had never engaged in in the past. They had met only along one facet of their characters. The fact that they could now talk like this brought her closer to him, made her more vulnerable. But it did not seem to affect his attitude to her. Hope knew she might be setting herself up for bitter heartache, but she could not resist the temptation of the discovery of Jude's character, even though it entailed the risk of revealing her own.

Life was not easy for Jude. The hard facade with which he had always dealt with the world was being dismantled, not by opposition, but by kindness. In the past he had asked no quarter, had given none. Opposition, if it affected him at all, had only made him stronger.

The architectural community had been shocked and appalled at Jude Daniels' conviction. In spite of their sometimes violent dislike of him, very few had really believed that Jude Daniels had gone ahead and put up a building knowing that it was unstable. Those who had followed the trial had assumed that he would be acquitted: to experts the evidence incontrovertibly pointed towards his innocence, and even those who would have loved to see Jude Daniels nailed to the wall for some dereliction could not be comfortable watching a man of integrity destroyed in such a way. Slowly, over the time of his trial and imprisonment, this view had spread through the profession and solidified.

So he came out of prison determined to prove his innocence, only to discover that for most people, his innocence was taken for granted.

He had two close friends from university days. Both had visited him regularly in prison. He had not been exactly surprised that they stuck by him; nevertheless, the gratitude he had experienced because of it had always worked to counter the prison-induced hardening of his character. So in spite of his bitterness, there had always been a crack in the facade. It was through that crack that kindness could now enter.

Whatever else happened, he was determined not to allow Hope to enter. Jude struggled to treat her politely and distantly, because when he shouted at her, when he expressed the sense of betrayal he had felt, when she explained the world to him in different colours than he had been used to seeing, he could feel the crack widening. It was best when he presented her with the blank wall of his indifference.

This task was hardest at the times when she painted him. They needed the money a successful show would bring in, and Daniel Johnson had been clear about what the show needed. Jude was artist enough to understand the necessity for the cycle to be completed. If he had still been in prison, then an "unfinished cycle" would have been appropriate. But he was free. They were married. She needed something to reflect that.

So he sat for her. It was August again, and the month was as usual hot and muggy. For the first painting, Hope set an armchair in front of the patio doors leading onto the roof terrace. He sat there, facing out while she faced him. Later, she would put him on the terrace and paint him from behind, inside the room.

Wearing jeans and a short-sleeved shirt, he sat for her in the evenings, in the hours before sunset. It was a dangerous time of day. Birds sang of summer, insects chirruped, wind gently stirred the leaves of the trees that enclosed the terrace in green, and blew in over his face, reminding him that he was free. For a year past, he seemed never to have felt the wind. Now it blew as if for him alone.

He remembered this room. It had been her bedroom a year ago. Once they had made love here, he could not remember the how or the why. She had brought fresh grapes up from the kitchen, cold from the fridge and beaded with water. He could remember the sight of them in the bowl, how their sensual beauty had almost hurt him.

Everything had had the power to touch him then, to move him. All his life he had been defended, closed. He had learned to protect himself very early. But she had stripped him bare for the first time in his life; he had had no defences against her. He had been as open as a child at the breast, drawing pure pleasure from her.

Watching her now, intent with concentration as her eyes flicked back and forth between him and the canvas, he had to fight against the thought of those other times, against the sense memory this stirred in his blood. He remembered the post-coital heaviness of his limbs with an immediacy that seemed to mock the sharpness of sexual need that he now felt.

Sex was a basic human need, as urgent as food and warmth. He did not want *her*. But when he remembered those moments, a year ago, when she would put down her brush and come to him, or he would get up from the bed or the floor and take the brush and palette from her hand...then his body made no distinctions.

For Hope, the world was very, very different. The feeling that she had been betrayed had lasted only long enough for her to do maximum damage to Jude's case. In the end, when the effects of shock had worn off, she had not really blamed him for not telling her about Corinne. They had hardly spoken during the short intense weeks of their love affair—why should he have wasted words on past history? She had not.

What had been less easy to forgive was his refusal to understand the reasons she had failed him. Less easy to get over, too, was his rejection of her. She had been deeply and fundamentally hurt when he told her to go away, when he ignored her letters. That hurt, over time, had escalated into an anger that had sometimes seemed close to hatred. When he had not communicated even at her father's death, that had been the final stroke for Hope. So when she discovered Gig Young's résumé, she had gone to Jude not out of any desire to see him, but from an impersonal sense of justice.

Later, driven into this sham marriage with him, sexually rejected when she had briefly weakened, she had really believed that her own angry indignation was now the sum total of her feelings for Jude.

Bit by bit, however, the mask was coming off her feelings. Since they no longer had the escape of sex, the vital energy that was still between them began to express itself in words. A year ago, she had believed that she "knew" Jude, through the physical, better and more deeply than words could ever have expressed, but the trial had proven her wrong. If she had known him, she would not have doubted him, even momentarily.

She was learning now, through words and silences, who he was. When he unconsciously revealed himself to her, she saw the terrain of a character that had been wary of trust until he met her, and then had broken down every barrier at once. To a nature like Jude's her fumbling doubt of him on the witness stand had been the worst and deepest kind of betrayal because it had proved that she did not trust him, while he had trusted her with everything he was. In his eyes, she had shorn the lamb that was his soul and then thrust it naked into the lashing hail and storm.

Because she understood that, she found it difficult to maintain the mask that hid her feelings from herself, even though she slowly began to fear that what was underneath would only bring her pain. To open herself up to him now, when he was a blank wall—that would be the act of a fool.

She was most at risk because of the physical pull she still, and always, felt. She knew that he had conquered or destroyed whatever desire he had once felt for her, because if he had felt any shadow of the deep, painful need that washed over her whenever her guard was down, he would have come to her in the night.

He watched her as she painted him, and she saw nothing to give her hope. His eyes were hard and wary, with no hint that the remembrance of things past ever assailed him.

"Jude! Hey, *Jude!*"

The voice called his name as Jude stepped down from the train into a blast of wind-driven rain. He turned in the direction the call had seemed to come from, but by then she was right beside him, small and confiding.

"Hi, remember me? Don't tell me we've been on the same train all the way from Toronto!"

He did remember her, though not immediately her name. She was a volunteer, working with a prisoners' help organization. Small and wiry, with a mop of tightly curling blonde hair, she was divorced, he knew, but that was all he could remember about her. She had poured out her heart to him during the course of a prison Visitors' Day in June. He hadn't seen her since.

"Rita," she said.

"Hello." He turned and together they fought their way along the platform against the driving rain.

"Congratulations on making...*parole!*" The last word was hissed into his ear, so as not to be overheard by the other commuters. "It's really great, eh? You must have been so excited!"

He opened his mouth, but no answer was necessary. Rita leapt to the most obvious topic. "Gosh, this weather, eh? It came up so suddenly! I'm soaked to the skin! I've got the car here, can I give you a lift? You'll never get a taxi in this!"

"Thank you. I'd appreciate it."

They made their way through the station and then faced the storm again, Rita laughing as the wind blew her against Jude, hanging on to his arm as they struggled to her car.

Inside the car at last, she ran a hand over her hair and face and shook the water off. "Wow! I feel like a drowned rat!"

She didn't look like a drowned rat. Her hair curled wetly against her scalp, and her lightly freckled skin, washed clean of make-up, and the remnants of her mascara, smudging the area around her eyes, made her seem young and vulnerable. Her thin blouse stuck to her, revealing tanned skin and small neat breasts inside a white bra.

Jude's shirt also clung to him, and his jeans were dark with wet. Water dripped off his face and hair, and he, too, wiped a hand over his head to take off the worst of it.

"So, where're you going?" Rita asked, starting the engine. "The halfway house?"

Once a week, on Friday, Jude returned to Kingston and spent the night at the halfway house. The terms were light—he had to check in by midnight, and could check out again at six the following morning.

"Thanks. If it's not out of your way."

"It's not out of my way," she said, pulling out onto the road, "but—have they got a laundry room in that place?"

"I don't know. I've never needed one."

"Well, mister, you need one tonight."

"I'll manage."

"How will you manage?" she challenged him. "Unless you've got your dinner packed in your overnight bag, which I doubt."

"I'll eat in a restaurant."

"In soaking wet clothes, or your pyjamas?" She tossed him a grin, and, the windshield wipers doing hard labour, peered through the windshield to negotiate a turn.

"In wet clothes," Jude said. "It won't kill me. The storm will pass soon."

"I've got a better idea. Why don't you come to my place and dry your clothes in the dryer, and we can order in Chinese, or go out, or whatever. And I promise to get you home by midnight, Mr. Cinderella."

Her tone was light, but Jude got the message. He turned his head and they exchanged a glance.

"That sounds good," he said, and Rita smiled.

She had an upper duplex in a pale yellow clapboard house with white shutters and trim. It was a nice enough neighbourhood, and the flat was big and airy, and decorated with an attempt at bohemianism. He did not know why he suddenly felt sorry for her. The place somehow made him think she was lonely, yet she seemed so cheerful.

"Right, okay! Guest bedroom's there, there's a bathrobe behind the door, and if you bring me your clothes I'll toss them in the dryer. Oh, and here's a towel."

He didn't need a towel, but he took it anyway. When he came out again, in the man's white towelling bathrobe he had found, the towel tossed around his neck, the gas fire was alight in the sitting room, warm and welcoming against the weather, and Rita called from the kitchen.

"Can I get you a drink?"

Jude walked to the kitchen. She was wearing a dark blue velvet bathrobe out of a fifties movie, tight to the waist, the skirt deeply flared to the floor, with voluminous sleeves that fell back to reveal her arms as she reached into a high cabinet for glasses.

"Just toss those in the dryer." She nodded to where the dryer sat with its door open, and he bent and shoved his jeans and shirt inside, closed the door, and gave them twenty minutes on the dial. "Wine, beer, something stronger?" Rita pursued. "I'm having a glass of white, but there's red open, and I have whisky and brandy."

"Whisky on the rocks, please," he said.

He looked at the slender athletic musculature of her arm, and then at the curve of her back under the bodice of her velvet robe, and thought of running his hand from neck to waist, but did not.

She got ice from the fridge, keeping up a light chatter, but whether for the sake of his nerves or her own he couldn't be sure. Her hair had been towelled dry and left attractively tousled, she had replaced her mascara but added no lipstick.

"There!" she said, handing him his drink, then picked up her wineglass and a plate of chips and crackers and led the way back to the sitting room. "Isn't this nice?" she demanded, settling on the sofa. She meant the fire, the cosiness of the room against the already diminishing storm.

"Very nice," Jude said, and sat beside her.

It was exactly what he needed. It was what she wanted. He sat down eighteen inches from her and, under the excuse of setting the plate of snacks on the floor between them, Rita closed the gap to eight inches. Then she took a sip of her wine and leaned her head confidingly against his chest.

Jude lifted his arm and put it around her. They sat in silence, staring into the flames that leapt and danced around the imitation coal, while outside the wind subsided.

"I wish it would keep on blowing," Rita said. "I love to be all cosy inside when there's a storm. It makes me feel safe."

Then she lifted her mouth for his kiss.

Her lips had a slightly bitter, slightly soapy tang that was not unpleasant to him, and he set down his glass and held her more tightly as the kiss moved into second gear, and he felt his loins stir.

It was that stirring, oddly enough, that told him he could not go through with it. He didn't know why. Perhaps because she was so clearly vulnerable and he was not. All he knew was that he lifted his lips and his hand came up to caress her cheek as he said quietly, "Rita, I'm sorry."

She smiled and snuggled against him. "Don't be sorry."

In the kitchen the dryer stopped spinning and beeped. He cleared his throat. "I'll get my clothes."

He saw the hurt, uncomprehending frown settle on her brow. "Jude?"

"Rita, it's just not…I'm sorry, I thought it would."

Now she understood. "Oh, *Jude!*" she wailed a protest, her face crumpling like a child who has learned to expect disappointment. "Why? Don't you—I mean, if we went on a little it would work. I'm sure it would."

He smiled gently at her, feeling pity tear at his heart, another feeling that had somehow slipped through the barriers without him noticing. "It's working just fine already, Rita," he said. "But I—I can't, that's all."

"Aw, Jude, you're such a decent kind of guy. The others get mean afterwards and say things, but you—I know you'd be different. Are you sure?"

He hated himself for not having foreseen his own reactions. For not having recognized her vulnerability behind that slightly hard exterior. He'd had no right to think of using a woman like this for his own ends—one way or the other he had been bound to hurt her.

He looked for the least hurtful excuse. "Rita, I'm married," he said, thinking it was a convenient excuse until he heard his own voice. A part of him asked, *Well, if that's not the real reason, what is?* but he turned a deaf ear.

"Yeah, I heard," she said despondently, sitting up straight. "Lots of guys, that doesn't make any difference. They figure they've got a lot of catching up to do."

The unspoken confession of what her life was stirred his pity unbearably. He said roughly, "Why do you live in Kingston? Why don't you go to some other city, somewhere where you can meet men who aren't ex-cons?"

"I don't know," she said quietly, dropping her head. "I guess I just got used to it."

He stood up and moved into the kitchen, where he pulled his clothes out of the dryer. "I'd better be going," he said.

She jumped up. "I'll drive you."

"The rain's stopped. I can walk."

She stood looking at him, her head on one side, her eyes wistful. "Would you—you still have to eat, right? Could we just go for a meal together, and then I'll drop you back? Please? That's all, just a meal. I hate eating alone all the time."

He wondered how much of a fool he was being. "Sure. I'd like that."

Rita smiled at him, her eyes sparkling with what he knew were tears. "I'll be ready in a sec!"

Five minutes later they stood at the door, dressed and ready to leave. As he reached for the handle, she put her hand on his arm. "Jude," she said, "would you just hold me? Not sexy or anything."

She came into his arms like a child, and he wrapped her and held her for a long time. At last she sighed deeply and drew away. "That's so good!" she exclaimed. "That's really what I miss, you know. Just being held like that."

Jude picked up his bag and opened the door. He felt torn from every direction. He seemed to have lost all his defences. He'd been so sure every feeling was dead in him, and now there was nothing but confusion.

Chapter 14

Roger Beatty leaned to open his briefcase and pulled out a sheet of paper. "So far, we're in luck," he said.

Hope leaned forward excitedly. "Really? You've found something?"

Jude, his eyes on the detective, simply watched.

"Something, yeah. We've found out the name of his wife."

"Oh," said Hope, unable to keep the disappointment from her tone. She thought it would be more than that.

"George Henry Young—" the detective took a sip of his drink and lifted the page "—is married to one Kimberley Bridges."

Now he had their full attention. "What?" said Jude.

Beatty nodded. "Yeah, we should have guessed it. Of course they kept it in the family. Kimberley Bridges is Bill Bridges' niece. Uncle gave her husband a job when the firm he was working for went under during the recession." He drank again. "Looks like Uncle Bill called in his debts."

"You're right, we should have guessed something like this," Jude said reflectively. "What else?"

"A few things. He's got two kids, pre-teen. He hasn't flown out of Pearson Airport during the past month. The address on the c.v. was false, but he was listed at that phone number up to a year ago. Young complained of hang-up calls and they got a new unlisted number under her name."

Jude's eyes were narrowed, taking it in. "You've got the address," he said.

One eye consulted the paper again, but it was only for show. "We've got the address. Nobody there at the moment. The house is shut up. Not unusual in August, according to the neighbours—they go up to the cottage every year."

Hope's heart was beating uncomfortably hard. It was a strange feeling, knowing that they were closing in on the man. She licked dry lips. "Do you know where it is?"

"That's next on the agenda. It won't be too difficult."

"Do you think that's where he is?"

"If he's not, the wife and kids probably are. It'll be easy enough to throw a scare into her and get her to spill the beans."

"Pre-teen children," Hope said. "You'll be careful, won't you? Don't scare them."

"Don't you worry," said the detective.

Jude frowned, catching the glibness. "She means it," he warned. "Don't talk to the mother if the kids are around."

Jude and the detective measured glances. Beatty lifted a hand in the symbol of surrender. "Right."

"They came and arrested my mother in front of me," Jude said. "Kids don't forget." He didn't know why he said it, except that everything was upside down in him. If he tried to say one thing, something else got said.

When the detective had gone, Jude returned to where Hope still sat in the sitting room. He paused in the doorway and she looked up at him.

"I didn't know that," she said. "How old were you?"

"Five," he said shortly.

"Did you ever see her again, after that?"

"She died in prison." It was something he never talked about. He was going to change the subject, but instead heard himself say, "They said a heart attack, but my father knew it was under torture."

She gasped. "Did he tell you?"

"Not then. Later, when we had finally escaped from Czechoslovakia. I was twelve when I learned for sure what it was. But I knew from the first something terrible had happened."

"From the first?" she repeated.

He shrugged. "When Stasi came to arrest someone it was not like an ambulance picking up someone ill. And when I asked my father when my mother was coming home he would not answer."

He walked over to the drinks tray and absently refilled his glass. He stood with his back to her, staring out the patio doors to the green and gold of the garden.

She muttered something. She wanted to encourage him to talk, but couldn't think of anything to say except to ask him to tell her what it had been like.

It was enough. "After that, everything was cold." He was caught in the toils of remembering now, he had no more thought of resisting whatever it was. "I don't know why, but that's what I remember. The flat seemed cold. Even food was cold. That's what I remember, although that must be wrong. Why would it be cold?"

"Maybe it's not wrong. Maybe your father was so depressed he forgot to put on the heat."

Jude nodded. "Yes, I remember now." He hadn't thought of that period of his life for years. "He wasn't there in the daytime the way my mother had been. Maybe the heating needed regular attention, maybe you're right and it really was cold.

"My grandmother lived with us." He had almost forgotten that, too. "She was very old and ill, I remember, she could do nothing. We sat together in the flat, holding each other for warmth." He frowned as distant images clarified behind his eyes. "She cried and talked to people from the past, she rarely spoke to me or saw me."

He fell silent for a long moment, then turned around and faced Hope. He only half saw her. He was straddling two worlds. "She spoke to my mother. 'Katia,' she would say, looking over my shoulder. But when I turned to look, my mother wasn't there. When I asked her, 'Where is my mother, where is Katia?' sometimes she heard me. She would say, 'She is in a prison cell.' 'Why doesn't she come out of the prison cell, Grandma?' I would ask. And then she would say, 'She can't come out, little one. She can't open the door.'

"I remember I thought I was also in a prison cell. I also could not escape, I could not go outside because I couldn't open the door. I sat all day with my grandmother and prayed for my mother to open the door, until my father came home."

Tears burned her eyes and spilled down her cheeks as she listened. "Oh, Jude, what a horrible thing for a child so young."

He focused on her. "Was it? Was it worse than other children experienced?" He really did not know.

"Yes, of course it was. Spending all day every day with a woman in the grip of senile dementia? My God, Jude, that would be hell even for an adult!"

"Yes, that's it," he said in some surprise. "Senile dementia, that's what it must have been. It's funny, I never put a name to it before. But my father was worse. He was not insane, but he trusted no one after that. He would tell me, 'What do you tell your friends? Be careful what you say.' And he would look at me—Christ! the way he looked at me!"

Hope stood up and crossed to where he stood. Gently she removed the glass from his hand and set it down, then put her arms around him. "I'm sorry you had such an awful time. I wish I could make it better, Jude."

He saw with astonishment that she was weeping for his pain. He looked down into her face.

"How can you make it better? You made it worse. The next time I saw that look in someone's eyes, suspicious, as if I—they were your eyes, Hope."

She sobbed once and bit her lip, and his next words were torn from him.

"Why did you look at me like that? That look in your eyes, that was how my father used to look at me, as if I might have betrayed him to the same people who had taken away my mother! Why should he think that? I loved him! Sometimes when he looked at me I thought—I saw him wonder if it had been I who betrayed my mother, whom I loved more than anyone! And then you, wondering if I had betrayed you! How could you imagine it?"

He closed his eyes and tried to take her arms from around him, but she resisted. "I'm sorry," she said. "It came at the worst possible time, and I know you can't forgive it. But Jude, remember that we didn't know each other very well…"

"Didn't *know* each other?" He pushed her away and glared at her in furious disbelief. "I loved you as if you were my own heart! You were what I loved and my own ability to love at the same time! Because of you I knew that God existed and that God is another word for love! And for you we didn't *know* each other?"

His voice was raw, ragged, cutting her heart like a jagged piece of tin. "Jude, I loved you, too," she cried. "I was weak, but please remember that I did love you!"

His heart seemed torn from a thousand directions. Feelings and memories long dead buffeted him, washed through him, tried to tear him adrift and fling him headlong into the storm.

"Did you?" he asked bitterly. "Did you love me, Hope?" He snorted one breath of mirthless laughter. "What a rock your love was, eh? Or perhaps you were confused about what love is! Perhaps for you it was only physical! That should have been enough, shouldn't it?" He smiled cruelly down into her tear-damp face. "Yes, I shouldn't have asked for the moon! Sex like that doesn't grow on bushes! Why should I ask for your heart when I had your body and it was so good!"

Suddenly the desire that he had been so easily able to resist two days ago boiled up in him, deep and overwhelming, and his blood shouted that now was the time and here was the place. Wildly, desperately, he fought it, because this was not the woman, this could not be the woman.

She felt how desire flooded his being, felt how he resisted it even as he wrapped her in his arms, and then his mouth was cruel on her own. Then he understood that what he had believed was violence in him was desire. Whatever he had imagined, whenever and for whatever reason he put his hands on her, it could only have changed into this.

Her head fell back under the savagery of his lips, and she moaned as his hands pressed her and his tongue plunged hungrily into her. His body was hard everywhere it met hers—hands, arms, chest, thighs, sex.

He pulled his mouth away, held her head, and forced her to meet his eyes. "It's not you!" he warned with a low growl, wanting to make her turn away, to resist this thing that was now unleashed again between them, because if he could not resist, she must. "I have not had a woman for a year, Hope. So if I take you now it's because of that, because you are a woman, any woman! Don't imagine anything more!"

Her skin was awash with sensation, shivering along her arms, down her back, over her breasts. Inside, a deeper sensation, a hot, slow melting of stomach, womb, sex, and beyond that the deep, spiritual hunger of need for him. She thought she should resist the clamour, should not give in to him in this cruel mood. But her body ached for him, her soul cleaved to him. Her blood rushed in her ears, she was weak with yearning. She was the beggar at the feast, hungry for any crumb.

"I don't care!" she cried. "Oh, Jude, touch me! Hold me!"

The last straw of his resistance was washed away in the flood that her words unleashed. His tortured cry of submission rose to heaven, railing at its failure to give him strength to resist in his hour of temptation. He pressed his mouth to her throat, then swung her up in his powerful arms and carried her to the same sofa where he had first made love to her, a long lifetime of suffering ago.

She knew, as he lay over her, naked now, his muscled arms holding his body above her—in the moment that he thrust into her, hard and burning against her flesh—in that moment she knew that she had been waiting for this, nothing but this, for all of the past year.

She cried out with the exquisiteness of the pain as his flesh found its home in her for the first time in an endless series of agonized, yearning nights. She could not remember anything now, not the pain of his betrayal, nor the agony of hers, not the thought of his anger—she knew nothing now, except that the waiting was over.

And then she knew nothing at all, because he drew out of her and then rammed home again, and everything went black with pleasure.

She cried his name. She was in another world, fainting, dreaming, lost. Her arms were around him, her hands pressing against his muscled back, his tightly clenched buttocks, pulling him in towards her again and again, thrusting up to meet him if he delayed for a second.

"Open your legs," he cried hoarsely once. "I can't get at you." He groaned aloud. "Oh, how I have wanted this!"

The wild hunger in him melted her. Everything melted her. She bent her knees and tilted her hips to make room for the full length of him, and whimpered as she felt him reach his depth in her at last. The cry of his satisfaction at being there ricocheted through her.

"I can't last!" he cried. "Too long, it's been too long!"

The hoarse cry was enough to send her over the edge, and the pleasure billowed up in her, its tendrils gripping muscle and sinew, brain and bone till she shuddered and wept with reaction. It was too much for him. Jude thrust hard into her and, with another cry, gave her at once the seed and fruit of his own pleasure.

They lay in silence, their bodies heaving for breath. Then his hand buried itself in her hair and he turned her head to look at him.

"Jude," she whispered.

He was appalled at what he had done, what he had allowed to happen. He did not know why it had happened, now, with Hope, when he had wanted it to happen two days ago with Rita and it had not. He did not understand why he had told her those things that no one knew, or why the telling had released such a torrent of uncontrollable feeling in him.

"It means nothing, Hope," he warned fiercely. "It changes nothing. Don't imagine that anything has changed between us. It's only because there was no other woman," he said, pretending to himself that it was not a lie.

Hope's heart clenched with pain. Tears burned her eyes and she closed them and tried to turn away. His hand in her hair prevented her.

"What's the matter?" he demanded, almost angry. "Did you hope this had changed something? What kind of change did you imagine?" He did not understand what he wanted from her, what kind of admission he was driven to hear.

"I don't know," she said, opening her eyes and gazing at him without shame now. "I only know we nearly touched something, and now we haven't."

At these words he was struck by a deep, primitive fear, nameless but menacing. He drew back physically and mentally. "There was nothing we nearly touched, Hope, not if you mean some hidden emotion in me. That is not hidden but dead. It was killed at the root."

"Jude," she protested, pushing herself up on her arms and looking down at him, "it was a momentary doubt, a momentary weakness, instilled deliberately by that woman—Jude, she's an expert in the manipulation of witnesses! What did I know? Anybody can be made to doubt anything for a moment!"

He swung away from her abruptly and sat up. He reached for his shorts, then, methodically, his jeans, and pulled them on. Then he turned to her, barefoot, bare-chested, but his eyes shuttered. "That was no momentary doubt, Hope. Why are you lying now? What good can it do you to lie? I already know the worst, have suffered all that I am going to suffer at your hands. What can be saved now by a lie?"

She felt the contempt in him strike her hard, like cruel hands beating her. She shivered and sat up, reaching for the clothes that he had torn from her body and tossed aside in his anguished passion. Now she needed clothes as armour against what was coming. She pulled on briefs, shorts, then the long T-shirt to cover her breasts that still ached and sang with his kisses.

"I don't know what you're talking about, Jude. You'd better tell me," she said then.

He was already at the drinks tray, dropping another ice cube into his whisky. He turned, eyeing her as if she were lying and they both knew it.

"Come on, Hope, we were both there. Why do you ask me to tell you what you know?"

She didn't know what was coming, but she thought suddenly that clothes were insufficient armour. Alcohol seemed like a good idea. The white wine she had been drinking was in an ice bucket. Not knowing where she had put her last glass, she crossed to his side and filled a new one.

"Tell me."

He shrugged, but his angry pain could not turn away from the invitation. "Hope, when your father said those words to you, what did you think? Did you believe in me then, or did you think it was of me that he spoke when he said, *He's lying about the letter?*"

She could not meet his eyes as despair settled around her. "Jude—" she began. Her breath came out in a sigh as she shook her head. "Ah, Jude—how was I to know what my father suspected?" she said helplessly, hopelessly. She heaved another sigh of despair and tried to explain. "Jude, it was the middle of the night, I was at a pitch of despair because of you and thinking my father was going to die the next minute, and suddenly—he was looking at me, speaking to me." She set down her glass and pressed both hands to her eyes. "I was completely emotionally destabilized by that point. I don't know what I thought just in that moment, Jude."

"No?" he asked ironically.

"Why do you say it that way, as if I doubted you?"

"Because of one little factor, Hope. Because you did not tell me or Nicholas Harvey, or anyone, about that moment. That's why I look at you as if you had doubted me."

"Jude, don't you understand that I really never thought of it again? What came after just drove it out of my mind. Maybe I wondered for one second if he meant you, but that wasn't why I kept quiet. I didn't think it was important, I didn't think anyone could ever know what he had meant, so how could it be important? That's why I never mentioned it.''

"But because of that, because you doubted me, it became important, didn't it, Hope?"

She could not deny it. She looked at it squarely for the first time and saw that he was right. If she had really, fully believed in Jude's innocence, she would have gone running to Nicholas Harvey or Jude to report her father's words, because if her father was so certain that Bill Bridges was lying, that might have meant there was some clue somewhere, something he had seen...but she had not been sure. She had wondered whether he meant Bridges or Jude.

"You're right," she said, and her eyes overflowed with tears. "I'm sorry. I was weak at all the wrong moments, and you paid the price."

"Now maybe you can understand why that moment in the court was the end for me. Don't ask for it back, what we had, Hope. Don't wish for it. It's dead, finished."

She looked at him without speaking. "Yes?" he urged, wanting to make her admit it, to submit and accept what he had just said, as though then he would know that it was the truth. But she only returned his gaze gravely, and made no answer.

Chapter 15

"Jude, this is Gig Young," said Roger Beatty.

The draughtsman and the detective were sitting on the same side of the table in the cheap cafe that still had the old-fashioned kind of enclosed booths with bench seating. It was a place Roger Beatty was used to patronizing. He sometimes found it useful to have whoever was doing the grassing locked in against the wall by his own body. It made sure they didn't bolt without warning, and often the very lack of an easy escape resigned them to staying to spill their guts.

Jude stood tall and bulky beside the table, in a thin T-shirt. Gig Young was grateful for the presence of the detective that separated and therefore protected him from Jude.

"He's got something to tell you," said Roger.

Jude raised one eyebrow without saying a word, and Gig Young trembled.

"Hi," he said. "I guess you remember me."

Jude sat down on the opposite bench, in the middle. Still he said nothing.

"He wanted to talk to you," said Beatty. "He'll tell you, no one else."

Jude's mouth moved. "Good," he said.

"I guess you wouldn't have had a detective on me if you didn't already know most of it," Gig Young babbled. "But I, uh—" He put both hands up and rubbed his face. "Hell, I've been wanting to tell someone, to confess, ever since it happened. I felt like hell when you got a conviction."

"But you managed to restrain yourself," Jude said.

"I got a wife, I got kids," he said sullenly. "He got me into it without me knowing what it was about, see? It wasn't supposed to be anything except covering his ass! That's what Bill told me. That was all it was! If I'd aknown, nothing would've...but it was too late by the time I found out. I didn't know the building was going to go like that, kill someone!"

Roger Beatty laid both his hands flat on the table and examined them. "Maybe you should start at the beginning," he suggested without heat.

"Yeah." Gig Young sniffed and wiped his nose with his hand. "My wife's uncle gave me a job when Fairmax went under—you remember that?" he asked Jude.

"Ninety-one," said Jude.

"Yeah. So many of us out on the street looking for work at the same time. I knew nothing about glass, but it was easy enough to learn. It wasn't hard to make the transition."

He paused, lost in his thoughts. "Go on," ordered Jude.

"Something went wrong with that order we were making up for you on the Rose Library. I never knew what, I didn't have anything to do with that project, I just—well, you could feel there was trouble."

"When?"

"Maybe a half, two-thirds of the glass was poured and

shipped? Anyway, alls I knew was, Bill was suddenly sending them all off to be tested again. That was alls I knew until he called me into the office one day and showed me an ad you were running for a draughtsman and said he wanted me to answer that ad and get the job."

"What made him think you would be able to?"

"I got the idea he felt he could ask Hal Thompson for a favour and get it. Not that he was owed or anything like that, just, he could say to Hal Thompson, 'Give him a break, Hal, he wants to get back into architecture, he's bored here, my niece is nagging me to find him something,' something like that, you know, and he'd do it. That's what I figured, anyway. And I went and got the job, still not putting two and two together. I just did what I was told."

"And what were you told, in the end?" Jude asked in a flat, unemotional voice, as if he had heard it all before, the story of the failure of a conscience.

"That was the weird thing, it seemed so simple. He told me to get into our file—that's the Environmental Glass file—at the Thompson Daniels offices and remove the test results we sent you on that glass for the Rose Library. I couldn't figure what was happening at all."

"And you did that."

He sniffed again. "Yeah, I did it. It wasn't so hard. You know, I could say I was looking for some specifications if anybody asked me what I was doing in the filing cabinet, but I did it at lunch when hardly anyone was there. Nobody said anything. It was a little harder making sure there wasn't another set of the figures in some other file. You had a set in your office, but they were right there with all the Rose Library paperwork, you know, and I told Bill that was all I could do. I couldn't go snooping everywhere, or somebody would notice."

"Is that it?" said Jude, dropping his hands down onto the table. The detective made a quick warning signal, and he relaxed again. "What else?"

Gig Young stared down at the tabletop in shame. "Then he asked me to *plant* that other set of figures, and I don't know why, but it wasn't till then that I started to see the light. I argued with him, but hell, he's my wife's uncle! He said nothing would ever happen, it was just like an insurance policy that would never be paid. So I did it."

"The letter was dated August first and stamped August sixth," Jude said, frowning. "You left July twenty-second."

"Yeah, that was the big compromise I got out of Bill," Young said with self-loathing. "I said if that letter was dated to the period I was there working for you, somebody would guess if anything ever happened. So he postdated it."

"Ah," said Jude.

"Yeah, and then I *mis*filed it, see, figuring that it wouldn't be found till long after August first, and then someone would just file it in the right place without looking at it. That was my idea," he said, half pleased at his shrewdness, half ashamed of its success. "I put it in the dead files, you know. The girls didn't go in there much, I noticed. The women, I mean."

"You stamped and initialled it."

"Yeah, I did that," he nodded. "I did that. I read all about the problems with that at your trial and I hoped that would get you off. I didn't know the two stamps were different, and Lena's desk was easier because she had her own office, I could get in there and get the stamp out of her desk and change the date on it, whereas Hope's desk was right out there in the main office. I didn't even think about whose signature, I just picked up the nearest letter and copied it, and it turned out to be Hope's."

"And then your job was done and you could resign."

"That's right. I went and told Hal Thompson some story and he said okay, no harm done, and I got out. And then five-six weeks later, when he'd promised me nothing would *ever* happen, but if it did it'd be years, five little weeks later the glass in the Rose Library blew.'' There was a long pause.

"Bill said he was sorry," Gig Young said levelly. "Somebody was dead, somebody else was injured, to save his bacon. And he was sorry. I have never held my head up since. I want you to know that."

"Yeah, I notice how troubled you were when I went on trial for manslaughter," Jude said mercilessly.

"So help me God, I didn't think they could possibly convict. Bill didn't tell me he was gonna testify against you, tell all those lies about talking to you...I swear I didn't know. And Bill gave me and my wife a surprise cruise in the Caribbean and when we came back, it was all over and you'd been—" He lifted a helpless hand. "I know I was a coward. You don't have to tell me. A million times I thought about writing the police a letter."

Jude ignored that. "What was wrong with the original test results?" Jude said.

Gig Young shrugged. "I don't know. We were supposed to send it to an independent lab for testing in the first place, I know that much, but Bill—somebody screwed up on the estimate, that much I do know, because the shit hit the fan when Bill realized. It was gonna cost a bundle to send that stuff out for testing, and it hadn't been costed in, because some cretin forgot that every single different shape had to be tested. He only costed in for the one shape. You follow me? So you had there—what?—ten, twelve different shapes making up those petals? Bill was gonna have to pay for those tests out of his own pocket."

"So he didn't have the tests done? Were those first results false?"

"No, they were tested, but he did it a sneaky way. We bought some new equipment so we could do all the tests on site, yeah? It wasn't independent, but it was thorough, it was rigorous, I could swear to that!"

"Not rigorous enough. When did he discover that the tests were inadequate?"

Gig Young looked at Jude. "You know, you must be right. You gotta be right that that's what happened. And yet, I could swear to you that that isn't the way it was. I don't know what happened, Bill never told me, he never told anyone. Just one day, something happened, and the factory was making another one single piece of every shape and we sent them out to DeMarco to be tested independently after all." He lifted his hands in a *you tell me* gesture. "He told me that he'd been wrong to do it the other way and he was morally obliged to get the glass tested independently like he promised. And that's when he got me to go and take that job with you guys."

Jude watched the man through narrowed eyes. "It doesn't fit together," he said, lifting a hand to count off on his fingers. "First, there was a mistake on the estimate because someone omitted the costs of testing."

"That's right."

"So contrary to our agreement, Bill did the testing on site and sent me those results."

Gig Young nodded.

"When two-thirds of the glass was shipped, the balloon went up that there was a problem. So then Bill sent all the glass for independent testing at an outside lab."

"Yup."

"And when the tests were done he put you in our office to destroy one set of tests and plant another."

Young nodded. Jude shook his head. "It doesn't fit. How the hell did he find out the testing he did was inadequate? Was there some fault discovered in one of the pieces of testing equipment?"

Young shook his head emphatically. "We were still testing glass for other sites on that equipment right the way through. We couldna done that if there was a problem. There was no problem."

"All right, is that everything?" asked Jude. He knew there was something that didn't hang together, but whether the man was lying or not he couldn't be sure. Something didn't fit.

That afternoon a representative of the Rose Library trustees arrived at the office to talk to Jude "unofficially."

"Have you been down to the site since you, ah... were released?" he asked.

"Yes, I've had a look around." The building was surrounded by scaffolding and the entire thing shrouded with tarpaulins. "I take it you haven't been able to decide what to do with it yet."

"Oh, I wouldn't say that. No, we've decided—most of us, it's not unanimous yet—what we'd like to do, but everyone was pretty much of the opinion that it won't do to proceed too fast. We wanted to wait for public opinion a bit."

Jude looked at him. "I see," he prompted, but this elicited nothing further. The man sat half-smiling and nodding like an animated Buddha statue. "What exactly do you want to do with it?"

"Well, we want you to complete it as designed," the man said, still nodding. "That is, all of us except one are agreed. We don't need a unanimous decision on this, but when you're presenting something controversial it's best not to have a dissenting voice. So we've been—wearing her down by attrition."

Jude stared at him. "You want me to complete the Rose Library as designed? Are you all nuts?"

"Oh, good heavens, there have been buildings that have lost glass before, Jude, you must know that, and even caused deaths! It's not as though this was deliberate on your part, even if you were guilty as convicted. Public opinion has to be looked at, of course, but so many people now agree that your trial was—well, that's really why I dropped by. The trustees are wondering if you're still appealing your conviction, Jude, even though you're now a free man.''

He thought wonders would never cease. Jude gazed at the apologetic little man in front of him, who looked the type to wimp out at the first breath of opposition.

"Did—did you hear my question?" he asked shyly now.

"Yes," said Jude. "Ah—yes, my appeal is going ahead. We have a date now in about six weeks."

"Good, good. Well, we just wanted to ascertain that. It'll make life easier for us, in the short run, if you're successful, but we'll have to consider whether to announce the trustees' decision before or after your appeal is heard. You understand."

"Yes," said Jude blankly. Clear as mud.

"If you win, everything's tickety-boo. But if you were to lose—and I'm sure you feel you have to face that possibility just as we do—might it be better for us to have run the gauntlet in advance? That's the issue. Otherwise we might be in the position of having to wait out that extra little puff of hostile opinion we'll get."

"I understand," said Jude, who, just at this moment, didn't think he would ever understand anything again.

So Hope had a lot more to digest that night than the meal of grilled chicken breasts and scalloped potatoes. She was delighted, but much less surprised than Jude at the decision of the Rose Fund trustees. The confession of Gig Young, though, naturally got the lion's share of their attention that night.

"What exactly doesn't fit?" she asked, when he had tried to express his doubt about the story Young had told.

"I can't put my finger on it." Jude shook his head. "Look: once the testing is done and Bill Bridges accepts that it's accurate, there's no reason for him to go over it again. Now his focus is on manufacturing and shipping the glass. What Gig Young says is that, with two-thirds of the glass shipped—that means we had half of it installed already—Bridges suddenly discovered a problem with his onsite testing that made him send every single shape off for another round of tests.''

Hope chewed thoughtfully for a moment. ''Maybe he discovered a problem with one piece right after they got it off the production line—maybe it shattered right there on the factory floor or something—and for some reason he decided to have them *all* retested.''

''If that's the scenario, the piece that proved to be weaker than the others during the DeMarco testing, the same piece that shattered on site—31AA—should have been the one that had the kind of problem you suggest at the time of manufacture. Would you agree?''

Hope drank and swallowed. ''Yes, that has to be the case, doesn't it?''

''According to this scenario, the shape that shattered on the factory floor was being shipped at about two-thirds of the way through, yes?''

''Yeah, that's right.''

Jude nodded. ''The *actual* problem piece—and the experts and I agreed that the shape that stressed and shattered spontaneously was the same as the one with the different test results—the others broke essentially because they were smashed by pieces of flying glass or because the structure destabilized—all the pieces of shape 31AA were manufactured, shipped and already installed long before Gig Young says the balloon went up at Environmental Glass.''

Hope took another sip of wine. ''Jude, that's weird.''

''So what could have happened at the lab *after* it was *already shipped* that would tell them there were problems with that shape that hadn't shown up on the tests, when at that time there wouldn't have been a piece that shape anywhere on the factory floor?'' He speared the last bite of meat on his plate and chewed appreciatively.

''Do you want some more?'' Hope offered.

Jude nodded and reached for the last piece of grilled garlic chicken, then lifted his plate as she gave him more potato. He still hadn't got used to how good food tasted in the real world.

"What we need is the original test papers from the Environmental Glass lab," she mused. "Do you suppose they discovered they left out one area of testing on that one shape?"

"Gig Young says he thinks all evidence of that first set of tests, and of the fact that the testing was ever done on site, was destroyed. Everything in the test laboratory goes straight to a computer and he's pretty sure that whole record was deleted."

Hope sat up as a thought slipped into her mind. "But someone had typed up those results on letterhead and sent them to you, right? I wonder if they remembered that in their purge of the records?"

Jude frowned. "What are you saying?"

Her eyes opened wide as the picture formed behind them. "I'm sure he remembered to wipe the lab computer. Do you think he remembered to wipe the *secretary's* hard disk?" she asked slowly.

There was a photograph of Hope and her mother, taken when Hope was age five or six, that sat on the drinks chest in the living room. It showed a smiling, pretty woman with long, straight blonde hair, parted in the middle, a necklace of painted beads and small feathers at her throat, pretty feathers hanging from silver earrings. Standing inside the embrace of one arm, her little hands holding her mother's wrist with the certainty of always being able to do so, stood Hope, the sunlight glinting off her tousled red curls, her mouth open, her eyes curving with laughter.

Sometimes Jude found himself studying the picture, but what was he looking for? He didn't know. Beside it was another picture of Hope, taken a decade or so later, a few years after her mother's death. The difference between the child and the teenager was striking. Gone was that serene knowledge that her world was indestructible, gone even the full sense of herself. The girl who looked out of the portrait at age fifteen had made a compromise with the world that had cost her some part of herself. The sort of compromise, Jude thought, that most people do not make until much later in life. She looked older than her years.

Sometimes he felt, in a wordless way, that the clue to why Hope had betrayed him was in these two photographs. Sometimes he felt that if he studied them for long enough he would find an answer.

One night, working on the Whalley and Sutton project in his study, he found himself at a creative standstill, tossed his pencil aside, got up and went downstairs to pour himself a drink.

Hope was upstairs working in her studio, and the house was silent. Outside twilight was closing in, crickets were singing, and the smell of the dying summer was rich in the air. Jude poured his whisky, and stood looking out the window as he sipped it. After a moment his eyes wandered to the photographs. He picked up the picture of Hope at fifteen and slowly, almost unconsciously, moved to the sofa and sat down.

She was not physically attractive, the girl in the photograph. Her hair was neither short nor long, her clothes so plain it could not be an accident, and her posture, with one arm bent to clasp the other near the shoulder, hiding the new young breasts, showed none of the blossoming, awkward sexual awareness that made teenage girls so painfully sweet to watch. This girl neither desired to attract nor believed she had the power, although there was a human understanding behind the eyes that was at once attractive and interesting and too old for her years.

When he had first been invited to this house by Hal Thompson and listened to the older man speak of his much

loved daughter, as he did sometimes, Jude had formed a
clear picture of the little rich girl who hadn't had the de-
cency to tell her father that she didn't care for a career as
architect, and was flitting through the capitals of Europe
instead of getting down to the serious business of life.

One day Hal had pointed this picture out to him, and
Jude had been astonished that this damaged, grave child
was the social butterfly they were discussing. Then he had
met her, and had lost sight of this picture in his estimate
of her. The contrast between this girl and Hope as she was
now was a mystery. Yet a mind like this did not simply
disappear, even under the weight of powerful feminine sex-
uality, rich clothes and well-cut hair.

Jude stood up and collected the other picture, that of the
child and her mother. He held the two pictures, one in either
hand, and looked back and forth between them.

He realized, with the shock of sudden insight which only
proves that the truth has been there all the time but that the
mind has hidden from it, that Hope at fifteen was the person
who had looked at him from the witness stand and doubted
him. She was the person who had looked at him the other
day when he had accused her and then made love to her.

He sat still. Even his heart seemed to stop beating as he
absorbed it, and tried to see what it meant.

"Hi. All finished?" said Hope, coming into the room,
and he looked up from the photograph and saw this girl
there, in the wariness behind her eyes. She looked at him,
only him, now, as she had once used to look at the world.

A smile teased her mouth. "What are you doing with
those?" she asked.

He didn't answer that. He said, holding up his hands, the
framed photos lying one on each, "What changed you from
this happy child to the girl here?"

She shrugged and turned away. "Oh, lots of things." She
bent to open the refrigerator compartment of the drinks
chest and drew out a bottle of white wine.

"Your mother died," he offered, behind her.

"Yes, that was a big part of it." Hope poured wine and mineral water into her glass and added an ice cube, then turned and came back to him, reaching out a hand for the photo.

"And you had a limp after the accident, I think," he pursued.

"Dad told you a lot, I guess." She moved to the armchair that cornered the sofa, sat, looked at the photo and smiled as sad memories tugged at her.

"He did not tell me enough to explain this change. Tell me," he commanded.

Hope leaned forward to set the photo down on the coffee table. "Is that all he told you—that I limped?"

"He said you were having an operation to cure you of a slight limp. But you still have it sometimes. The operation was not a complete success?"

"The operation was an amazing, a miraculous success." She smiled again, and looked at him. "I don't know why my father didn't tell you the truth. I had a very ugly limp and a hip that kept me in constant pain." She flicked her eyes to the picture again. "This photo was taken just around the time that I finally realized what it meant: that I could never have a sexual relationship, never get married, would never have children."

Jude frowned, his eyes involuntarily dropping to the pictured face again. "My God," he breathed.

She nodded wordlessly. Even now, the remembered anguish of that discovery could bring tears to her eyes.

"When did this change?"

"After the operations two years ago."

"*What?*"

She smiled quizzically. "What did you think?"

"But your father told me how popular you always were, what a good time you were having…"

"I was popular. All through high school I was one of

the guys. Until my operations, however, I had hardly even kissed anyone.''

"Surely it didn't hurt to kiss," he protested. He wasn't sure why this revelation was so shocking to him. One by one, every preconception he had had about Hope seemed destined to be turned on its head. He had been prepared to hate her, and instead he had loved her. He imagined a woman who had no respect for her father and he had found one who adored and worshipped him. He had thought her a dilettante and she was an artist of power. He imagined that she had always been rich and protected from life, and here was the history of the kind of prolonged and deep suffering from which wealth can never protect.

And if this was true, what must now happen to his belief that she had loved so often it was cheap to her, that she had betrayed him because she neither understood nor respected true love?

"No, it didn't hurt to kiss," she was agreeing. "In an earlier generation, I guess I'd have got a little romantic experience before the sword fell, but for us—even at thirteen we knew kisses led to sex, didn't we? I told myself I could never risk having a boyfriend, in case he got angry when the day came that I had to explain. Maybe if my mother had been alive, she'd have taught me another way. Raoul Spitzen—the surgeon who cured me—said that in certain positions sex would have been possible, and I guess if I'd had the courage to date a boy who liked me, who knows? Maybe if he'd been patient I'd have learned to trust him, and then—certainly if I knew a girl in the same situation I wouldn't advise her to do it the way I did. But I never thought of asking Dad about things, I just took it on the chin.''

Almost unconsciously Jude leaned forward to pick up the photo again, and looked between the cherished, confident child and the tragic teenager.

"But I was not your first lover," he said after a bit. He

couldn't have been that insensitive, not to have realized it if he had been.

"No, not technically, but emotionally, as good as," Hope said, and something struck him hard over the heart so that he lost his breath. He grunted with the unexpected force of it, yet when he searched he could not find what feeling it was.

"You had no experience of…love?" he said slowly.

"Virtually none."

"So when they told you that…I had pretended to love you so that you would commit perjury for me, when Corinne said that she and I were engaged—you were a girl with no previous experience. You didn't know what we had, how special it was."

She sat motionless, looking at nothing, as his voice washed over her. "I knew it was special for me," she said.

"But not for me?"

"You had never said anything in words. And you didn't say you loved me when I asked you at the detention centre. That was what I remembered, that you hadn't said it."

His voice was rough with regret. "A man can't say *I love you* to a woman when he might be convicted of manslaughter!"

"No?" She looked at him at last. There was no blame, only deep sadness in her eyes. "Still, I wish you had. I wish I'd heard it once, whatever happened after."

Her chin quivered, her lips trembled in a smile, and his heart seemed torn from its moorings. He no longer knew who he was, what he felt, what was certain.

"Yes," he said, the words coming from him without his will. "I should have said it. I should have said it at the beginning. A man should tell a woman how he feels while he has the chance."

Chapter 16

The moonlight fell across her pillow as he stood in the darkness watching. It illumined a soft curl of hair on the pillow, a pale shoulder where a scrap of lace lay against her skin, the slender form under a thin sheet.

He had awakened from a dream of her to find himself alone in his bed, and thought himself back in a barred cell. How many times he had awakened thus in the year just past, aching to hold her, burning with need, turning to her, and then had seen the bars against the window, remembered all over again where he was, reminded himself with ruthless accounting why she could never be his again...

Tonight he had awakened, prepared to remember the bars, and there were none. Tonight, for the first time, he had awakened to remind himself that he was free. And then his eager flesh had demanded hers, and he had been driven up out of his bed to come and find her.

He stood like a thief, watching as a cloud moved against the moon, so that the soft glow seemed to caress her. His yearning, his need, was unbearable. All that time behind bars he had somehow been able to fight it, to control it so that he was not driven mad by it. Each night he had ruthlessly reminded himself of her betrayal, and calmed his desperate flesh that could never remember that she was lost to him. But now she was here, and the gulf that lay between them was harder to remember.

She turned her head on the pillow, and the moonlight kissed her full lower lip, and he felt that touch of light on flesh as a knife of need in his gut.

No. He could not give in. He had been weak once and it had been torment and punishment to him, and cruel to her. Jude put up his hand and gripped the doorpost and wrenched his gaze from her.

"Jude."

He heard the pleading whisper of his name as it ignited his skin to flame, and something in him cracked from side to side, and he knew that he had lost. Silently he turned, silently he stepped across the carpet to the bed, and looked down.

Her eyes were shut. As he watched, she frowned and twisted her head. "Jude, Jude!" she wept, and then the sound of her own voice woke her. Her hand lifted to her eyes. "Oh, God!" she muttered.

He said her name, and she gasped and looked up. The moonlight fell across his face. "Jude?"

He was too hungry now to speak. He slipped down to sit on the bed beside her, wrapped his arms under her, and pressed his starving mouth to her breast, then her shoulder, then lifted it to smother her mouth.

He felt the response in her, felt the ease with which his presence ignited her own hunger, and his body clamoured to appease her hunger and his own. His hands moved to enclose her head and he held her as if she had tried to escape, his mouth hard and hungry with need.

Hope wrapped her arms around him and moaned as his lips crushed hers.

His mouth lifted then, and laid a trail of sparks down her throat to the lace at her breast. "I need you!" he said hoarsely.

She felt passion pour through her being as floodgates opened somewhere above her, and knew the force would sweep her away to her doom. "No," she breathed. "No."

He was almost beyond hearing, but he heard. "Hope, don't say no to me," he begged. "I need you. Do you know how many times I woke in that place, dreaming of you, and you were not there? And now you are here, I am here, don't say no, Hope."

But she remembered the pain when she had given in to his need last time. *It means nothing,* he had said then. *Only that there was no other woman.*

She reached out and found the switch of her bedside lamp. They both blinked in the sudden soft glow. Hope struggled to sit up. Jude's hands gripped and then released her, and he sat back to look at her.

"Do you love me, Jude?" she asked.

His jaw clenched. He could feel shutters come down inside him. "Hope," he said gently, "don't ask me this question."

Tears burned her eyes. "Don't ask me for meaningless sex."

He looked at her. "What meaning would you like it to have, Hope?"

She said, "I don't believe there's no other woman you could have, Jude, if you went looking. So why don't you ask yourself why you don't go looking?"

"What are you trying to say?" he asked cynically, as all his anger rushed to the ramparts. "That I'm cherishing a secret love for you that I'm afraid to tell you about?"

His tone hurt, but she stood her ground. "Maybe you're afraid to tell yourself," she said softly.

But the challenge was too dangerous, too soon, he was not ready for it. Unable to face the new truth, he hid behind the old certainties. "The one who is afraid to face the truth is you, Hope," he said. "You are afraid to face the truth that this was always meaningless sex—for you. Why should it not be so again, now that I also understand the rules?"

All the fire died in her, and she shivered under the freezing rain of his words. "When you can tell me why you want me, Jude, you come to me again. When you've really looked at it and know the truth."

"You are very sure the truth is something you will want to hear," he said.

"I am not going to make love to you again and then listen to blame. I'm not a masochist. Either you love me and forgive me, or you have to leave me alone. I'm not a punching bag."

He felt threatened by some nameless thing, and his heart beat light and fast, urging flight. "Good night," he said, as if that were his answer, and left her.

Behind him, in the room, the tears she had been holding back gushed out of her eyes. Was she a fool? Had she been wrong to send him away? If he did not love her, he would never come to her again. Hope bent forward, her hands on her upbent knees, her face in her hands, and, knowing herself to be a starveling, sobbed for the half loaf she had been offered and had turned away.

"You can't ask me to do it!" Gig Young pleaded hoarsely.

"Oh, I can ask a lot more than that," Jude replied, in a soft tone that terrified the draughtsman.

"I should never have talked to you! Bill would kill me if he knew. And if I take you in there—what if he finds out?"

"He will find out if you don't," Jude said, his voice harsh with threat. "Because then I will go to the police and the records will be subpoenaed and you will be called as a witness."

"I'm going to end up in jail! I know I am! I've got kids to think of!"

"It is late to think of your children. But now at least they have the chance to see their father an honest man who confessed and tried to put justice right instead of a villain who thought of nothing except—"

"Shut up! You think because you're the one who went to prison you're the only one who suffered? You had it easier, let me tell you! You at least knew you were innocent! You haven't been looking at the face of a moral coward in the mirror for the past year!"

Jude's gaze remained steady on him, saying nothing, and Gig Young's eyes fell.

"Tell me again what it is you want," he muttered.

"We want to go inside the offices at night and search for evidence in the files and on the computer."

"I told you, he wiped everything! He shredded the evidence!"

"If you are right, then no proof exists anywhere. If you are wrong, if he overlooked something, then it is there. Yes?"

"He'll kill me. The son of a bitch will kill me," Gig Young said, but there was resignation in his tone and Jude knew he had won.

"My dear, let me say that this is all absolutely wonderful!" the too-thin woman discreetly gushed at her. "A *marvellous* show, Daniel!" She reached past Hope to grip Daniel's sleeve. "What a talent! What a discovery!"

"Hope, let me introduce Veronica Taggart. Veronica is an interior designer, and one of my best customers."

"How do you do?" Hope said.

"I particularly adore you in semi-mimetic mode! Those—*Empty Bed,* isn't it, and what's the other—those are unreservedly fabulous! Well, and of course, the nudes!" She twinkled conspiratorially at Hope to indicate that they both adored naked men, flicked a nervous glance at Jude. But her courage failed her there. "Now, Daniel, I'm definitely having one of those, so you must come and tell me which one I should take. And then I *think* two more for clients." She put her arm on the art dealer's sleeve with the utter confidence of a regular buyer whose taste is impeccable and who will not be rebuffed. "Oh, by the way," she said to Hope as she led him off, "it was my son who bought your father's Picasso for his new place in the Romanoff! Justin McCourt! You remember! He was absolutely thrilled about it!"

"Oh," Hope said. But luckily, no more was expected of her. Veronica Taggart had gone.

The gallery was as full as it could stand. The buzz of conversation, the clink of glasses and the smell of success danced on the air. After only one hour into the private viewing, there were at least four red dots on pictures around the room. Daniel Johnson had already confidently stated that every picture would sell by the end of the two-week run.

Every picture except one. In the end, she could not part with the painting of Jude the Lion. The notice beside that read, "From the artist's private collection" to signal that it was not for sale.

Beside her, Jude, handsome as a devil in a black dinner suit, lifted his glass. "That woman is even worse than someone having an architect design her house," he muttered.

Hope laughed and sipped from her own glass. Pure mineral water, because she would need a glass in her hand all night to give her confidence and she didn't want to get drunk.

"Thanks for coming tonight, Jude."

"But you didn't need me, after all," he pointed out, his eyes wandering over the well-dressed crowd. Of course she had been frightened that no one would come.

"I'm sure half the people are only here to see Jude Daniels in the flesh," she said.

His eyes glinted down at her, with no message except the amusement of the moment. "Well, they can do that with or without me, can't they?"

Hope gurgled with laughter.

"You're the artist, aren't you? I wonder if you would come and tell me about one of your pictures," a middle-aged woman said beside them.

"Yes, of course," said Hope, and with a smile at Jude moved off. She was wearing black, a simple ankle-length dress with plain scooped neck and short sleeves that emphasized her slimness. Her red hair was caught up in a loose knot on top of her head, and her long neck held her head like a flower on a stem. Silver earrings dangled from her ears, catching the light. She was pale, he thought suddenly, and looked fragile, not glowing with health and vitality as she had been when they met.

He watched her bend to hear a question and then smile gently, nod and speak. He guessed that the question was naive, not very insightful, but she listened to the woman with the perfect humility of one who might hear genius.

Then his vision did a curious thing, shifting forward and back like a camera, as if to get her in better focus. And now he saw her as he should always have seen her—as a human being who has been tempered by deep suffering and whose heart is open to the pain of the world.

The shock he experienced was not the shock of surprise, but that of someone who has stared at an optical illusion which suddenly flicks into place. Why had he not seen this before? Why had he never put all the pieces together? He saw that whatever he had slowly learned about her, even as he fell in love with her, he had not seriously adjusted his first impression of her as a frivolous, somewhat shallow woman. And although he had never consciously formed the thought before, the deep reason why he had never told her he loved her was because of a fear that she was incapable of returning his love at the level he had wanted from her.

She was right: they had not known each other. If he had known her, if he had understood the sensitivity of that soul, he would have understood the look he got from the stand that day as self-doubt, and not doubt of him. If he had known her—if he had known himself!—he would have committed to her emotionally as well as physically, long before tragedy overtook them.

Behind her head the large canvas she had done of him most recently hung on a burlap-covered room divider. It was placed last in the chronologically arranged sequence, in such a position that the viewer came on it unexpectedly. It had been finished only days ago, was still unvarnished, unframed.

She had placed him on the terrace outside her studio, on a white plastic garden chair. She had stood behind him, just inside the patio doors, and he had sat three-quarters, his back to her, looking out past the treetops. That was all it was, a barefoot man, blue jeans and a polo shirt, through an open door. But somehow, he did not know how, she had captured the feeling of the wind against his face, so different from any prison breeze. Captured both the wind and its meaning for him.

Wind, she had titled it. Now, seeing her and the painting together, he understood the message that she was trying to send him through this.

To truly love another is to know oneself. Had he heard that somewhere? Jude was ashamed. He had not known himself until this moment. He had accused her of not loving him. The truth was, it was he who had not loved her.

"I've told the night watchman I'll be working for a couple of hours and he can relax," Gig Young hissed. "He doesn't know I'm not working here anymore. He's at the back watching television. For God's sake, keep your voices down! If he sees you, I'll have a lot of explaining to do.''

Jude and Hope nodded silently, slipped through the door and followed him past rows of desks. Down a short corridor they saw light falling through a doorway, and it was there that he was leading them. Once inside the office, he closed the door.

''This is Bill's office,'' said Gig Young.

A computer sat on a console at one side of the room, glowing with life. ''I've put the computer on,'' he said needlessly. ''This is the only computer on the floor that is connected to every other computer—the factory, the testing lab, all the office computers.''

There were two chairs in place in front of the computer. Jude held one for Hope; Young sat in the other. ''So, what do you want first?'' he asked.

''The secretaries' document files directories,'' Hope said.

One wall of the room was filled with filing cabinets, and as Hope and the draughtsman bent to their work, Jude moved over to them. They were locked, but he had guessed that they would be. He moved to the desk. It, too, was locked.

''Have you got a key for this desk?'' he asked quietly.

Gig looked up. ''No, he's very careful about keys. The filing cabinet keys are usually in the desk, but he has his desk key on his key ring.''

Without another word Jude reached into his pocket and pulled out the Swiss army knife he had put there. ''If you do that, he's going to know!'' Young protested, but it was the protest of one who has already lost the argument. Jude flicked a look at him and away, and Young turned back to the computer.

For the next hour there was silence in the office, as Hope flicked through the document files looking at anything that might have been the typist's file copy of the original test data and Jude combed through the desk and the filing cabinets. Beside the computer a laser printer now and then hummed into life as Hope took a copy of various documents she found.

At last Hope sat back, blowing upwards to dislodge a damp tendril of hair that flicked her eye. "Well, I don't think there's anything here."

Jude crossed silently to stand beside her. "No?"

"As far as I can see, the document files are arranged exactly like ordinary files: they open a client folder, and then every letter they write relative to that client is saved in that folder. We've checked every computer in the office, and there's only one Thompson Daniels file. That's got a copy of that letter dated August first as the last letter on file, and no previous letter referring to test data."

"And the others?" Jude asked.

She bent to pull the pages out of the laser printer. "The file for DeMarco Labs has the letters you'd expect relative to the testing in June and July and the test results they used in court. I've checked for other labs, too, but there's nothing. I've looked for ROSE and LIBRARY, in case whoever was typing had chosen a file name that Bill Bridges didn't know about. I've checked every file that has a curious file name, that might be code. I'm about out of inspiration. Nothing."

It mirrored his own findings among the paper files. Hope stood up to stretch, and Jude slipped into the chair she had vacated. On the screen was a directory with three choices: OFF, LAB, FAK.

"Right," he said to Young. "Let's go into the lab files."

They had agreed in advance that Hope would check the office files; but Jude would have better experience and feeling for the test laboratory records.

Another age passed, the silence broken only by the click of the keyboard, a muttered question, the sound of drawers and paper. There was one document to reflect the preliminary test done on the prototype shape. At last Jude admitted defeat and abandoned the lab computers, punching the directory back up onto the screen.

OFF, LAB, FAK. This time he noticed that it was a *K* and not an *X*. It was a curious misspelling of *fax*, his brain suggested, as though trying to bring the third option to his notice. "Fax!" he whispered, as an idea brushed him "Does this have a computer-generated fax system on it?" Computer-generated fax systems saved all faxes sent and received in a separate file.

But Gig was shaking his head. "Nah, that's not *fax*, it's the factory. Bill got the factory computers on-line a couple of months ago. He didn't have the capacity before, but this is a new computer."

Jude stared at Gig Young, then at the screen, then back at the draughtsman again. "All the equipment on the factory floor is computerized," he said, as if to himself.

"Oh, yeah, it's years since we had that."

Jude said, "Let's take a look at the actual manufacturing programs for the Rose Library glass."

"Hell, that won't tell you anything."

"No," Jude agreed, not sure what his brain was trying to tell him. "Let's look anyway."

Gig Young reached in front of Jude and pulled the keyboard closer to himself. He began punching in codes. Suddenly the screen was full of long lists of numbers. He shook his head.

"The jobs are all saved under the factory code," he said. "I got no idea how the codes are assigned. The guys on the floor know the codes for whatever job they're working on."

"There must be some kind of master document," said Jude.

"I guess so."

Hope, abandoning her fruitless re-search of the paper files, drifted over to look over Jude's shoulder. *8192A. 5593. 6694C. 41295A. 7696A. 111296B. 2197D. 3397A,* she read at random. She frowned, bending down over Jude, and her eyes quickly scanned the screen. The second-last digit of every number was a nine; there was no final digit higher than seven. No letter higher than *D*. "Those are dates, aren't they?" she said.

The two men stared transfixed at the screen as gibberish transformed itself into sense.

"So they are!" breathed Gig Young. "The Start Date! I'm always hearing the guys asking for the Start Date Number to be assigned to a job. *A, B, C,* and *D* would be used if more than one job was started on the same day. I don't think we have the capacity to start more than four in one day unless there's a couple of very small jobs."

"The Start Date for the Rose Library job must have been late April or early May that year," said Jude, and all three bent their heads closer to the screen in sudden excitement. "Is this day month year or month day year?"

"Day month," said Young.

20596A. 20596B.

Gig's finger pointed out the figures. "That'd be two different jobs started on the same day, see!" he said excitedly.

23496. 24496. 27496A. 27496B.

Jude said, "When there's no letter suffix, what does that mean?"

"Only one job started that day, probably."

6596B.

May 6, 1996. Jude frowned. "Why is there no 6596A?"

"Hard to say." Young shook his head.

"Because he wiped it," Hope offered simultaneously.

Jude exchanged glances with her and nodded. "Because he wiped it," he agreed.

"Can you call up one of these files?"

"I can try." Young hit several keys.

The screen filled with the recognizable gibberish of a computer programme. They heaved a simultaneous sigh.

"This is the instructions to the computer that controls the blast furnace," said Jude. "Why did Bridges wipe the Rose Library program? It's meaningless without a reference, in any case."

"I don't understand what this is," Hope said.

He twisted to look up at her. "It's just temperature and timing control during the manufacture. It's telling the furnaces how to temper the glass. To hold it at a certain temperature for a certain period. To reduce the temperature over a certain period. Why did he wipe this information?"

"Just being thorough," Gig Young guessed.

"Maybe," said Jude. "Maybe not." He stared unseeingly at the screen as light seemed to form in his head. "This is the one thing I never thought of," he said slowly. "The most obvious thing, and I overlooked it. There was a problem in the actual manufacture of the glass."

He sat silently brooding while the other two waited and watched his brain work behind the broad brow.

"Hope," he whispered after a moment. "Now I see it. They made a mistake in the computer instructions to the furnace. The first shape off the production line—31AA—was flawed, but nobody realized. By the time they noticed it, we had the glass installed…and it was going to cost Bridges if he told us about it…."

"A lot?" Hope asked.

"Enough." Jude came out of his reverie. "What we need are not the test documents, but what was probably filed here as 6596A: the computer instructions for the furnace for every shape of glass that was poured for the library consignment."

"Wait a minute," said Hope in a different voice that made both men look at her. She turned to Gig Young. "Can you go back into the OFF files, please?"

Jude stood up to make way for her to sit in front of the computer while Gig Young summoned up access to the office hard disk.

Dir/p, Hope typed, and again the screen was filled with a list of codes. She hit a key at random several times, then paused. "There!" she said.

SD3-em<DIR> the screen read.

cd/SD, Hope told it.

C:/SD> replied the computer.

dir/p, she requested.

All three held their breath.

The same long list of number codes flashed on the screen, the 92s, then the 93s...Hope hit a key to flash each succeeding page of the directory until they came to those numbers ending in 96 and a letter. The codes ran through February, March, April, May. ..

6596A

6596B

Gig breathed a curse. "There it is! 6596A. He musta wiped it off the factory computer but forgot there was a matching record in the office files. This should have the original instructions that they used to program the factory computer as well as the actual program."

Her heart pounding with almost unbearable excitement, Hope instructed the computer to open the 6596A file.

THOMPSON DANIELS, ARCHITECTS

THE ROSE LIBRARY, the computer announced unemotionally, but it seemed to its three interlocutors that it screamed the words.

Chapter 17

"It's past four o'clock already," Gig Young said nervously. "Can we get out of here? The guys in the factory start coming on at six."

Jude pushed back his chair and stood up. "I've seen all I need to see." He picked up the sheaf of laser printed pages he had been poring over and glanced at where Hope stood taking more pages out of the printer.

"Have you got everything, Hope?"

"Three copies," she said. "You found it?"

He smiled grimly. "Easy when you know what you're looking for. Let's get going."

The sky was already growing pale as they emerged from the front doors of the building, so it wasn't difficult to see the flashing lights of the police cruiser as it screeched to a halt a few feet away, nor the guns in the hands of the uniformed men who piled out of the car, leveled their aim and ordered them to put their hands up.

She heard Jude sigh beside her as the three of them obediently came to a halt. Just ahead of her, Gig Young was cursing in a high, nervous voice.

Beyond the police cruiser, another car entered the factory parking lot and pulled up.

Bill Bridges stepped out. He looked first at her, frowned in incomprehension, then at Jude. His face hardened into concentrated ugliness. "Jude Daniels!" he spat. Then his gaze moved to the third member of the party, and the look on his face shifted between shock and rage.

"You little bastard!" he shouted. "You damn stinking coward, what the hell are you doing here?"

One of the police officers looked at him. "Do you know this man, Mr. Bridges?"

"Sure he knows me," Gig Young said excitedly. "I'm his nephew. I work for him. I've got keys. It's not a burglary!"

Out of the corner of her eye, Hope noticed a third man, in jeans and a jacket, slide out of the back seat of the police cruiser. He lifted his hands and she heard the whirr and click of a flashless camera.

"Not anymore he doesn't!" Bridges snapped. "This is breaking and entering. Arrest them all."

"I've got keys!" Young shouted triumphantly. "I'm a registered keyholder for the alarm company! You can check the record! We didn't break and enter, we used my keys."

"Is that right, Mr. Bridges?" asked one of the uniformed men. "Is he a keyholder?"

But Bill Bridges ignored him and addressed his nephew again. "You bastard!" he said again.

"Not him, Bridges," Jude said with a contempt that froze them all where they stood. "You. You're the bastard."

Bridges turned to look at him and smiled. "You got any evidence of that?" he asked insolently, as if he knew the answer.

"Oh, yes," said Jude. "We have the evidence. You

missed one file in your purge, Bill. The one that proves form 31AA was three hours short in the annealing time."

The change that came over Bridges' face now was ludicrous. Anger, shock, incredulity, horror.

"I'm Art Foster, *The Express*," interjected the man who had got out of the police cruiser. "Aren't you Jude Daniels, the Rose Library architect?"

"That's right."

"I followed your case last year. I've just been with these guys here—" he indicated the uniformed police with a negligent thumb "—looking for something to fill up a slow night. Think I just found it," said the reporter.

Art Foster's exclusive was blazoned across the front page of the first edition. Jude Daniels Proves Innocence the headline read. Underneath was an unflattering photo of Bill Bridges, his mouth open, his eyes narrowed menacingly. He looked coldly sinister.

> "Bill Bridges early this morning at his glass factory listens to architect Jude Daniels tell him he has gathered the proof from Bridges' own files that the glass that exploded in last year's Rose Library disaster was defective and the evidence covered up by the manufacturer. Jude Daniels served a prison term for manslaughter of the night watchman who was killed in the tragedy. He has always maintained his innocence."

"Trial by front page," remarked Jude.

He had been released from police custody in time to come home to a late breakfast. During the ten minutes in which the police had questioned them all, prior to arresting Jude for parole violation, the journalist had got his story.

Hope nodded. "They don't actually say anywhere that he's guilty, but no one reading this is going to be in any doubt, are they? 'More pictures, page three.'" She turned the page to find a large shot of

> Jude Daniels, his wife, and the Environmental Glass employee Gig Young at the glass factory where they uncovered the evidence reproduced below. Gig Young, an employee and relative of Bill Bridges, alleges that he was forced by Bill Bridges to take part in the cover-up. He took a job at the firm of architects Thompson Daniels allegedly to plant false evidence of negligence that later convicted Jude Daniels.

The bottom half of the page showed photo reproductions of two documents they had printed from the computer, copies of which Jude had given to the reporter as well as the police. She read the caption.

> The document on the left records the correct manufacturing process. On the right, the figure circled in red shows that the glass shape manufactured to these specifications was tempered for an inadequate length of time. At Jude Daniels' trial, it was shown that it was this shape that exploded, causing all the other pieces of glass in the Rose Library to shatter.

Hope smiled tremulously at Jude across the table. "Congratulations, Jude," she said.

The phone rang, the first of many times.

Bill Bridges did not crack. The factory foreman did.

"Here's what they've got," Nicholas Harvey said. He leaned back in his leather chair and steepled his fingers. "The accountant doing the costing estimates on the Rose Library glass failed to take into consideration that more than one shape had to be tested. Their estimate to you was low. Now, that's where Bill Bridges' greed took over. He decided to do the testing in his own labs to keep his costs down. And that should have been the end of it.

"But then something else happened during the manufacturing process. As you saw from the records, somebody on the factory floor misread a number and cooked—whatever you call it—"

"Annealed," said Jude.

"Annealed the glass for an inadequate time. That was only the one shape, but of course every piece of that shape was made to the same program and came off the line stressed."

"Right."

"By the time anyone realized, the rose was already half complete. Now, we're at crisis of conscience number two for Bridges. And what he does is manufacture another piece of glass with the same specifications as the *stressed* pieces he shipped to the site—you get me?—and runs that through the tests in his own lab."

Jude nodded as he saw the lawyer's point. "To find out how much danger there was of the stressed glass exploding immediately."

"That's right. And he finds out that the stressed glass isn't as dangerous and volatile as he feared. It hasn't got quite the same specifications as the correctly manufactured glass, but it might be years before anything happened, if ever. So what does he do? He now gets an independent lab—DeMarco, as it happens—to test *all* the glass shapes, including the stressed shape, as if they were the routine tests."

Jude frowned with amazed incomprehension. "What?"

"That's it. Meanwhile he asks Hal Thompson to hire his nephew, and the nephew plants the evidence in the office and removes the original docu—"

"No." Jude shook his head. "No, this is impossible. That glass was stressed. It didn't just have greater thermal movement, it was stressed due to faulty manufacture.

DeMarco *would* have picked it up. Whoever is telling this story is still lying when he says the stressed glass shape was tested and found not to be too far out of line with the others. When Bill Bridges tested that badly manufactured shape it exploded right there in the lab, I guarantee it. It had to.''

Jude considered a moment. ''What he then did was deliberately develop another shape which they called 31AA and was close in shape to the real 31AA, but which was designed to have slightly more thermal movement. *This* is the shape he sent to DeMarco for testing.''

The lawyer stared at him. ''Jude, are you sure?''

''Bill Bridges could be morally certain that glass would not hold up,'' said Jude. ''Stressed glass is unpredictable. It didn't need a heat wave. It could go anytime. Anything might have triggered the explosion.''

''Right. I'll pass that on.''

''Your Honour, the prosecution does not intend to offer any argument in this appeal. In fact, we join with defence counsel in urging you to direct a new verdict of acquittal, and with the Court's permission, we would like to take this opportunity to tender the Crown's apology—and I would like to add my own personal apology—to Jude Daniels for what I'm sure Your Honour will agree has been a miscarriage of justice...'' said Sondra Holt.

''...and this Court of Appeal therefore orders a directed verdict of acquittal to be entered in the records, and for Jude Daniels to walk from this courtroom in the knowledge that his entire innocence of the crime has been established to the satisfaction of this court and the people of the land....''

''Isn't it funny how everything can just be over like that?'' Hope said softly that evening. The nights were closing in; the smell of winter was in the air. A bright half moon climbed up the sky, and Venus winked and blinked at them in solitary splendour, a wishing star. Hope was both happy and sad at the same time.

"Just like that you're not on parole anymore—technically you were never convicted. And now the city will have to withdraw its claim against us for damages...and pretty soon I guess it'll be as if we'd never married, either. You don't need the charade anymore."

Jude watched her thoughtfully without speaking. His steady gaze made her nervous.

"It almost seems as though everything should suddenly be perfect again. But you still spent a year in prison, whatever the court records say, and Dad...well, it won't bring him back, will it?"

She did not say that it would not bring back what she and Jude had once had, nor his trust of her, because there was no point in saying it. But it was in her mind.

"No," he agreed, and it seemed as if he were agreeing with her unspoken thoughts, agreeing that nothing could bring back his feeling for her. "No, it won't bring back perfection. Everything changes, everything has to move on, one way or the other, Hope."

Outside a yellow leaf fell from its anchorage and drifted down onto the grass.

She looked down at her clasped hands. "I guess there's no point in saying I'm sorry again. But I really, really am, Jude."

He looked at her and saw in her face the shadow of the girl in the picture, making up her mind that she could never have what she most wanted.

"I guess we'll have to decide what to do about the house," she went nervously on, afraid to stop babbling nothings in case she began to beg. "Now that you're back in business I guess...I mean, I won't be able to afford it, but would you like to keep it?"

"Yes," he said. "I'd like to keep it."

She shrugged and nodded as if she had expected it, but in fact she had hoped he would want to sell quickly. To leave him in the house would hurt, but it was not within her rights to complain. It had been left to them equally. He could raise a mortgage and pay her her half share, but she couldn't possibly offer to do the reverse. And if he didn't want to continue to share the house she doubted if her father's will gave her the power to force him to do so.

"I suppose you—would you consider dividing it into a duplex? We could make a separate entrance with an outside staircase and I could have the attic and the third floor. It wouldn't be too hard to put in a kitchen." She grinned in an attempt at lightness. "You should be able to come up with a nice 'architect-designed renovation.'"

She knew she was a fool to suggest it. She was storing up heartbreak for herself, living in the same house, watching him, waiting for the night that would never come, the night when he would come to her again, love her again…but she herself had made that impossible.

"Hope," he said, and the flat, unemotional tone terrified her.

"I know you want a divorce, now that it's all over I know you want your freedom, that's okay, so do I. Also I want to get back to France, get down to some real painting, you know?"

"Do you?"

"Yes, but I'd like to know this place was still here, I could rent out my half if we—" she swallowed, running out of steam "—if we made it self-contained, and then I'd always have somewhere to come home to."

She fell silent.

"Is that what you want?" he asked. "Somewhere to come home to?"

She met his eyes, tried to smile, and looked away.

"Hope," he said, in a hoarse, raw voice, and now she could hear how he battled with emotion. "Is it too late to tell you the answer to the question you asked me that night?''

''Is it—what?'' she said, unwilling to believe what she thought she had heard.

''Don't leave me, Hope. Don't make me live without you again. I learned to do it last time by teaching myself to hate you for what I thought you had done.''

She closed her eyes. ''You succeeded.''

''No,'' he said. ''*No!* I didn't succeed. I thought I had...'' He squeezed his eyes shut. ''How you haunted me in that place! Night after night! But I told myself—I don't know what I told myself to keep sane. Hope, you asked me to forgive you, but I also need to be forgiven. I'm sorry. I hurt you, my blind stupidity made an intolerable year much worse hell for both of us. I'm very sorry I misunderstood you, and myself, and everything. Do you forgive me?''

''Yes.'' Tears burned her cheeks, and she brushed them impatiently aside.

''I love you. That's the answer to your question, Hope. You were right. I love you. Look at me.''

He got up and was standing over her chair. Hope lifted her head and met his eyes, and what she saw in them now lifted her heart to the sun.

''Do you love me?'' he asked.

''You know I do.''

''Not until I hear you say it. Say it,'' he half begged, half commanded, and then, before she could speak, reached down and drew her to her feet, into his arms.

''Say it, Hope. Say I am not too late.''

''I love you,'' she said. His hold tightened painfully around her. ''Oh, Jude, I love you!''

''Hope, will you be married to me, and live with me, and be my wife?''

She sighed as his breath brushed her cheek. ''Oh, yes!'' she began, but Jude could not wait to hear the words, and bent to take her answer from her lips.

Jude led his wife to the bedroom and the bed which he had never yet shared with her. He lay down and drew her gently after him, and then he wrapped her in his arms and held her for long, silent moments in which they both understood more than words could say. His desire was painfully tender in him now, and he felt that he would cherish and protect her all of his days. He kissed her, and stroked her forehead and her hair, smiled down at her and kissed her again, as tenderly as if she were newborn.

Hope felt the tenderness in him, felt how her heart trembled and opened under its impact. The desire that flooded her now was not sharp, but full, rich, and trusting. She wrapped her arms around his neck and gave herself up to his embrace with an openness that shook him.

Slowly, without haste, he unbuttoned her shirt and slipped it from her shoulders, lifting her body to take it from her. Gently he stroked her bare flesh, kissed her as though she were a flower bud. His love was all new to him, though it had been part of him almost since the first moment of seeing her. It was new because for the first time he was not afraid of it; not afraid of how love would make him vulnerable.

He undressed her, bit by bit, and then lifted the quilt as she slipped naked into the warmth of the bed. When he had taken his own clothes off, he followed her, and took her in his arms again, and kissed her, and held her.

"I love you, Hope," he said.

"I love you," Hope replied, smiling softly up into his face.

"You're my wife," said Jude, and she blinked back tears.

Then slowly, gently, he began to make love to his wife, loving her, desiring her, needing her body and soul, and knowing it. He made her tremble and cry out with pleasure, and drank in her responses like nectar. When at last her hands held and begged him, he rose over her and pressed his way home, feeling how much trust her acceptance of his body signified, how deeply she trusted him, and he her, and he shuddered as feeling shook him.

He smothered her mouth with a kiss, wanting to take her into himself, wanting to be part of her, wanting her to be part of him, feeling that deeper, truer union that this act was the physical image of.

"Hope," he whispered, and she was: she was hope to him. She always had been.

He pushed into her again, and then wrapped her tightly in his arms, kissing her face, her mouth, her hair as sensation enveloped them. They had had passion, and would have it again, but not yet. Now he felt a tenderness so strong it could hardly be borne as he moved in her and felt how her body accepted his.

For Hope it was a nearly unbearable pleasure, a pleasure that tore at her heart and made her weep with love, with sadness, with happiness, with forgiving. When he moved in her he touched her soul, and her soul answered with a yearning ache, a profound need of him that would never leave her.

Slowly, slowly, the need built in them both, and he raised himself over her and began that rhythmic motion that would not be denied, as the rain of pleasure built up in them. Then, like a flooded river, it burst its banks, and the floodwaters rushed through the valley of their two selves to nourish and moisten what had been parched and dry.

There was so much that he had never understood before. Jude lay beside Hope, clasping her to himself, and felt how love consumed him, altered him, and knew that it was this that he had feared: that one could not hide behind walls, and love. He had tried to have both—his invulnerability and his love of her, but love that withholds itself is not love.

He had feared her because love had stripped him of armour. It was he himself, not she, who had not trusted their love. If he had trusted himself and love, he would have bound her to him from the beginning, instead of allowing their love to be a thing understood but not spoken.

To say ''I love you'' is to admit to a vulnerability that he had been afraid to admit. He had had no right to expect her to take for granted something that he himself did not confess.

''I'm sorry,'' he whispered awkwardly, for words did not come easy to him. ''I was wrong. I should have told you I loved you, Hope, long, long ago.''

She smiled tenderly at him as deep, loving contentment spread through her in the aftermath of his lovemaking and his words. ''It doesn't matter anymore,'' she said, and he knew that she was right.

Only the future mattered now.

* * * * *

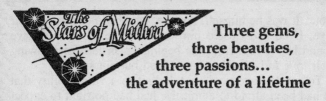

The Stars of Mithra

**Three gems,
three beauties,
three passions...
the adventure of a lifetime**

SILHOUETTE·INTIMATE·MOMENTS®
brings you a thrilling new series by
New York Times bestselling author

Nora Roberts

**Three mystical blue diamonds place three close
friends in jeopardy...and lead them to romance.**

**In October
HIDDEN STAR (IM#811)**
Bailey James can't remember a thing, but she knows
she's in big trouble. And she desperately needs private
investigator Cade Parris to help her live long enough to
find out just what kind.

**In December
CAPTIVE STAR (IM#823)**
Cynical bounty hunter Jack Dakota and spitfire
M. J. O'Leary are handcuffed together and on the run
from a pair of hired killers. And Jack wants to know
why—but M.J.'s not talking.

**In February
SECRET STAR (IM#835)**
Lieutenant Seth Buchanan's murder investigation takes
a strange turn when Grace Fontaine turns up alive. But
as the mystery unfolds, he soon discovers the notorious
heiress is the biggest mystery of all.

Available at your favorite retail outlet.

Look us up on-line at: http://www.romance.net   MITHRA

Take 4 bestselling love stories FREE

Plus get a FREE surprise gift!

Special Limited-time Offer

Mail to Silhouette Reader Service™

3010 Walden Avenue
P.O. Box 1867
Buffalo, N.Y. 14240-1867

YES! Please send me 4 free Silhouette Intimate Moments® novels and my free surprise gift. Then send me 6 brand-new novels every month, which I will receive months before they appear in bookstores. Bill me at the low price of $3.34 each plus 25¢ delivery and applicable sales tax, if any.* That's the complete price and a savings of over 10% off the cover prices—quite a bargain! I understand that accepting the books and gift places me under no obligation ever to buy any books. I can always return a shipment and cancel at any time. Even if I never buy another book from Silhouette, the 4 free books and the surprise gift are mine to keep forever.

245 BPA A3UW

Name	(PLEASE PRINT)
Address	Apt. No.
City	State	Zip

This offer is limited to one order per household and not valid to present Silhouette Intimate Moments® subscribers. *Terms and prices are subject to change without notice. Sales tax applicable in N.Y.

UMOM-696 ©1990 Harlequin Enterprises Limited

SILHOUETTE WOMEN KNOW ROMANCE WHEN THEY SEE IT.

And they'll see it on **ROMANCE CLASSICS**, the new 24-hour TV channel devoted to romantic movies and original programs like the special **Romantically Speaking—Harlequin™ Goes Prime Time.**

Romantically Speaking—Harlequin™ Goes Prime Time introduces you to many of your favorite romance authors in a program developed exclusively for Harlequin® and Silhouette® readers.

Watch for **Romantically Speaking—Harlequin™ Goes Prime Time** beginning in the summer of 1997.

If you're not receiving ROMANCE CLASSICS, call your local cable operator or satellite provider and ask for it today!

Escape to the network of your dreams.

See Ingrid Bergman and Gregory Peck in *Spellbound* on Romance Classics.

©1997 American Movie Classics Co. "Romance Classics" is a service mark of American Movie Classics Co.
Harlequin is a trademark of Harlequin Enterprises Ltd.
Silhouette is a registered trademark of Harlequin Books, S.A.

RMCLS-S-R2

As seen on TV!
Free Gift Offer

With a Free Gift proof-of-purchase from any Silhouette® book, you can receive a beautiful cubic zirconia pendant.

This gorgeous marquise-shaped stone is a genuine cubic zirconia—accented by an 18" gold tone necklace.

(Approximate retail value $19.95)

Send for yours today...
compliments of ▼ *Silhouette*®

To receive your free gift, a cubic zirconia pendant, send us one original proof-of-purchase, photocopies not accepted, from the back of any Silhouette Romance™, Silhouette Desire®, Silhouette Special Edition®, Silhouette Intimate Moments® or Silhouette Yours Truly™ title available at your favorite retail outlet, together with the Free Gift Certificate, plus a check or money order for $1.65 U.S./$2.15 CAN. (do not send cash) to cover postage and handling, payable to Silhouette Free Gift Offer. We will send you the specified gift. Allow 6 to 8 weeks for delivery. Offer good until March 31, 1998, or while quantities last. Offer valid in the U.S. and Canada only.

Free Gift Certificate

Name: _____

Address: _____

City: _____ State/Province: _____ Zip/Postal Code: _____

Mail this certificate, one proof-of-purchase and a check or money order for postage and handling to: SILHOUETTE FREE GIFT OFFER 1998. In the U.S.: 3010 Walden Avenue, P.O. Box 9077, Buffalo, NY 14269-9077. In Canada: P.O. Box 613, Fort Erie, Ontario L2Z 5X3.

FREE GIFT OFFER   084-KFD
ONE PROOF-OF-PURCHASE
To collect your fabulous FREE GIFT, a cubic zirconia pendant, you must include this original proof-of-purchase for each gift with the properly completed Free Gift Certificate.

084-KFDR2

SUSAN MALLERY

Continues the twelve-book
series—36 HOURS—in
January 1998 with
Book Seven

THE RANCHER AND THE RUNAWAY BRIDE

When Randi Howell fled the altar, she'd been running for her life! And she'd kept on running—straight into the arms of rugged rancher Brady Jones. She knew he had his suspicions, but how could she tell him the truth about her identity? Then again, if she ever wanted to approach the altar in earnest, how could she not?

For Brady and Randi and *all* the residents of Grand Springs, Colorado, the storm-induced blackout was just the beginning of 36 Hours that changed *everything!* You won't want to miss a single book.

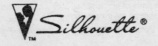

Available at your favorite retail outlet.

Look us up on-line at: http://www.romance.net   36HRS7